THE YEAR OF LIVING AWKWARDLY

EMMA CHASTAIN

SIMON & SCHUSTER

First published in Great Britain in 2018 by Simon & Schuster UK Ltd
A CBS COMPANY

Originally published in the USA in 2018 by Simon Pulse,
an imprint of Simon & Schuster Children's Publishing Division

1 3 5 7 9 10 8 6 4 2

Simon & Schuster UK Ltd
1st Floor, 222 Gray's Inn Road
London
WC1X 8HB

www.simonandschuster.co.uk
www.simonandschuster.com.au
www.simonandschuster.co.in

Simon & Schuster Australia, Sydney
Simon & Schuster India, New Delhi

A CIP catalogue record for this book is available from the British Library.

PB ISBN 978-1-4711-6048-6
eBook ISBN 978-1-4711-6049-3

Printed and bound by CPI Group (UK) Ltd, Croydon, CR0 4YY

MIX
Paper from
responsible sources
FSC
www.fsc.org FSC® C020471

Simon & Schuster UK Ltd are committed to sourcing paper that is made from
wood grown in sustainable forests and support the Forest Stewardship Council, the
leading international forest certification organisation. Our books displaying the FSC
logo are printed on FSC certified paper.

For *Anita Lawson*

Wednesday, August 10

OMG. I think Grady likes me.

Maybe! I mean, I'm not positive. But work today was *weird.*

It was hot, but there were big rain clouds overhead, so no one came to the pool. Grady and I sat on our stools in the concession stand, eating Twizzlers and talking about where we'd most like to live when we finally escape our hellishly pleasant New England suburb.

Grady said, "Probably Berlin, or Istanbul."

I said, "New York, definitely. Or maybe Bermuda, so I can ride around on a scooter."

He shook his head. "No way. It'd be too boring,

living there forever. We could go there on our honeymoon, though."

I whipped my head to the left to look at his face. My mouth was hanging open from the shock. He's never said anything like that to me before! He's a year younger than me! He knows I just got dumped by Mac, my pretend boyfriend who had a girlfriend but made out with me constantly anyway!

He looked a little nervous, but also pleased with himself.

"Sure," I said finally. "I hear they have pink sand."

The thing about Grady is, he's basically my height, so it's easy to stare into his eyes, which are deep-set, and to notice his eyelashes, which are so long they get tangled sometimes.

I see that he's handsome, but I don't feel it in my bones. Could I ever like Grady? Good old Grady, my co-worker, the guy who burps the alphabet for my entertainment when we get bored?

Thursday, August 11
OK, I think yesterday was all in my head. It was about a thousand degrees in the concession stand today, and I was dying.

"I'm sweating like a pig," I told Grady. "I think I forgot to put on deodorant."

He tried to smell my armpit and I pushed his head away.

"You definitely forgot," he said, fanning his hand in front of his face.

This is how we normally treat each other: like siblings. Disgusting siblings.

Then we talked about (a) whether or not dogs have a sense of the future, (b) gross smells we secretly like (gasoline, skunks), and (c) earbuds versus over-ear headphones. Hardly a sexy, tension-filled conversation, thank God.

Friday, August 12
Barf. Email from Mom.

> Dearest Chloe,
>
> I know you're angry with me, and I respect that. Don't feel you need to respond to this missive—but know I would adore a response, should you be able to muster one.
>
> Javi and I have settled into our new place in San Miguel. We've set aside a bedroom for you. In the evenings, we sit on the balcony and sip tequila while the lights come on, twinkling

across the mountain below us as if mirroring
the stars in the sky.

I've finished the first draft of my novel and have
put it in a drawer, where I intend to leave it for a
while before revisiting it with fresh eyes. While I
wait, I'll deepen my yoga practice. I've found a
charming little studio mere blocks away.

Well, darling, I think of you every minute, and
am sending you so much love.

Yours,
Ever,
Mommy

I started a draft.

Veronica,

Remember that time you ran away to Mexico
to work on your (probably terrible) novel,
abandoning me and Dad? Remember how you
pretended you were only going to be away for
a few months, when you knew you were never
coming back? Remember how you showed up

at our July 4th BBQ with your MUCH-YOUNGER
boyfriend, Javi, and humiliated me in front of
my friends and then told me you and Dad are
getting a divorce? Oh, wait, that all happened in
the past year, so you definitely remember it. I do
too. Don't email me anymore,

—Chloe

But then I deleted it. I don't want to give her the attention. She doesn't deserve it.

Saturday, August 13

Dad was washing the dishes and singing "The Surrey with the Fringe on Top." You wouldn't think it to look at him, since he's a middle-aged lawyer dad who wears collared shirts even on the weekend, but he's really into musicals. It must be hereditary, because I've always loved them too.

He felt me staring at him and stopped.

"Too loud?" he said.

"No, it's nice." I didn't tell him the truth, which is that I'd been standing there worrying about him. I worry about him all the time now. Mostly I picture him dying in a car accident. That's what scares me the most, maybe because it seems like it could actually happen.

Dad said, "I have to head out in a few minutes."

"You're going out? I didn't know that. I would have invited Tris over if—"

"Hang on, Chloe." He turned off the water and looked at me. "I'm meeting Miss Murphy for a drink."

"Oh. OK."

My voice must have sounded funny, because he said, "You did say I should ask her out again, so I thought . . ."

"It's fine. I don't care."

I dried a pan off furiously and then clanged it into a cabinet.

"Chloe. Come on."

"Just . . . Please don't go out around here. I don't want people seeing you and teasing me at school."

"Do you think they would?"

I picked up the colander and examined it. "There's still a bunch of pasta on this thing."

"Oh yeah. Give me a do-over."

I handed it to him.

"They would definitely tease me," I said. "Definitely."

"OK." He was bent over, working with the sponge. "We can drive a few towns over."

I folded the dish towel in half, then in half again. "You know she's my English teacher again this year, right?" I thought for sure she'd keep teaching freshman English, but no, apparently she's going to follow me through high school like a curse.

He nodded without looking at me. "I did see that on your schedule."

I waited, but he didn't say anything else. I don't know what I was expecting. Maybe something like, *I can see how awkward it would be for you to know that the person teaching your favorite subject is also boning your dad.*

After we finished the dishes, I walked upstairs slowly so it wouldn't seem like I was storming off. Why did I even feel like storming off?

I love Miss Murphy. She was mine before she was Dad's. She was my English teacher, and she thought I said smart things about *Ethan Frome*. And she cast me, a mere freshman, as the star of *The Sound of Music*! She's in her thirties, I think, but she still remembers what it was like to be a kid. She's funny and interesting and she used to be a Broadway director before she moved back here to take care of her mom. I admire her.

And I know my mother abandoned my father and started an affair, and what was Dad supposed to do, sit at home crying while she drank beer on the beach with a guy young enough to be her son?

But it still makes me slightly sick to think about them dating people who are not each other.

Sunday, August 14

I think some major sophomore class drama kicked off at the pool today. Reese was the lifeguard on duty. She's the queen of our grade, the kind of girl grown-ups refuse to believe is horrible because she fools them with her performance of bubbly sweetness and they can't perceive the darkness in her soul. She has two dimples she's constantly twinkling at everyone. She wears a lot of purple. Instead of saying something openly cruel, like, "Good gravy, Madeline got huge over the summer," she says something ostensibly kind, like, "I'm so *worried* about Madeline." She rules with an iron fist, but she wants everyone to think she's So Nice.

I'm terrified of Reese. I also desperately want her to like me. I am a disgusting person.

Anyway, a girl showed up at work today first thing in the morning, before it was busy, and immediately ran over to Reese. They both squealed and threw their arms around each other.

Grady elbowed me and tried to show me a sketch he was working on. "It's a giant octopus eating the concession stand," he said. "Look, I put you—"

"SHHHHH," I hissed. I didn't want to miss anything.

"Who is that?" Grady asked, looking where I was looking.

"I don't know yet," I said.

Then Reese shrieked, "How was Paris? Tell me everything!" and I realized.

"Wait," I said. "That's Noelle Phelps!"

Noelle had left for Paris about 90 pounds dripping wet. It was obvious why she was Reese's number two: she worshipped Reese, and she was pretty enough, but not Reese-pretty. She was scrawny and watchful and unsmiling, with mousy brown hair. The person now grinning at Reese was platinum blond and wearing huge glamorous sunglasses. Then Noelle said, "It's so hot I can't stand it!" and whipped off her cover-up.

"Oh my God," I said. "Noelle's boobs came in."

Grady nodded. "I've never seen her before, but she definitely has boobs now."

I covered his eyes with my hand. "Don't be a perv."

"You started it!" he said, and pulled my hand off his face.

Reese ran her eyes over Noelle. "You look amazing," she said thoughtfully, and I thought, *Noelle is screwed.*

Noelle sat next to Reese on the lifeguard chair for hours, which is definitely against the rules, and they talked and laughed the entire time, but I'm not fooled. Noelle is a dead man walking.

Monday, August 15

Grady's three-year-old brother, Bear, showed up at the pool with his babysitter in the afternoon and came tearing over to jump into Grady's arms. Then he looked at me and said, "I like your underwear."

"It's a bikini, buddy," said Grady.

Suddenly bathing suits seemed bizarre. We would never hang around in our undies, so why were we standing a foot away from each other, basically naked, just because we were at the pool?

"He's so cute," I said, watching Bear race over to the kiddie pool. "It's weird—you guys look nothing alike."

"Thanks a lot!"

"No, I meant—I didn't mean you're not cute."

"REALLY!" He made a Sexy Expression at me.

"Get your face out of my face," I said, and pushed him away.

"Bear and I have different dads," he said. "Thanks for making me feel awkward about it."

I gasped. "Oh my God. I'm sorry."

"I'm just messing with you, dork," he said, laughing. "I mean, he *is* my mom's kid with my stepfather, but it's fine. I've had three years to get used to it."

"You are incredibly annoying," I said.

"You love me," he said.

"I really don't."

"You love me so much you want to marry me."

"Stop trying to hug me! You're all sweaty and covered in sunscreen!"

God! He's so immature!

Tuesday, August 16

Dad had to work late, so I invited Tristan over. We ate crackers and cheese for dinner, sitting on a towel in the backyard, coated in bug spray.

"Would it be weird if I went out with a freshman?" I said.

"Who?" Tris said.

"No one in particular."

"Yeah, right."

"Imagine a normal, shortish guy. Would everyone make fun of me?"

Luckily, Grady has happened to be off work the few times Tris has visited me at the pool, or he would have instantly known who I was talking about.

Tris shrugged. "Probably. You know how people are. They'd say you were robbing the cradle."

"It's so ridiculous. No one cares when senior guys go out with freshman girls." I collapsed backward onto the towel. "I hate high school."

Tris collapsed next to me. "I hate it more."

We looked up at the sky, which was still pink.

"Roy's going to a club tonight," Tris said. "With all his new college friends."

I turned my face to look at him, and he turned his to look at me. We were two centimeters apart. I could smell his Tropical Twist Trident. "You're not worried, are you?" I said.

"No. A little bit. I don't know. We FaceTimed twice today. I think he misses me."

"I'm sure he does."

Tris sighed.

I asked, "Do you think your mom told your dad about you and Roy?"

"Probably."

"But you don't know for sure? If she'd told him, wouldn't he talk to you about it?"

Tris laughed. "Are you serious? That's the last thing he'd do. I bet I'll be coming home with my husband and kid in 20 years and he'll still pretend to have no idea what's going on."

"Does it make you sad?" I said.

He shook his head impatiently. "It's fine. Don't worry about it. Tell me what's going on with *your* dad."

"He's dating Miss Murphy again," I said. I wanted to keep asking Tris about his parents, but I didn't want to be annoying or nosy.

"No way. Are you upset?"

"Yeah, but I know I shouldn't be. She's great, or whatever."

"She's great as our director. Not as your stepmother!"

Stepmother!?! Perish the thought.

Wednesday, August 17

Grady spent the whole day quizzing me about high school. How do the locks on the lockers work, again? Right, left, then right, but at what point do you go past the first number? Has anyone ever actually shoved a freshman's head in a toilet and flushed, or is that a suburban legend? Do they hand out a map of the school on the first day? Do teachers get mad if freshmen are late to class because they got lost?

Speaking of questions, is there anything less attractive than someone nervously fretting? I know I was the same way last year. I freely admit it must have been hideously unsexy.

I keep thinking about Mac. I don't want to. I order myself to cut it out, but it doesn't work. It's just that he was so confident. And mean, and thoughtless, and not even very interesting. But the confidence! It canceled out all of his flaws.

Enough of this mooning around. I got over him. I need to *stay* over him.

Thursday, August 18

We got an email from the principal today with a bunch of reminders about parking passes, proof of a recent physical exam for student athletes, school email account access, etc., etc. All this nitty-gritty proof that classes are going to start again made me feel a little queasy, and I was about to delete the email when I saw a shocking announcement in the second-to-last bullet point: they're adding a dance this year! A HALLOWEEN DANCE! Immediately, I texted Hannah and Tris to alert them to this life-altering news.

I don't know if it's like this at every school, but at MH, dances are hotbeds of romance. People flirt. People make out for the duration of slow songs. People grind, which is against the rules, and get separated by a chaperone, only to start grinding again as soon as the chaperone leaves. People get their hearts broken and sob in the bathrooms. It's all very stressful and exciting, and you have to go, first because something amazing might happen to you, and second because even if it doesn't, you need to know what happened to other people so you can be up to speed on the gossip.

All I do is hide in my room and write in this diary. I want to change. I want to go to the Halloween dance, and I want something thrilling to happen to me there. Something I'll remember when I'm 90. Winning the costume contest, or jumping into the center of a dance circle, or, I don't know, making out with someone for the duration of a slow song. I'm writing it in all caps as a promise to myself: I WILL MAKE SOMETHING MEMORABLE HAPPEN AT THE HALLOWEEN DANCE.

Friday, August 19

I was standing by the edge of the pool today when Grady snuck up behind me, scooped me up, and threw me in the water.

"I'm wearing my sneakers, you goober!" I yelled at him when I came up for air. He'd dropped to the grass and was rolling around laughing hysterically. What a child.

My sneakers squished for the rest of the day.

I'm surprised he can lift me. Those pipe cleaner arms are stronger than they look.

Saturday, August 20

Got my revenge on Grady today! I waited until our shift was over and he'd put on his T-shirt. We were walking toward the parking lot, talking about our least favorite customer, a little demon named Paxon who pays for his treats with fifties, when without warning I pushed him into the pool right at the five-foot mark. Oh, the shocked look on his face! I wish I had a picture of it.

Sunday, August 21

Told Hannah about the saga of the pool pushing. She smiled through the whole thing and then said, "That sounds pretty flirty."

"What? No, no, no. It's not like that at all."

"Are you sure?"

"Yes!"

She still looked skeptical. In the spirit of being honest with her, which I wasn't always last year, and which led to us drifting apart, I said, "I guess there's a tiny possibility he likes me."

"And you don't like him?"

"No. Not at all."

She examined my face. "If that's true, you shouldn't flirt with him."

I groaned. "I'm not flirting with him, Hannah."

"You pushed him into the pool."

"Oh my God! Call the romance police!"

"If he really does like you, it's not fair to get his hopes up."

I was about to say something rude, but it occurred to me that as annoying as it is to listen to her lecture me, she's always right about this stuff, so I said I'd think about it. Then we went back to watching YouTube hip-hop tutorials in preparation for the Halloween dance.

Monday, August 22

I went to work determined not to flirt with Grady, which was easy, because Reese was the lifeguard on duty, and first thing in the morning she yelled across the pool, "You guys are so adorable in there! You look like you're playing house!" so of course Grady and I were too embarrassed to even look at each other for most of the day.

During an adult swim, when Reese got a break, she wandered over to steal a Tootsie Pop.

"You know Noelle, right?" she asked me.

"I think so," I said, trying to be cool, although what's so cool about pretending not to know someone who's been in your class since kindergarten?

Reese unwrapped the lollipop. "It's scary how much people can change in such a short time. She's one of my best friends, but I feel like I don't even know her anymore. I'm, like, the last person to slut-shame, but I'm sorry, I don't think it's right to have sex with multiple guys on vacation. I just worry about her health, you know?"

In our bullying workshops, the teachers talk about taking the side of the victim. I could have said, "It sounds like you *are* slut-shaming Noelle, actually." Joking is another option, or "disarming the bully with humor," if you want to get fancy about it. I could have said, "Wow, where do I sign up for a trip to Paris?" I knew all this, but I nodded and said nothing.

Then Grady said, "What's wrong with having sex with multiple guys on vacation?" Either he was truly curious or he's a great actor.

Reese laughed. "You're hilarious, Grady. Anyway,

it's not just that." She looked around like she was checking for eavesdroppers, then leaned forward. Grady and I both leaned toward her. "She hung out with Nevaeh and Nick last night, and Nevaeh said she was fully hitting on Nick. She was wearing this low-cut shirt and Nick couldn't stop staring at her chest. It wasn't his fault. If she doesn't want people to look, she shouldn't flaunt it."

Reese shook her head and gave the lollipop a contemplative lick. "We already had our costume planned for the Halloween dance, but I texted her and told her she needs to find someone else to go with. Which is so sad, but I don't think I can be friends with someone like that."

After she'd gone, Grady whispered, "She is ice cold."

"Right?!" I said. "I knew she wasn't going to stand for a smoking-hot best friend."

"Is Noelle going to take her on?" Grady asked.

"What, like try to dethrone Reese?"

He nodded. He really is fun to talk to about this stuff. He's much gossipier than Hannah, and almost as gossipy as Tristan.

"I would be shocked," I said. "Noelle is basically a sweet person, and Reese is like one of those Roman ladies who poison their enemies. Noelle wouldn't stand a chance."

Grady shook his head. "Poor Noelle. Do you think she really banged a bunch of French dudes?"

I laughed. "No way! No way. But it doesn't matter. She can't prove she didn't, right?"

We both looked across the pool at Reese, who was back on her chair, her face shadowed by her baseball cap, looking serene and beautiful.

Tuesday, August 23

I feel so terrible that I didn't stick up for Noelle even a tiny bit. What's the worst that could have happened? Reese could have decided I'm an enemy and made the next three years of my life a living hell.

That's why people don't take on bullies. Self-preservation. Or just plain selfishness, I guess. I wish I were brave enough to think, *So what if she hates me? I'll live. Standing up for this person is more important than trying to save myself.* That's what a strong, confident person would think. I'm weak and scared. It's gross.

Maybe that's what I could do to make the Halloween dance memorable. I could march up to Reese and say, in front of everyone, "Excuse me, but remember that time you made up a lie about Noelle at the pool and then judged her for something she never even did? That was wrong!"

Yeah, it needs some work. But the basic idea isn't bad.

Wednesday, August 24

Another email from Mom.

> Dearest Chloe,
>
> It is your privilege, as my child, to show me
> you're angry by refusing to respond to me.
> It is my responsibility, as your mother, to
> keep showing you how ardently I love you
> by continuing to write to you even in the face
> of your silence. I'll be in touch soon, whether
> or not you are.
>
> Your faithful correspondent,
> Mom

She is ridiculous. I'm ignoring her.

Thursday, August 25

Hannah and I went to Tris's house after dinner. Hannah's mom dropped her off, pulling up in her SUV right as I arrived on my bike.

"Honey, you should have said you needed a ride," Mrs. Egan cooed out her open window. "I'm always happy to pick you up."

"I like riding my bike. Thanks, though," I said, taking off my helmet. I was lying, of course. Riding my bike is humiliating, and I'm counting down the seconds until I can get my learner's permit. But I know how much Mrs. Egan enjoys pitying me because my mom's away and my dad works late some nights, and I don't want her stupid pity.

Tris and Hannah and I sat in Adirondack chairs in the backyard, watched the stars come out, and tried not to look at our phones too much.

"Do you realize school starts a week from today?" Hannah said.

"I've been so bored all summer," Tris said, "and now I'd give anything to have another two months off."

"School won't be as scary as it was last year," I said. "I mean, it can't be. Right?"

"We know where everything is now," Hannah said.

"And there'll be a new batch of freshmen!" I said. "Automatically, they're lamer than we are."

"True," said Tris.

"Maybe being sophomores will be great," I said, getting into it. "We're past the worst year, but we don't have to start panicking about the SATs or college applications yet."

"I'm panicking about the SATs," Hannah said.

"But by choice," I said. "You enjoy panicking about them. Tris and I can wait until we're juniors."

"I ordered a PSAT prep book last night," Tris said.

"You haven't started studying yet?" Hannah said. "We're taking it in October!"

"Stop! We still have a week of summer left! You're both ruining it!" I said.

"You're right," Tris said. "Let's talk about sunburns or fireworks or something."

We tried, but it was too late, and we wound up discussing the PSAT 10 versus the PSAT/NMSQT until it was time to leave.

Friday, August 26

I think our discussion last night came as a big shock to Hannah. She must have realized Tris and I aren't up to her organizational standards, because she called a planning meeting today.

"What are we planning?" Tris said. It was 4 p.m., and we were sitting in Hannah's living room. She'd made us drop our phones in a woven basket on our way in, and I think she must have hidden the remote controls, because I couldn't find them anywhere.

"Various things!" Hannah said. "I printed out copies of the agenda."

Friday, August 26

Sophomore Year Planning Session

Attendees: Hannah Egan, Tristan Flynn, Chloe Snow

Discussion items:

    Academic goals

    Extracurricular goals

    Personal goals

    Short-range goals (Halloween dance, PSATs)

"How do you even know how to do this?" I asked her.

"I read a blog for parents who want to help their kids do well in school." (Of course she does.) "This one post said it helps to write down your intentions at the beginning of the year so you can refer back to them and make sure you're on track. Here . . ." She passed out notebooks and pens. "OK, first item. What are our academic goals?"

"Stay awake during math," I said.

"Chloe! This isn't going to work unless you take it seriously."

"Fine, Mom," I said, and then instantly felt bad. My actual mother wasn't here to nag me, and my father was too busy to do it. It *was* nice that Hannah was helping us with this. It was more than nice: it was generous and thoughtful.

"Sorry," I said. "I do want to improve in math, for real. And I want to study for the PSATs."

"What GPA do you want to maintain?" Hannah said.

"Um, what's an A-?"

"A 3.7," Hannah said. "OK, write all that down in your notebook. Tris?"

"I want to move up to honors English. And I'll say 3.7 too."

Hannah said she wants to maintain her 4.0 and excel in chemistry and trig so she's set up to get into AP Calculus and AP Chemistry, and possibly AP Bio.

"Moving on to extracurriculars!"

"Do I have to be modest?" Tris said.

"No, be honest," Hannah said.

"I want to be a lead in the musical again," Tris said.

"Me too," I said.

"I probably won't get a good part, but I'll try out for the musical too," Hannah said. She didn't sound self-pitying. She sounded matter-of-fact. "And of course I'll keep volunteering with youth group."

"Can we do personal goals now?" I said. "Because I have a bunch. Number one: I want to learn to drive! Number two: I want to stop thinking about guys so much and focus on more important things." I could feel Hannah and Tris struggling not to give each other meaningful looks. "And number three: I want to be a better friend. Less selfish." I was hoping they'd say, "What are you talking about? You're not selfish!" but they just looked thoughtful and nodded, which made me feel kind of sick.

Tris said, "I want to be low-maintenance with Roy, so he doesn't think of me as a whiny annoyance he has to feel guilty about not calling more."

"I want to abide by my own religious beliefs," Hannah said, and if you didn't know her like Tris and I do, you wouldn't know she actually meant "I don't want to have sex again until I'm married," which makes me worried she's feeling guilty for no reason, but which I didn't say anything about, because hey, it's her goal, and who am I to judge?

We wrote it all down. It felt great, like just by putting our goals on paper, we'd already started carrying them out.

"On to short-range goals," Hannah said. "What are your thoughts on the Halloween dance?"

"Here's what we need to do," I said. "Number one: decide if we're doing a group costume or not. Number two: find out if anyone's having a pre-dance party."

"I want to skip the whole thing," Tris said, before I could get to number three.

"WHAT? You can't!" I said.

"It's going to be too sad, watching everyone else slow-dance and thinking about Roy."

We spent the rest of the night trying to convince him he has to go, and never got around to discussing the PSATs, which was fine by me.

Saturday, August 27

I rode my bike over to Hannah's today without texting first, and who should be there but Zach Chen, guitar-playing dreamboat! Last year, when I was a mere child and had never even kissed anyone, I put him on a list of guys I wanted to make out with. Now here he was, sitting in the kitchen with Hannah and her mom, help-ing Mrs. Egan snap the ends off of green beans (Mrs. Egan is the type of mother who plans meals for the whole week on Sunday and preps dinner ingredients right after lunch is over). "Hey, Chloe," he said when I came in.

"Chloe! Hi! Did we have plans?" Hannah said. She looked terrified.

"No. I wanted to surprise you," I said.

"Are you OK?" Zach asked Hannah. She'd gone pale.

"I'm fine. Chloe, can you show me that thing . . . with your bike?"

"Uh, sure," I said.

We walked out to the garage in silence.

"What's going on?" I asked when she'd pulled the door shut behind us. "That bike ruse was quite some-thing, by the way. You would make a terrible spy."

She looked confused. "You're not mad?"

"About what?"

"About Zach!"

"What, that he's sitting in your kitchen clearly in love with you?"

"You think he's in love with me?" She sounded thrilled.

"Hannah, he's prepping vegetables for your mom. Case closed."

"And you really don't care?"

"This is the kissing-list thing? You don't get to claim someone for all eternity by writing his name down in your diary."

She still looked sick. "You don't . . . you don't like him, do you?"

I put my hands on her shoulders. "Hannah, I swear to you, I don't like him. He's all yours."

"OK. Thank goodness."

We smiled at each other.

"How long have you two been hanging out?" I said.

"We haven't been. This is the second time I've seen him. He picked his sister up from ballet yesterday and wound up giving me a ride home too. Then he texted me today asking if he could stop by. It could turn out to be nothing."

"Uh-huh."

"It could! I don't want to get my hopes up."

"Well, I'll get my hopes up for you."

She gave me a big hug.

Now Hannah will almost certainly have a date for the Halloween dance. I should be happy for her. And

I am! Or if I'm not, I will be soon, as soon as I get over feeling disappointed that we won't get to go in a group of three, like we'd planned.

Sunday, August 28

School starts this Thursday. Summer's essentially over. Why, oh why, did I spend so much of it staring into my phone? Why didn't I work out so I could amaze everyone with my physical transformation? Why didn't I take some hip-hop classes? I could have shown up at the Halloween dance with the moves of a video vixen! And now most likely Miss Murphy will pick *Chicago* and I won't get the lead because I can't handle the choreography. Actually, I should have spent the summer getting up to speed on math. Geometry's coming and I never even grasped the point of algebra. I'm letting down my entire gender being so stereotypically bad at anything STEM-y. What a waste of the two best months of the year! All I did was work on my tan, read, read some more, chat with Grady, eat Dad's dinners, and hang around with Tris and Hannah.

I changed my mind: it was the perfect summer, and now it's over forever.

Monday, August 29

I know what I should have been doing this summer, and I'm embarrassed it took me this long to realize it: I should have been marching, or resisting, or doing something socially conscious. I'm like a satire of a privileged person. What is my problem, exactly? My parents are getting divorced. Whoop-de-doo, it happens to literally half of all kids everywhere. True, not everyone's mother moves to another country, but at least I have a mother. And a father who loves me. I'm not persecuted because of my sexual orientation or gender identity or race. I'm rich compared to almost everyone else in the world. And yet all I do is whine and obsess about myself. I want to do more, or at the very least, I want to remember how lucky I am every single minute.

Tuesday, August 30

Uhhhhhhh, Mac texted me.

> - whats up sophomore? Hope ur good. Miss you kid.

A thoughtful text wondering how I'm doing and expressing affection? Did someone steal his phone?

Maybe college has already changed him! That's a thing that happens. Maybe he's realized he made a mistake, messing around with me and then abandoning me. People make mistakes. I certainly do! And you have to forgive people, not hold a grudge against them forever.

I texted back, *I miss you too!* I keep making my screen dark and then unlocking my phone so I can look at the exchange again, like it will have somehow changed in the 30 seconds since I last studied it.

There's no reason to feel so sick with excitement. Nothing has changed. Mac is still a grade-A sleazer who broke my heart. He still has a girlfriend. He's still away at college.

But he texted me!

Wednesday, August 31

Something awful happened.

Grady and I were at work. It was hot and still. No breeze. The trees drooped over the pool, looking exhausted. I kept zoning out and missing what Grady was saying. The third time I asked him to repeat himself, he said, "What's wrong?"

"Oh . . ." I contemplated lying, but then decided, *Eff it.* "Mac texted me yesterday."

"Mac. Your boyfriend from last year."

"Uh, not my boyfriend, exactly, but yeah."

Grady stared across the pool. Reese was sitting on her white lifeguard chair near the shallow end, rebraiding her hair while she watched some kids play chicken.

"What did he say?"

"Nothing. Just that he misses me."

"What did you say?"

I glanced at him. He wouldn't meet my eye. The whole conversation felt like it was happening in a dream. Grady sounded so serious and quiet, and I knew why, and I didn't know what to do about it.

"I said . . . I said I missed him too."

"So you still like him."

"No. I mean, I don't want to. And I don't. I don't know. It's confusing."

He turned to look at me. *Don't say it*, I thought. *Don't, don't, don't.*

"Chloe, you know I like you, right?"

His deep-set eyes. His tangled eyelashes. Plus crazy cheekbones and a full mouth. And more than that, his niceness, his funniness, his easy-to-talk-to-ness. But when I look at him, I think, *You're sweet.* When I looked at Mac, I thought, *I want to put your entire body inside my mouth.*

"Grady . . . ," I said, and I saw from his expression he knew what I was going to say next.

"OK," he said. "I had to tell you. Don't worry about it."

"You're one of my best friends."

He flinched. I should have stopped talking, but I couldn't.

"I really like talking to you," I said. "And being with you."

"I know. You've been flirting with me all summer," he said, sounding angry.

"I have not!" I said, even though of course I have.

"Whatever."

How long had this conversation been going on? It felt like the summer had ended, a year had passed, and we'd slogged through a whole other summer.

I tried to count backward from 10 to calm myself down, and gave up at 7. "You're a lot younger than me. I don't see you that way."

He barked out a laugh. "Yeah, OK. I get it."

"Grady."

"It's fine, Chloe. Let's talk about something else."

But we couldn't. We barely said two words to each other for the rest of the day.

Reese came over during the last adult swim and said, "Look at you two in here. So cute! When are you going to make it official?"

"Do you want a Popsicle or something?" I said.

"No thanks. I'm good. Can you believe this is our last day of work? Wait, let me get a selfie with you guys. My little pool buddies!"

When she left, Grady said, "The worst," and I said, "The *worst*," and we almost smiled at each other, so that was good, but oh, Grady.

Thursday, September 1

First day of school. Smiling teachers, clean classrooms, everyone hugging and saying hi in the halls. It'll all fall apart within two weeks, but it's nice for now.

I was dreading seeing Grady, but when I finally did, right after the last class of the day, it was fine. He was with some friends, and he was wearing his cutoff Dickies, Vans, and a black T-shirt. It was strange to see him fully clothed. I said hi first, but he said it back right away. For a second, after we'd passed each other, I thought I might cry. Probably the trauma of being back at school had gotten to me.

Grady's friends were loud and cute and dressed like him—punk/skater types. I wonder where they fall in their class's social system. If I had to guess, I'd say they aren't popular and they claim not to care about being popular and for the most part they genuinely don't care. Because they're confident and have a distinct style, they're probably respected by the aristocrats in their grade, and will gain power over their four years of high school as everyone in their class slowly realizes that the jocky, purportedly cool kids have excellent hand-eye coordination and are great at making other people hate themselves but are otherwise talentless and boring. But it's just a guess.

After dinner, I took Snickers for a walk. We went past the pool. The gate is pulled shut and locked for the season. Someone—probably Reese—had taped up an 8.5 x 11 sheet of notebook paper Sharpied with SEE YOU NEXT SUMMER! and a smiley face. It's odd knowing

I won't see Grady at work anymore. I keep thinking of things I have to tell him and then remembering I won't get the chance. I guess I could text him—we have each other's numbers—but we've never texted anything beyond *running late see you in 10 min* or *forgot to cash out can you do it?*

I looked down at Snickers's little Boston terrier butt, waggling along without a care in the world. I wish I were a dog.

Friday, September 2

The only thing scarier than seeing Grady was seeing Miss Murphy. I walked into honors English today feeling like there was a 67% chance I was going to develop anxiety diarrhea.

Miss Murphy was leaning against the whiteboard saying hi to everyone, and when I came in, she said "Nice to see you, Chloe" in a friendly, plain way. No extra eye contact, no meaningful look, no apologetic tone in her voice.

As an icebreaker, she asked us to go around the room and say our name, our favorite book, and our favorite word. When it was my turn, I said, "I'm Chloe Snow. My favorite book is *Prep*. My favorite word is 'moxie.'" Miss Murphy smiled and said, "That sounds about right."

I studied her as she stood in front of us, laughing

and crossing her arms while she listened. She was wearing a white Oxford shirt, green pants, and brown loafers. She didn't have makeup on. She had a tan. She also had some wrinkles around her eyes, but they looked nice, like she got them from being a happy person.

I miss my stupid mother.

Saturday, September 3

As we were eating lunch yesterday, Tris lowered his voice and said, "Did you hear Noelle had a threesome while she was in Paris?"

"Oh my God," I said. "That never happened."

"You don't have to bite my head off," Tris said.

"You can't spread this rumor. You have to promise me," I said.

"I promise," he said. "Are you suddenly friends with Noelle or something?"

"I've probably said five words total to her in my life," I said. "But Reese is trying to destroy her, and it's not right."

"Reese wouldn't do that," Hannah said, sounding shocked.

"She's already doing it, Hannah," I said. I crumpled up my brown paper bag. "She's not even a good liar, but it doesn't matter! A *threesome*? Next she'll say Noelle banged some guy at the top of the Eiffel Tower while eating a baguette and wearing a beret, and everyone will believe her. And why are people so judgmental? If Noelle had a threesome—which she didn't—but if she did, good for her!"

"I agree! Geez!" said Tris. I texted him and Hannah later to apologize. I wish I hadn't snapped at them. If I'm going to snap at anyone, it should be myself. Maybe I could have nipped this whole thing in the bud by standing up to Reese at the pool that day.

Sunday, September 4

Tris is in Rhode Island with his parents for the long weekend, so Hannah and I had a girls-only sleepover at my house. We made ice cream sundaes, which we've been doing since we were eight. She puts peanuts on hers, because she's a mutant. We were sitting at the island in the kitchen, and I was halfway through my sundae (extra whipped cream, no peanuts, for the love of God) when I noticed she was sitting there staring into space, not eating.

"Are you OK?" I said.

"I think I messed up with Zach."

"Go on," I said.

"He stopped by again today, and we sat on the back porch, and it was really fun, and we were kind of flirting, and we started talking about our exes."

I nodded. I know the old talking-about-your-exes

move. Not that I have any exes to talk about.

"So he was telling me about Ellie Rajavi and complaining that she hated going to Deposed Monarchs shows, which is crazy, because they're an amazing band. I really think Zach could be a professional musician. Anyway, and then he said, 'Didn't you come to a show last year with Josh?' and we started talking about Josh, and I kind of got carried away."

She poked a peanut with her spoon.

"Carried away how?"

"I told him how much I loved Josh, and how amazing he is, and how I'm almost positive he cheated on me at Prospective Students' Weekend. And how I lost my virginity to him."

She looked at my face to see how I was reacting.

"You think I shouldn't have said that stuff, right?"

"What? No, it's fine! It sounds like you feel comfortable with him."

"I do, but maybe it was too soon to be so honest."

I said, "How did he react?"

"He said, 'Oh, uh, OK.' Like that. Kind of shocked and quiet. And then he said he had to go."

Snickers came into the kitchen and flopped down at our feet dramatically, like he knew it was too much to hope for that we'd share our food, so he was going to preemptively die of sadness on the floor.

Hannah said, "Do you think he'll stop liking me because I'm not a virgin?"

"If he does, he's not good enough for you."

"I wonder if he'll tell anyone."

"He wouldn't," I said, even though for all I know, he might.

"I hate thinking about people finding out," she said. "Not because I'm ashamed. Because everyone would be so surprised, and so excited to be surprised. 'Hannah, the super-religious girl? No way!' People love finding out they had the wrong idea about you all along."

"No one has the wrong idea about you," I said. "You still *are* a super-religious girl."

"I guess that's true," she said, and started eating her sundae.

Monday, September 5

Another email from Mom.

> Hello darling,
>
> We had a massive thunderstorm here last night, and the internet went down, so I'm writing to you now from the library, which has a small, stuffy computer room and two tiny machines

that can access the world wide web verrrrry
slowly, as if they're hobbling through it on
walkers. Ah, the sacrifices I make to (attempt to)
reach my sweet daughter!

This morning it occurred to me that today is
Labor Day, and Americans everywhere are
soaking up the last drops of summer. It's
always odd to remember these holidays here,
where they go unremarked and uncelebrated.
I hope you're putting your day off to good
use: reading, walking, contemplating. Don't
waste the sunshine watching old movies with
your father! I wish I were there to exhort you
in person.

All my love,
Mom

For one thing, she definitely went to the library
because she's addicted to the internet and couldn't make
it one day without checking Twitter. Emailing me had
nothing to do with it. For another thing, I went for a bike
ride *and* walked around the arboretum this morning, and
Dad is outside mowing the lawn right now, but I'm going
to force him to come inside and watch *An American in*

Paris with me before it gets dark, to spite her. For a third thing, if she wished she were here so much, she could be. It's called an airplane.

Tuesday, September 6

I saw Grady getting books out of his locker today, and without thinking about it, I went to talk to him.

"How's freshman year? As bad as you thought?" I said.

"It's OK."

"No one's flushed your head in a toilet?"

"Not so far."

Was he mad at me, or just being quiet?

We stared at each other without speaking. At the pool, when a silence fell, it wasn't stressful, because we knew we were trapped together for eight hours and of course there were going to be silences sometimes.

He closed his locker. "I'm headed upstairs. You?"

Even though I *was* headed upstairs, I said no, because our conversation was so stilted and I couldn't take the contrast between happy-chatty-sweating-summer Chloe and Grady and awkward-quiet-chilly-September Chloe and Grady.

Wednesday, September 7

Roy tweeted a GIF of a sobbing animated Ariel from *The Little Mermaid* and captioned it "missing bb like . . ."

Tris was beside himself with joy. I wonder what it's like to know you have a boyfriend and he loves you.

He's still saying he doesn't want to go to the Halloween dance, and I'm trying to respect his feelings, but if Hannah winds up going with Zach, and Tris won't go at all, that means I'll have to . . . go by myself?! I mean, I guess technically I could, but how would that work? Would I inch up to groups of people and hope they turn around and say, "Oh, hello, Chloe! We didn't see you there! Would you like to join our conversation?" I want to have the courage to go alone. Maybe I can find it. I still have a month and a half left to transform myself into a confident, unself-conscious person.

Thursday, September 8

I did something a tiny bit brave today. Classes were over, and I was getting my stuff together at my locker. Noelle was a few lockers away talking to Harper, the only one of the popular girls who still associates with her. I have a sixth sense for Noelle now, maybe because I feel so guilty about not defending her, or maybe because her platinum hair makes her noticeable. I'm constantly spotting her in the halls, and I have to say, she's an impressive sight. When everyone was talking about me last year, I scuttled around staring at the floor, trying to make myself invisible. Noelle walks with her shoulders back and her eyes straight ahead. She always has her hair blown out and her eye makeup on. She looks tense, but dignified.

As I put my math book in my backpack, Reese rounded the corner with her friend Lianna, spotted Noelle, and came right up to her.

"Noelle, so sorry to interrupt, but Lianna and I have something private to discuss with Harper."

I could tell from Lianna's excited, surprised face that Reese was making this up on the spot and that there was no private thing at all.

Noelle flinched, but said, "I'm talking to Harper right now." She looked at Harper for backup, but Harper wouldn't make eye contact.

"Um, it can't really wait," said Reese. "So if you could give us some privacy?"

Noelle stood her ground for another moment, but then she lost her nerve. "Whatever," she said, and turned to leave.

"Hey, Noelle!" I heard myself calling, before I'd had time to think it through.

Everyone turned to look at me. I slammed my locker shut and jogged over to Noelle. I linked my arm through hers, pulled her down the hall, and whispered, "Laugh."

"What?" she whispered back.

"Ha! Ha! Ha!" I said. "That's *hilarious*!"

"Hahaha!" she said, catching on. Her fake laugh was much better than mine. "Are you serious? That's so funny!"

We didn't look back, but I could feel Reese burning holes in our heads with her eyes.

We turned the corner and kept laughing for a while, then kept walking in silence, but with our arms still linked. Finally we stopped outside an empty classroom.

"Thanks," Noelle said. "That was nice of you."

"No problem," I said. "My friend did the same thing for me last year. I just stole his idea."

She looked like she would have smiled if she weren't so miserable.

"I'm sorry Reese is . . ." I paused, not sure how to finish my sentence. "Punishing you for being beautiful"? "Torturing you"? "Singling you out because tyrants need enemies to maintain their grip on power"? I couldn't figure it out on the spot, so I abandoned my opening and said, "Are you OK?"

She toggled her hand back and forth like so-so. "I've been better."

"I don't know if you know this, but all the seniors hated me last year because I hooked up with Mac Brody."

"Yeah, I wanted to ask you about that."

It's hard to explain how weird this conversation was. In high school, everyone pretends not to know what's happening outside of their immediate friend group, even though we all know what everyone else is doing and who they're dating and who got moved down a level in history because he was flunking out of AP. Noelle and I have never been friends. We don't even say hi to each other in the halls. And now we'd admitted we know all about each other. I think being alone after school had something to do with it. It felt like we'd stepped out of time, and so it was OK to talk about real stuff.

"Sure, ask me anything," I said.

"What did you do when everyone was gossiping about you? Did anything work?"

"Nothing made people stop talking. But I deleted Facebook and Twitter and everything for a while. That helped."

"Yeah, I should probably do that. My mentions are a freaking disaster."

"Don't even look."

"You're right. I shouldn't."

She fidgeted with her backpack strap. "Sorry I didn't say hi to you at the pool this summer," she said. "I don't know why I didn't."

It had never occurred to me that she would say hi to me. Of course she wouldn't—I'm a nobody. I was shocked that it had crossed her mind, and even more shocked that apparently she felt guilty about ignoring me.

"I know why!" I said. "Because you're popular."

She laughed. "Not anymore."

Normally I would have contradicted her, to be nice, but since we were being honest, I said, "What does it feel like? To be popular and then not?"

"It sucks!" she said. We both laughed.

"I have to go," she said. "But put your number in my phone."

After I did it, she took it back and texted me: *It's Noelle.*

I texted her back, *It's me Chloe the person standing right next to you.*

She texted back, *Bonjour.*

Then we texted smiley faces back and forth, and then we smiled at each other in real life, and then we really did leave.

Friday, September 9

I think I might be friends with Noelle now? After school she texted me, *What are you up to*, and I texted back, *Creeping on you* with the googly eyes emoji, because she happened to be in my line of sight in the lobby. She looked up from her phone and came over.

"How was your day?" I said, and she said, "Horrible," so I knew we didn't have to revert to being polite and fake even though we were no longer in the magical empty minutes inside the magical empty hallway. We leaned against the wall while she told me Harper's no longer speaking to her. "She gave me this apologetic expression as she walked past with Reese and everyone, and it was like, you obviously don't feel that bad or you'd come over to say hi."

Noelle said she had to go or she was going to miss her bus, so we went outside, but the buses were already gone, so we sat on the curb and talked about her options for feeling better. I said she must have friends besides the popular kids, and she said Lauren Englander, Maisie Tillinghast, Yvette Brown, a few other kids. "And the popular guys probably still like you, right?" I said.

"Maybe. But none of them are my *friend* friends."

"What about Thalia Rosen?" Thalia is this girl Reese banished last year for supposedly having a crush on Reese's brother, which Reese said was "crossing a line" and "such a betrayal."

Noelle sighed. "I guess."

"What's wrong with Thalia?" I asked.

"Can I tell you something?" she said. "It's kind of boring, hanging out with the B-list."

"WHAT!"

"You hate me, right?"

"No, I just can't believe you're admitting it. Wait, am I B-list, or C-list?"

She looked at me like she was considering it. "It's like you're not on a list." I started to freak out. "No, but in a good way! You were the lead in the musical last year. That was weird, but kind of interesting. People know your name. I don't associate you with a particular group."

"That's because I have, like, no friends. Before yesterday, what did you think when you heard my name?"

"The musical . . . senior drama . . . had sex with Mac."

"I didn't!"

"No?"

"Seriously, no! Is that what everyone thinks?"

She shrugged. "It's not a bad thing."

"I know. I'm just surprised."

"What did you think when you heard my name?" she asked.

"Popular . . . second banana to Reese . . . kind of shy. But that was last year. After you got back from France, I would have said popular and hot. What happened to you in France, anyway?"

"I didn't have a threesome."

"I know that! I'm just saying, you seemed like a different person when you came back."

"My mom's friend and her daughter took me shopping, and maybe it's shallow, but I kind of do feel like a different person when I'm wearing French clothes. And obviously I changed my hair."

"It looks amazing," I said, and she said, "Thanks"— but fast and almost bored, like she was expecting the compliment. For a second I remembered why she was popular for so many years, and wondered if I could ever actually like her. But then she said, "I don't know . . . it's not just that. I hung out with all these French kids while I was there, and went to the Louvre and read a book in the Luxembourg Gardens, and I realized, oh, our high school isn't the only place in the universe! You know? Like, all these little dramas and whatever, they're that— they're little. They're tiny."

"So is it helping you now, to remember that?"

She laughed. "Not really. But if I can't sleep at night, I tell myself, 'You can move to Paris someday.'"

We talked for almost an hour, sitting there on the curb.

Saturday, September 10

It was boiling hot today and we already have hours of homework thanks to our sadistic teachers, and yet Dad still made me help him with yard work all fricking day.

"I hate this," I said, dragging a garbage bag full of sticks past him and toward the garage.

"I know," he said cheerfully. "Hey, you're sleeping over at Hannah's house tonight, right?"

"Yes," I said. "Why?"

"Just wanted to make sure you'd be all right if I go out."

I was sweaty and covered in grass clippings and dirt. My hair kept falling out of my elastic and into my face, and I'd ripped my beloved OTTER TAIL COUNTY FAIR WEST T-shirt while pulling a dead branch out of a tree. Meanwhile, Dad was literally whistling.

"Who are you going out with? Miss Murphy?" I asked spitefully.

He'd been crouched down, trying to free a shovel from where it was trapped behind the lawn mower. In the few seconds it took him to slowly stand up and turn to face me, I had time to deeply regret asking the question.

"I am," he said. "Is that OK with you?" He wasn't being a dick. He was genuinely asking.

Is it OK with me? I mean, no. Not at all. I want Dad to stay single forever. I want him to keep going on runs by himself and grilling two steaks for us on Saturday nights and fighting with me about whose turn it is to walk Snickers. If he falls in love with someone else, everything will change, and he'll really never get back together with Mom.

"It's kind of weird," I said.

He gripped the shovel gently, like it was the hand

of someone he likes. "I've been thinking about it, and here's my plan. Number one: she and I won't have any sleepovers," he said.

"DAD!" I said, and pretended to throw up.

"Hang on. We won't have any sleepovers, and you won't have to spend time with her outside of school. And I won't bring it up—dating her—but you can ask me anything you want."

"No sleepovers and no hanging out until when?" It was nice, it was considerate, but it also made me furious. He was going to be her boyfriend but hide it from me? What was I, some baby he had to protect from real life? And how long did he think this would work? Were they going to get married secretly and not invite me in case it hurt my feelings?

"Uh, until we all feel comfortable," he said.

I stomped off and swept the back patio so vigorously I think I pulled my groin.

I have to stop this and pull myself together. Mom lives in Mexico! I like Miss Murphy! What is my problem?

Sunday, September 11

It's still uncomfortably hot (thanks for ruining our planet, previous generations), so Tris's mom drove us to the mall and went off to look for work clothes at Ann Taylor while Tris and I strolled around keeping an eye out for cute guys.

"You didn't tell your mom about my dad and Miss Murphy, did you?" I asked.

"No," he said.

Tris's mother isn't like Mrs. Egan—she wouldn't immediately text all her friends, saying, *Did you hear about Charlie Snow and that English teacher? Poor Chloe.* But she might talk to Mr. Flynn about it, and they might agree that my dad and Miss Murphy make sense as a couple, or that it seems a little soon for him to be dating, or that it must be awkward for me at school, or whatever. It doesn't matter what their analysis is. The point is, to them it's something interesting to discuss over dinner, whereas to me it's a disaster.

Monday, September 12

As I was passing Grady's locker, Reese came along in the other direction. I thought she might be out to get me after I publicly sided with Noelle, but apparently I got away with it, because she crossed traffic to dart over and pull me and Grady into a hug. "POOL REUNION!" she squealed. She smells amazing, like things that are so fancy I don't even know they exist. Honey roses. Cloud soap. Sea diamonds.

"Chloe, you're friends with Hannah, right?" she said, staring into my face. She's like a snake charmer: when her eyes are on you, you feel you have to do whatever she asks.

I nodded yes.

She gripped my upper arm. "She was at field hockey tryouts yesterday. She's really good. And she's really, really pretty!"

Classic Reese: subtly reminding me she's already co-captain of the field hockey team, even though she's an underclassman, then saying something that seems nice (Hannah is pretty) but might be an insult (does she mean I'm ugly?), or might simply be a statement of fact (Hannah IS pretty!), and why are you so insecure and paranoid that you interpret every offhanded remark as a dig at you?

"You smell amazing," I blurted out. Groveling at her feet like a peasant! Gross!

She threw her head back and laughed, showing us her blindingly white teeth. "You are so adorable," she said. "I've got to run, cuties." She made intense eye contact with me, then with Grady, then sashayed away.

Grady and I looked at each other. "I hate her," I said.

He shook his head. "I'm glad I'm not a girl."

Tuesday, September 13

Hannah called tonight and said Zach is being polite to her in the halls, but he doesn't talk to her alone and he hasn't texted her at all. "I should never have told him I'm not a virgin," she said.

I went bananas. "If he's not interested in you anymore because you're a woman of the world, then FORGET HIM. What is he, some kind of saint? Is *he* a virgin?"

"I don't know."

"He probably *is* a virgin, and he's probably intimidated by you. Well, his loss!" I was pacing around my room, shouting.

"You can't blame him for the way he feels."

"Oh yes, I most certainly can! I blame him big-time! Your sexual history is none of his business."

I kept ranting like this for a while, but it didn't have any effect. She was as sad and quiet when we got off the phone as she was when she called. God, I hate our stupid backward hypocritical woman-hating slut-shaming puritanical culture.

Wednesday, September 14

Tris and I were cutting across the baseball diamond to pick Hannah up from field hockey practice and I was checking for new likes, but subtly, with my phone by my hip, because it drives Tristan insane when I look at my phone when we're talking (which I get, because I hate it when he looks at *his* phone when we're talking), and when I looked up, there was Grady, a few feet away, walking toward us.

Something about Tris by my side made me feel

confident and show-offy, and being outside reminded me of summer, before everything got awkward and we started wearing actual clothes, and Grady looked so Grady-ish, and, well, I found myself rushing up to him and squeezing his face.

"Hi, Chloe," he said. He looked confused.

"Hi! What are you doing here?"

"Coming back from the clearing."

The clearing is a little plot of land hidden by the trees lining the fields. The skaters and potheads and emo kids go there to smoke cigarettes and weed, which the teachers know about but don't bother to crack down on, I think because the kids are at least being respectful enough to hide.

Was Grady smoking cigarettes and weed already? The thought of it stressed me out.

"I'm Tristan," Tris said.

"Sorry," I said. "Grady, this is my friend Tristan. Tris, this is Grady."

"Whoa, Tristan!" Grady said. "No way. I feel like I'm meeting a celebrity. Chloe talks about you constantly."

"Oh!" said Tris, looking delighted.

"I gotta run, but it was nice to meet you, man." He looked at me without smiling. "See you guys around."

Tris and I walked away in silence. I was dying to strike up a sparkling conversation, so Grady wouldn't think we were waiting until he was out of earshot to start talking about him, but I couldn't think of a single thing to say, probably because of the barrage of meaningful glances and elbow prods coming from Tris. "Stop!" I hissed. What if Grady turned around and saw Tris madly poking me in the ribs?

"Who was that?" Tris hissed back.

"Shhhh."

"Is that the freshman you were talking about?"

"SHHHHH."

Finally we made it a respectable distance away, and I said, "That's the guy I worked with at the pool, OK?"

Tris turned around to stare at his retreating back. "Are you serious?"

"Yeah. So?"

"Chloe, he's hot!"

"You think?"

"Yes. Obviously. It's not subjective."

"I guess."

"I cannot believe you didn't tell me about this before. So what happened? Did he turn you down?"

I was kind of offended. "No, he likes me," I said. "Or he did, anyway. He told me on our last day of work."

"And?"

"I told him I see him as a friend."

Tris stopped dead in right field. "WHAT?"

"It's the truth!"

Tris stared at me for a while. When we finally started walking, I said, "Also, Mac had just texted me saying he misses me."

We stopped walking again. At this rate, we were going to be two hours late to pick up Hannah. "You're not serious," Tris said.

"I know, I know, I know."

"I'm going to show up at Mac's school and break all his fingers so he can't use his phone. You realize it's never going to work out with you and him, right?"

"You think he doesn't really miss me?"

Tris groaned. "Maybe he did miss you in that moment. Or maybe he was bored, or drunk. He's playing college football! Imagine what his life is like right now. He probably has to wheel a giant suitcase full of condoms wherever he goes. And besides, remember what happened, like, four months ago? Remember how he crapped all over your heart?"

"Even if Mac didn't exist, I wouldn't be into Grady. He's not my type, OK? He's too young and short and . . . Those are my reasons."

"First of all, too short? He's probably not done growing!"

"Gross."

"Second of all, could you be any more shallow, please?"

I know he's right. And I don't actually care about Grady's height. Objectively speaking, Grady is way cuter than Mac. If a mom saw a picture of Grady in a year-book, she would say, "Whoa, who's that handsome kid?" *and* he likes me, *and* he's smart and interesting and nice. So it makes no sense that I'm not into him. I'm not even sure why I feel the way I do. I just know that Mac makes me light up like a Christmas tree, and Grady doesn't.

"Maybe it's shallow," I said, "but he's not for me."

"If that's how you feel, that's how you feel."

"It is."

"Fine. As long as you're not choosing a meaningless text over a nice guy who actually likes you."

We started walking. I scuffed my feet through the grass angrily.

"You don't even know Grady," I said. "You just like him because he called you a celebrity."

"You're right. I don't know him. He seems nice, but we only talked for a few seconds. Is he a jerk? Or weird, or moody, or conceited?"

"No, he's great."

Tris pointedly didn't say anything.

When we got close to Hannah, we saw that she was talking to Reese, who was wearing a skintight athleisure top and tiny shorts/underpants.

I was hoping Reese's outfit would distract Tris from

Grady, but no, as soon as the three of us were alone, he said, "Hannah, do you know about this Grady thing?"

Hannah said, "Grady from the pool? The really cute one with the hair that sticks up?" which didn't help at all.

Thursday, September 15
Have I made a huge mistake?

Friday, September 16
Tris shakes his head sadly whenever he sees me, sometimes when I'm in the middle of talking about something important, like global warming, or how many likes my latest Instagram got.

Saturday, September 17
My long-running and formerly witty group text with Hannah and Tris has devolved into Tris sending around pictures of Grady's face, creepily screengrabbed from social media.

Sunday, September 18
Noelle invited me over after lunch, so I rode my bike to her house. I felt nervous. We've been talking between classes, and texting a little bit, but hanging out on the weekend is a whole other step.

Her house turned out to be close to Tris's—a McMansion, like his. All of the furniture was white and gray, and there wasn't much of it. The shades were pulled halfway down, and the air smelled stale. I asked Noelle if her parents were out, and she said her dad lives in Maryland and her mother was away on a business trip. "She's a consultant for tech start-ups, so she travels a lot."

"Who stays with you while she's gone?"

Noelle gave me a weird look and said, "No one," which made me feel like a baby, since I hate being home alone even for one night.

I'm desperate to talk to anyone whose parents are divorced, because I want to know what it's like. So I asked, "Is it tough, having your dad all the way in Maryland?"

But she just shrugged and said, "I'm used to it. Want a Diet Coke?"

She grabbed two cans from the fridge, and we went outside to sit on the deck. She got out a pack of cigarettes. I shook my head no when she offered me one. I can't believe anyone smokes. Apart from the lung cancer, etc., it gives you wrinkles! I'm not cute enough to risk that. I need all the help I can get.

"How long have you smoked?" I asked Noelle.

"Oh, I don't, really," she said. "I'm just having one."

But she looked very practiced and efficient. She got through her cigarette fast.

She still scares me a little.

We spent most of the afternoon talking about Reese. Noelle said they've been friends since they took a dance class together in kindergarten, and every four years or so, Reese turns on her. "But this time is different," Noelle said. "Making up rumors about me, spreading them all over school? I'll never forgive her."

Noelle answered all my burning questions. Yes, Reese keeps up the nice act with her friends. Yes, she talks about everyone behind their backs, but under the guise of being concerned about them. Yes, she hates everyone who's not in her squad, although she'd never admit it. Yes, she's turned down most of the popular guys in our grade, and several juniors and seniors.

It was an interesting conversation at the time, but now that it's over and I'm home, I feel gross, like I read back-to-back issues of gossip magazines all afternoon.

Monday, September 19

I happened to see Grady at his locker today.

"Hey!" I said, grabbing his arm.

"Hey."

"What do you have next period?"

"Spanish."

We talked about Señora Friedman and her Shakira obsession for a few minutes, and then he said he had to go.

"I feel like I never see you anymore!" I said.

"Besides nearly every day at school?"

"No, but I mean *see* you, see you."

He didn't say anything.

"I thought you were one of my besties," I said, and instantly loathed myself. I've never uttered the word "besties" in my life, and only used it with Grady because I was feeling so awkward and nervous that I was trying to transform into some other person on the spot.

"I am," he said. "But, Chloe . . ." He stopped, looking upset.

And then one of his skater friends came along and said, *"Vamos a clase"* in a terrible accent. Grady hesitated but then headed off to Spanish class.

"But, Chloe" what??? Now I'll never know.

Tuesday, September 20

Grady found me right before fourth period and said, "Can I talk to you for a second?"

"Sure."

The girl at the locker next to Grady's turned to look at us, like she was excited to hear what he'd say next.

"Um, hang on." Grady put his hand on my lower back and guided me down the hall.

Grady is touching me. Grady is touching me. Grady is touching me, my brain announced. I don't know why it seemed so different, when I spent the entire summer pushing him out of my way and feeling nothing but irritation whenever his sweaty naked torso got between me and the freezer, but it did.

We wandered around for a while without talking and finally ducked underneath the open staircase. Class was starting and the hallways were emptying out. We were going to be late, but I didn't care.

"Uh, how are you?" he said.

"Oh, fine, fine," I said. "And you?"

"I'm just dandy," he said. We smiled at each other, and for a second it felt like we were in the concession stand again.

"Don't freak out," he said. "I'm not going to tell you I like you again."

"OK." I should have felt relieved, but I didn't.

"I get that you're not into me. And that's fine. I mean, I have no idea why you'd turn down all of this." He swept his hand around his body like a game show hostess showing off a prize. It was so nice of him, to go to all the effort of making a self-deprecating joke at such a tense moment.

He looked into my eyes. "But, Chloe, I don't think I can be friends with you right now."

"Oh." The inside of my chest got icy. "Why not?"

"I don't know. I wish we could go back to the way things were before, but I can't."

I'd never heard him sound this serious before. It made him seem older.

He said, "It just makes me feel like garbage, seeing you and, like, flirting at our lockers." He looked into my eyes. "You understand, right?"

"I guess."

"It's like being starving and staring at a big pepperoni pizza you're not allowed to eat. Not that I think you're a pepperoni pizza. You know what I mean."

I nodded.

"Obviously I still want to say hi to you in the halls. We don't have to ignore each other or anything."

I nodded.

"Are you all right?" he said, maybe because it was obvious I was trying not to cry.

I nodded.

"OK," he said uncertainly. "Well . . . sorry if this was awkward."

We stared at each other, and he hugged me quickly, and pulled back to look into my eyes again, and then walked away.

Wednesday, September 21

I called Tristan, and then I called Hannah, but I didn't wind up telling either of them what Grady said. I'm not sure why. I couldn't.

If he's starving for pizza, that means he still likes me, right?

He *is* nice, and he *is* cute, and I *do* love hanging out with him. But he doesn't make me feel sick with excitement, the way Mac does! I want to feel sick.

What is wrong with me?

I wish I could keep hanging around Grady's locker and squeezing his face and flirting with him until I figure out how I feel about him. But of course I see how unfair that is. Mac did that to me, and it was awful.

Maybe I make Grady feel as sick as Mac made me!

I shouldn't be happy about that.

WHAT IS WRONG WITH ME?

Thursday, September 22

Saw Grady in the hall today and we nodded at each other with somber faces, like we were crossing paths at a funeral. I guess this is how things are going to be from now on.

Friday, September 23

Tris and Hannah and I went to the football game tonight. I don't understand the rules, I don't care about any of the players now that Mac's in college, and I know the sport causes brain damage and mental illness, so why do I enjoy the games so much? I love everything about them: Showing up at school in the dark and heading toward the floodlights in a crowd of happy kids and parents. Sitting on the metal bleachers. Buying a snack. Watching the halftime show—all those earnest kids marching around in red-and-white uniforms, bravely risking getting teased to do something they enjoy (and why do people tease them?! They're amazing!). Talking to people in my class I don't know very well. Running back to Hannah and Tris when I need a break from talking to people I don't know very well. Whispering to Hannah and Tris about Grady and Roy and Zach. Seeing who's flirting and who's not speaking to each other and who's obviously having a fight even though they're keeping their voices down and trying not to look upset (Luke Powers and Danielle de Vincenzo). I even liked seeing Grady with his friends, because it made my chest ache in a way that almost felt good. He had his skateboard with him and was trying to do some trick that involved spinning it between his feet. He kept falling down and laughing and trying it again. He didn't look my way. Maybe he didn't see me.

Saturday, September 24
Of course he saw me. He didn't want to look at me, that's all.

Sunday, September 25

Went to Hannah's and we wound up stalking boys online, like we always do. She wanted to look at pictures of Judgmental Zach, which I discouraged, but you can't keep a girl with a smartphone away from photos of the guy she loves but shouldn't. Unfortunately, there was a new album showing Zach's band playing at a club. In one of the pictures he was singing with his eyes closed, standing under a blue light, with his face twisted up like he was in pain. He looked beautiful. "That's a nice one," Hannah said bravely.

Monday, September 26

Mac called me today at 9:13 p.m. I almost had a heart attack when his name came up on my phone.

"Chloe SNOW!" he shouted when I picked up. He sounded kind of drunk.

"Hi!" I said.

"Man, it's good to hear your voice. I miss you, kid."

"I miss you so much. How are you?"

"Dying."

He told me how hard practice is, and how crazy it is that they expect him to do problem sets when he's been up since dawn and his whole body hurts, and how unfair it is that he's not getting playing time just because he got in a fight with the O line coach during a summer workout.

After half an hour he said, "Hang on," and then bellowed, "DUDE! GET OFF MY ASS!" Then to me: "Sorry, Chlo. Some whiny little loser wants to leave for a party. GO WITHOUT ME, DICKFACE!"

I heard manly shouting in the background. Mac laughed and said, in the direction of the shouting, "SHE'S UNDERAGE. CALM DOWN."

Was this friend of Mac's talking about *me*? Was he asking what I look like?

It's embarrassing to be underage, but it's a good thing Mac's talking about me, right?

My heart was racing.

"I gotta go, babe. Be good, OK?"

After we hung up, my bedroom looked different to me. Mac and his friend were still echoing around it, making it strange.

Tuesday, September 27

I broke down and asked Dad to order me a PSAT prep book. He did a pretend double take, which I knew he would do. If parents weren't 100% predictable, they wouldn't be so annoying.

"Dost mine ears deceive me?" Dad said. "Did you say you want to prepare for a test?"

I moaned. "Dad, please."

"Have you been replaced by a pod person?"

"I don't understand your old-timey references."

"What's with the sudden interest in studying?"

I shrugged. "Tris and Hannah are a good influence."

"Thank God for that." He looked thoughtful. "Aren't they jumping the gun, though? I don't think I took the PSAT until I was a junior."

"Life is harder now."

He got out his phone and started scrolling. "This one looks good," he said. "Cookie9874 gives it five stars. 'Super detailed and has the new math info.'"

He tried to show me his screen. I saw an appalling brown-and-pale-blue cover and shut my eyes.

"Pick it for me," I said. "I can't look."

"This should be a great use of eight bucks," he said. "You know you're going to have to look at the book to use it, right?"

"I'll see it when it gets here," I said.

He spent at least half an hour reading reviews of different prep books while I ate string cheese. He is a good egg.

Wednesday, September 28

Dad sprang for one-day shipping, so I got to start the book tonight. This doesn't seem so hard! Finding an implicit meaning in a text? I do it every other day in English. Using a counterclaim to support a claim? My father's a lawyer. I've been listening to him lecture me about straw men since birth. Completing sentences? ____ of cake.

Thursday, September 29

Well, I've reached the math section. "You will be expected to solve a linear equation in one variable when there are an infinite number of solutions." Sure, no problem. Just an *infinite number of solutions!!!!!*

Friday, September 30

Tris was waiting for me by my locker after second period. He handed me his phone and said, "Look at this!"

It was a picture of Roy with someone I don't know, presumably an NYU kid. They were standing and smiling under the arch in Washington Square Park.

"Hey, that's where Sally drops Harry off in the movie!" I said.

"Look at this *hot guy*," Tris said, stabbing his finger at his phone. "His shoulder is pressed against Roy's shoulder! Don't you think that's suspicious?"

I studied the photo carefully.

"You have nothing to worry about," I said.

"Really?" Tris looked hopeful.

"They're barely touching. And they're so relaxed! They don't look like people with secret crushes on each other. Plus, Roy's not an idiot. Why would he post a picture of a guy he's into when he knows you'll see it?"

"That's true."

We looked at his phone together.

"I'm going to like the picture," Tris said. "To show how totally fine I am with it."

"Good idea."

He tapped the empty heart, and it turned red. I put my arm around his waist and gave him a little squeeze. It must be hard, being in a long-distance relationship.

Saturday, October 1

What the double F?

> Dear Chloe,
>
> I've finished rereading my novel, and I have thrilling news: what I thought was the first draft is actually very, very close to completion. A few touch-ups are needed in spots, but no major surgery is required. I hope to start querying agents within two weeks.
>
> After these long months of silence from you, I would fear for your safety were I not in contact with your father, who tells me you're thriving. As you probably know, he's insisting that we work

with this ridiculous mediator. What there is to mediate, I have no idea. I'm insulted that he thinks I'd be unreasonable about any of this. But *basta ya*; I vowed to myself that I would never speak ill of him to you.

I won't ask you to write, since my pleas fall on deaf ears, so I'll only sign off, with fondest love,

Your mother

Sunday, October 2

I tried not to take her bait. I tried to be unflappable and silent, like a sphinx. Then this morning, the smell of bacon woke me up, and before I knew it, I'd run downstairs in my pajamas and was yelling "WHAT'S A MEDIATOR???" at Dad.

He sighed. "Did Mom email you?"

"You can't not tell me this stuff! I have to know what's going on!"

He looked angry. "No, you *don't* have to know what's going on, and it's completely inappropriate to talk to you about the details of the divorce."

Mom hadn't used the D word.

"But you know I'm going to hear the details from Mom, so what's the point of keeping things from me?"

"Your mother and I agreed—or I thought we agreed—that we're not going to burden you with more information than you need."

"I'm not a child! Don't you know I think about the—about you and Mom constantly? It's making me sick!"

I ran up to my room crying, which I haven't done in a while.

Dad knocked on the door after about 20 minutes. My pillowcase was soaking wet.

He sat on the foot of my bed. "A mediator's a neutral third party who can help two people figure out the terms of their divorce."

I sat up and wiped my nose on my sleeve. "OK. Is Mom going to come back, then, for the meetings?"

"No. We considered that, but it wasn't feasible." He picked at a hangnail. "But I found someone willing to work with us over Skype."

"Oh. Weird."

He laugh-grunted. "Yeah, it is weird. Blow your nose." He yanked a tissue out of the box on my night-stand and handed it to me.

"How long will it take?"

"If everything goes smoothly, six months."

I started crying into the tissue.

"What's wrong, honey?"

"I don't know."

"Are you upset about the divorce?"

I nodded without looking up. The tissue was full of tears and snot.

He put his hand on my right foot. "Are you wishing we'd stay together?"

Mom skipping dinner to work on her novel. Mom hissing at Dad, throwing a spoon at him, pulling out a clump of her own hair in her fury. Mom never once asking me how that test went, or making a fuss when I got another A in English. Mom leaving me.

"No. I guess not."

He kept trying to get me to talk, and I wanted to, but my feelings were like a shapeless gray blob. I didn't know how to describe them. Finally Dad patted my foot and went downstairs. Now it's the middle of the night and I can't sleep. I keep picturing Dad driving on a four-lane road. He's listening to '90s rock and singing along, and then the guy driving the car next to him hears a notification, looks down at his phone, and veers into Dad, who gets bumped into oncoming traffic and hit head-on by a semi. I can see the blood and the bones. This isn't a vision of the future, is it? It's just my diseased brain torturing me?

Monday, October 3

I invited Noelle over, and we went through every guy in our class and discussed who's good-looking and who's repulsive. It was fun to hear some new opinions; I could recite Hannah's and Tristan's takes on everyone in my sleep. I almost told Noelle about the situation with Grady, but something made me hold back. Even though she's my friend now, I don't completely trust her. What if she made fun of me, or said she thinks Grady's lame, or did something else I could never get out of my head?

I asked her about the dance, and she said she's not going. "Reese and I were planning to dress up as the twin emoji—you know, the girls wearing black leotards and bunny ears? It was her idea. I'm terrible at thinking of costumes."

I said, "I'm sure you can come up with something," but she looked miserable, so I dropped it.

Tuesday, October 4

"We're starting Emily Dickinson today," Miss Murphy said, when we were all seated and quiet. "Get psyched! She's the mother of American poetry."

One nice thing about honors English is that you don't have to pretend to be bored. You're excited to learn about the mother of American poetry? Great! So is everyone else in the room. Go ahead and write "EMILY D!" in your notebook with huge stars all around it. No one will tease you.

Miss Murphy walked slowly back and forth in front of us. "This is a woman who never married. Rarely left Amherst. Rarely left her house, even. Became a recluse in the 1860s. And yet she traveled wherever she wanted to through books. Because of her reading, and because of her great mind, she was sophisticated, wry, worldly."

She told us more: Emily Dickinson loved Valentine's Day. Her father was a lawyer (like Dad!) and a congressman. Dickinson had a sister, Lavinia, and a brother, Austin. She had intense crushes on people who hardly knew she existed. (I can relate.) Her editor described her as "a little plain woman with two smooth bands of red hair and a face . . . with no good feature." (Her editor sounds like a real turd. Also, I looked her up on Google Images after class, and I think she was pretty! A little eyeliner would have helped, but who among us doesn't need a little eyeliner?)

Then we read a poem that starts, "Wild Nights— Wild Nights! / Were I with thee / Wild Nights should be our luxury!"

I jumped when the bell rang—Miss Murphy had just asked us to interpret "Might I but moor—Tonight / In Thee!" and I was wondering if anyone would have the courage to point out the obvious, which is that it definitely means "I wish I could bone you," and I was so engrossed, I had no idea class was almost over.

Wednesday, October 5

I spent hours reading Emily Dickinson and copying out her poems by hand. She uses tons of exclamation marks, which goes to show that grown-ups who make fun of teenagers' punctuation have no idea what they're talking about.

Thursday, October 6

Tris and I went to Hannah's field hockey game today. It was a perfect fall afternoon. Cool air. Lavender sky. Leaves the color of cherries. Smell of woodsmoke. Sometimes New England is so New Englandy.

I know field hockey players are attempting to get the ball into the goal, but that's where my knowledge of the rules ends. Still, I enjoy watching. It's like resting your eyes on a fire. And even I can tell Reese is amazing. She whips her stick through the air like it's a sword and races around with her ponytail flying behind her. Hannah seems pretty good too. She does a lot of screaming on the field, which surprises me, since she's so mild-mannered in real life.

Halfway through the game, Grady showed up with a friend of his—Elliott, I think his name is. They sat on the sidelines across the field from me and Tris. "What's Grady doing here?" Tris asked.

"I have no idea," I said. "I haven't talked to him in a while."

"Oh," Tris said, with a question in his voice. I got very focused on ripping up the grass next to my leg and constructing a circular pile with it. He took the hint and didn't ask me anything else.

Did Grady guess I was going to watch Hannah? Did he come to see me without officially seeing me?

I tried to catch his eye, but he pretended not to notice me.

After they won the game, Reese and Hannah jumped on each other like two puppies.

Friday, October 7

I bumped into Miss Murphy in the hall after school. We were walking in the same direction, so we continued together, awkwardly talking about English stuff. Or, no—I was awkward. She seemed fine.

When we got to the door leading to the parking lot, she hesitated with her hand on the push bar. "Hey, do you want a ride home?" she asked. I must have looked horrified, because she laughed and said, "It was just a suggestion."

"Oh—yeah. I'm OK. Thanks, though."

She smiled and said, "Have a good weekend."

What would people think if they saw me leaving school with her? That's all I need, for our entire class to decide I'm not actually good at English or acting—that

I'm just getting special treatment because I'm best friends with Miss Murphy. English and acting are my only two claims to fame! I need them to survive in this hellscape! And what was Miss Murphy going to do, drop me off and drive away like everything was normal? Or come in to give Dad a smooch?

Saturday, October 8

Asked Dad what's going on with the mediator. He said they're not having their first session for a while. He sounded so stiff and uncomfortable that I decided not to torture him anymore, and dropped it.

Sunday, October 9

God, if you exist, thank you for Tristan. He makes my whole life bearable. It was pouring today, but I biked over to his house anyway, and he gave me comfy pants and a T-shirt to change into, and we sat in his bed watching English comedies on his laptop for five hours, and I didn't think about Miss Murphy the entire time.

I was getting ready to leave when Tris said, "I was thinking maybe I should go to the dance after all."

I ordered myself not to scare him off by overreacting. "Oh yeah?" I said.

"Roy's busy taking selfies with hot guys. Why should I sit home by myself missing him?"

"That makes sense."

Yes yes yes yesssss! The Halloween Lifetime Memory project is ON!

Monday, October 10

No school—Columbus Day. I stopped by CVS on the way to Tris's house, and as I was walking out I saw Grady and Bear standing by the coin-operated horse in front of that stationery store two doors down. I was going to sneak by without saying hello, but Bear spotted me and solemnly waved, so Grady turned around to look.

"Hi, guys," I called, walking up to them.

Bear examined me. "You have a blue jacket," he said. "I have a blue jacket too."

It seemed rude to loom over him, so I crouched down. "You also have very cool sneakers," I said.

"They close with Velcro," he said.

"Wow." I looked into his perfect little face, and he looked back. Only kids can make the expression he was making: open, watchful, serious.

His eyes moved up to my hair. "Do you have a bun, or a ponytail?"

"Today I have a ponytail," I said.

"I like it," Bear said.

"You're barking up the wrong tree, dude," Grady said. "She's not into younger guys." His tone was neutral—he didn't sound angry or bitter or anything. My eyes jumped to his face. He was smiling, but then again, he was looking at Bear, which would make anyone smile.

"Dogs bark," Bear said.

"I have a dog," I said. "Do you want to see?"

He studied a Snickers snap on my phone and then said, "Do you have any pictures of fire trucks?"

Grady said, "No more pictures, bud. We have to go meet Mom. Give Chloe a high five, OK?"

Bear reached out, and I patted his little star of a hand with mine.

If he's joking around about me not being into younger guys, Grady must be thawing out, right? He must be changing his mind about being friends?

As an experiment, I'm going to ask him if he's going to the Halloween dance. It's merely a normal question one friend would ask another.

Tuesday, October 11

That was . . . confusing.

I did it right after homeroom, so I wouldn't lose my nerve. I found Grady at his locker and, after some preliminaries about how much I love Bear, said, "Do you have your costume all picked out for the dance?"

He instantly looked wary. "Uh, yeah," he said. "I'm going as a ghost."

"Cool. Classic," I said.

"Are you going?"

"Maybe," I said.

"OK, well, see you there, maybe," he said.

Wednesday, October 12

I've got it. It's perfect. I'm going to tell Grady I like him at the Halloween dance.

Thursday, October 13

I've examined this plan from every angle, and I can't find any flaws in it. I wanted to make the dance memorable, and this is the perfect way to do it. The PSATs will be over by the 29th, so I won't be distracted by having to study for them right as our relationship gets going. And most importantly, confessing my feelings at the dance will be romantic AF.

Friday, October 14

OK, so what exactly am I going to say? "Grady, I made a mistake." No. Start over. "Grady, it's true you're nothing like Mac, and I have to be honest, the age difference still worries me." Terrible! "Grady, can I talk to you for a second? I've been thinking about it, and I have a crush on you, too." That's not bad. But is it special enough? Will he remember it in 50 years?

Maybe I'll wing it. I'm sure something will come to me in the moment.

Saturday, October 15

DEAR LORD THE PSATS ARE ON WEDNESDAY HOW DID THIS HAPPEN WHAT WILL BECOME OF ME

I really do want to study, and I'm going to as soon as I very, very quickly check everything and make sure I'm up to date on new likes, retweets, and comments, and see if there are any new Grady pics since this morning. I need to get that out of the way before I buckle down, or I won't be able to concentrate.

Sunday, October 16

Emergency last-ditch PSAT study session at Tris's house with Hannah—called by me, since if I attempt to study alone I wind up staring at my phone for four hours. I wore one of Dad's old sweatshirts and my lucky pair of yoga pants. Tris was in head-to-toe fleece. Hannah was wearing a dress, since she'd come straight from her youth group meeting at church.

Tris and Hannah tried to explain quadratic equations to me for approximately two hours, but it's no use. Hannah started out by saying, "So we know a, b, and c are the coefficients, right?" in the same tone of voice you'd use to say something obvious, like, "So we know snow is cold, right?" Then they both looked at me like they were expecting me to say, "Right, of course," after which we could briskly move on to the hard part, but instead they saw the panic in my eyes and we had to go back even farther, until we'd regressed all the way to what exactly a square root is.

Monday, October 17

The PSATs are important, but not actually as important as the Halloween dance. I probably won't even remember my PSAT score when I'm grown-up, but if all goes according to plan, I'll remember the dance for the rest of my life. So it's crucial that I take a study break and make a list of possible group costumes, as well as a backup list of solo costumes, in case Tris and Hannah think that's the way to go.

Tuesday, October 18

I'm doomed! I went to bed at 9 p.m. so I'd be well rested for the PSATs, and now it's almost midnight! I've been thrashing around in bed for three hours! I'm going to be exhausted and brain-dead tomorrow, and I'm going to get a terrible score. Which doesn't even matter!! It's just a practice test! The word "PRACTICE" is in the *name* of the *test*! What's the worst that can happen? I'll get a

400 and my teachers will see it and decide I'm not AP material, and because I'm shut out of AP classes I won't get into a good college, and I'll never get a decent job and I won't be able to move to New York, much less afford my own apartment, and I'll wind up living with Dad and dying a virgin, like Emily Dickinson, but without the immortal poetry.

Oh my God, the last thing I should be doing is panicking into my diary as time marches on and the PSATs get closer with every passing second. Why can't I RELAX and GO TO SLEEP?

Wednesday, October 19

I survived. I even kind of had fun?!

We took the test in the cafeteria. Miss Murphy was one of the proctors, which should have been distracting, but which helped. I felt more and more nervous as she read through all the rules about calculators and form codes. By the time she got to the reading test instructions, I was in a panic, and when she said, "Open your test book to Section 1, read the directions, and begin work," and everyone started reading as fast as they could, I was on the brink of hyperventilating. But she caught my eye and gave me a firm nod, and I calmed down a little. And it was OK! It helped that the first passage was from *Ethan Frome*, which we read last year. The science excerpts were harder, but I think I basically understood them. The math part was an abomination and I doubt I got even half of the answers right, but maybe my belly flop there will be balanced out by a stellar performance on the writing and language section, which was soooooo easy and basically was like noticing people's terrible grammar on FB, but even more fun, because on the PSAT the whole point is to fix the mistakes, which unfortunately you cannot do on the internet.

And now I'm going to take some Tylenol for the massive headache pounding in my eyes like tiny hammers made of fire.

Thursday, October 20

The pre-PSAT stress was worth it just for this blissful feeling of knowing I never have to take the PSAT again.

Until next fall.

And then comes the SAT.

The next time a grown-up says, "Youth is wasted on the young," or "No taxes. No job. Enjoy it while you can," or "These are the best years of your life," I'm going to punch him in the junk.

Friday, October 21

I thought I would be so relieved to have the test behind me, and I am, but now there's nothing to distract me from the terror and excitement of my confession-at-the-dance plan.

Saturday, October 22

I've been trying to text Hannah and Tris about our costumes, and the conversation keeps turning to nonessential topics such as Señora Friedman accidentally wearing her sweater backward yesterday (Tris), or whether it's rude to call someone a "real so-and-so" (Hannah). If they knew what was at stake here, they would be taking this a lot more seriously. Which I do realize is my problem, since I haven't told them what's at stake here.

Sunday, October 23

I don't know why, but Mac keeps popping into my head. I'll be walking Snickers or taking a shower, and suddenly I see him in my mind's eye so clearly. I see him looking down at me, or throwing his head back to laugh, or driving his truck with one hand while squeezing my thigh with the other.

It's impossible that I still have feelings for him. Some primordial part of my lizard brain is trying to sabotage me.

I don't have to be 100% sure I want to marry Grady. I can go out with him and see what happens. It's fine. It's high school!

Monday, October 24

This might be my last week as a spinster. In a few days, I could be one of those people with a couple photo as a profile picture. I could be one half of Chloe and Grady (or maybe people will say his name first: Grady and Chloe). I could be one half of a couple mash-up name. Ghloe! Crady! Groe!

Tuesday, October 25

I finally managed to get Tris and Hannah over for a costume-planning meeting at my house after school by bribing them with candy pumpkins.

"We need to look cool, but like we're not trying to be cool," I said. I was pacing around the living room. "And cute, but not intentionally sexy."

Tris was licking orange dye off his fingers. Hannah was biting into a pumpkin stem-first.

"Guys!" I clapped my hands. "Any ideas?"

"I still think we should go as zombies," Tris said.

"Or what about puns?" Hannah said. "Like a deviled egg! I could make an egg out of construction paper and wear devil's horns!"

What part of construction paper egg did she think equaled cool and cute?

"Do you mind sitting down?" Tris asked me. "You're making me nervous."

"Chloe, what's wrong?" Hannah said. "Are you OK?"

"Yes. No," I said. "Grady's going to the dance."

They stared at me. "So what?" Tris said.

"I'm going to tell him I like him," I said.

"You *are*?" Tris said.

"Chloe, do not tell him you like him unless you're sure you do," Hannah said.

"I'm *not* sure I do!" I said. "I still think about Mac constantly."

Hannah was shaking her head with her lips pinched together.

"Is it so bad to try going out with Grady and see how I feel? Why is that a crime?" I said.

"It's not a crime," Tris said. "Hannah, stop. You're being ridiculous. We're high school kids."

"Youth is no excuse for treating people badly," Hannah said.

"Noted," I said. "Now can we please think of a costume that will make Grady like me back?"

The best we came up with was barnyard animals. I'm going to be a sheep, Tris will be a cow, Hannah will be a chicken, and we'll make a fence out of cardboard and hold it around ourselves. It doesn't exactly scream "effortlessly cool," but Tris convinced me nothing could be more adorable than a face-painted black nose.

Wednesday, October 26

Crafting session at Hannah's after school. I glued cotton balls all over the torso and hood of a hoody, Hannah taped dishwashing gloves to the ends of her yellow rain boots, and Tris cut black felt into wavy patches to sew on to his white T-shirt and white jeans.

"I have a good feeling about the dance," I said. "I think it's going to be exciting."

"Exciting for you, maybe," Tris said.

"It stinks that Roy can't come," I said.

"I wish Zach weren't going," Hannah said. "I'm dreading seeing him."

"You'll probably fall in love with some upperclassman we've never even met before," I said. "You'll see him from across the room during a slow song and your eyes will lock."

Tris snorted. "I *wish* there were upperclassmen we've never met before. I'm so sick of everyone. I'm even sick of everyone's clothes."

"Now imagine if you'd lived in this town since you were born," I said. Tris is an arriviste. He thinks *he's* bored?!

"You could have a boyfriend in three days, Chloe," Hannah said wistfully.

"I'm sure I won't," I said, but I was being modest. I probably WILL!

"What's Noelle going as?" Tris said. He was trying to scrub the dirt off his black-and-white Chuck Taylors, which he's wearing to complete his cow look.

"She's not," I said. "She was going to go with Reese, but obviously that's not happening anymore."

"She should come with us!" Hannah said. "She can be a pig or a duck or something!"

I don't know why I didn't think of that. It seems dangerous to me, somehow, trying to pull Noelle into my main friend group. What if it's awkward? What if no one gets along? But Hannah's right—I should invite her. She's lonely, and it's the nice thing to do.

Thursday, October 27
Noelle said yes. "But I'm not going as a *pig*. That's ridiculous. I'll be a sexy farmer."

Friday, October 28
Saw Grady in the hallway today. His handsomeness made me shy, and so did the secret knowledge of my plan. I waved and scurried away. Am I going to have the nerve do this tomorrow?

Saturday, October 29
187 minutes until the dance. Hannah and Tris and Noelle are on their way over to get ready. I slept for 10

hours last night, I did a mud mask when I woke up, and I'm feeling kind of scared but mostly excited. Here goes something, I guess.

Sunday, October 30

I'm shocked. I feel the same way I did when I was six years old and nearly got electrocuted while trying to plug Mom's hair dryer into an outlet: like I'm gently buzzing all over and my brain has been wiped off with a sponge.

I should have been suspicious when the night started off so well. The planning committee must have blown its budget, because the gym looked excellent, all draped in fake cobwebs and plastic bats that looked spooky in the low light. Everyone loved our costumes, and we posed for a million pictures, holding up our fence. Hannah and Tris and I looked pretty cute, I think. Noelle, who was wearing tiny cutoffs, a straw hat, and a plaid shirt knotted above her belly button, looked hot. Zach was there dressed as a police officer, and I thought he looked obnoxiously into himself, strutting around wearing mirrored aviator glasses with his jaw clenched, but naturally I didn't tell Hannah that, since she was gazing at him longingly. Then, from across the room, I saw Grady. He was covered in green body paint, and he'd made his hair green somehow. I didn't get it until Tris told me he must be Slimer from *Ghostbusters*.

"Are you going to talk to him?" he asked.

"In a second," I said. My heart was pounding, and I could feel myself blushing.

"The green really works on him," Tris said.

"You're not helping," I said.

"Who are you guys talking about?" Noelle said. "That cute guy over there? Wait, that's the kid from the pool, right?"

Hannah came back from the snacks table carrying four cupcakes on a paper plate. "Have you talked to him yet?" she asked me.

I was about to answer her when I saw Reese burst through the double doors with her squad trailing behind her, smiling like she was arriving on a red carpet, which in a way, she was. She had on a tight khaki romper unbuttoned to her sternum and high black boots. She carried a black plastic tube and wore a black backpack.

"What is she dressed as?" Tris said breathlessly. He was openly watching her stride across the gym. Everyone was.

Reese has a great walk. Her hips go bam, bam, bam, and she holds herself high, like a string is running through the top of her head up to the ceiling.

"She's a Ghostbuster!" Hannah said. "She's a sexy Ghostbuster!"

"That's a coincidence, when Grady's . . ." I said, and then I realized.

"They must have planned it," Noelle said.

When Reese got to Grady, she threw her arms around him. I could see him grinning over her shoulder.

None of us actually gasped, but there was a gasp-like vibe in the air.

"Don't leave," I said.

"We won't," Tris said.

But we should have left, or at least I should have. Still, show me the normal human who could have turned and walked away without waiting to see what would happen next.

What happened next was, a slow song came on. Reese took Grady's hand and led him to the center of the dance floor. At first they were swaying back and forth, talking and laughing with their cheeks close, occasionally pulling back to look at each other. Then Reese wrapped her arms tightly around Grady's neck and put her head on his shoulder. And then she lifted her head up, closed her eyes, and kissed him. He kissed her back, and kissed her back, and kissed her back. They were making out hardcore at the Halloween dance, and it looked so fun and so classically high school, and it could have been me getting green face paint all over my mouth, but it wasn't, because I'd messed up again.

"I can't watch this," I said, staring at Reese and Grady so hard my eyes felt dry.

"Let's go," Tris said. "Come on." He picked up my hand, then Hannah's, so I grabbed Noelle's, and the four of us marched toward the exit. I was doing fine at first, but suddenly I could feel the tears coming. I muttered that I'd be right back, and speed-walked to the girls' locker room. It was shockingly bright in there, after the dimness of the gym. One stall was open, and I locked myself in it and tried to cry as quietly as I could, so no one else would hear. I pulled myself together and dried my face off, but as soon as I'd finished, I started crying again. Finally I finished for real, flushed the toilet, washed my hands, and found Tris and Hannah and Noelle right where I'd left them.

"I hate her," I said, when we'd gotten outside. "I hate her so much."

"Yep," Noelle said.

"I'm sure she doesn't know you like Grady," Hannah said.

I'd forgotten for a second that Hannah and Reese are field hockey bros. "Did you know she was dressing up with him?" I asked. "Did she tell you they're—going out, or whatever?"

"No," Hannah said, sounding shocked. "I had no idea."

"Probably because she knew if she told you, you'd tell me," I said. "And she didn't want me to know, because then I might have skipped the dance and missed her big make-out party."

"I can see why you're upset right now," Hannah said. "But I think you're being paranoid. If you got to know Reese, you'd like her."

I turned to Noelle like, *Can you chime in, please?*

"Trust me, however bad you think she is, she's worse," Noelle said. I could see Hannah wanting to argue back but not wanting to be rude to a relative stranger.

"I'm going to walk home," I said. "You guys stay and have fun. Text me later."

"WHAT? No," Noelle said. "We're all going back in there and acting like nothing's wrong."

"I can't," I said.

"Of course you can," Noelle said. "And our costume is one-quarter suckier if you bail. Don't be selfish."

I looked at Tris and Hannah for help, but they were busy staring at Noelle with fear in their eyes. They don't know her like I do. To them she's still a mean girl.

"Hang on," Noelle said to me. "Your nose is smudged." She pulled a liquid eyeliner out of her bag and fixed me up. After she'd gone to all that effort, it seemed like it would be rude to leave.

We went back in and stayed until almost the end.

We posed for more pictures. We danced together. We fake laughed, or maybe the others were really laughing. Tris didn't look like he was pining away for Roy. Hannah and Zach waved to each other once, so that was exciting. I tried hard not to look at Grady and Reese, but twice I did by accident. The first time they were feeding each other cupcakes. The second time they were kissing again.

Oh, what a stupid, terrible night. I'm like that husband and wife in the monkey paw story who curse themselves by wishing for money. I wished for a memory, and I got one, and now I'm sorry I ever wanted it.

Monday, October 31
Reese posted a picture of Grady looking smoldering in his body paint and captioned it "green bae." Wonderful. And excuse me, but at what point did Grady decide Reese is the love of his life? Two seconds ago he was in the concession stand with me, agreeing that she's a fake-nice, actually-mean bully. Maybe her hotness cancels out her cruelty. Maybe that's how it works for guys.

Tuesday, November 1
What did I expect, that Grady was going to sit around waiting for me to make up my mind? That he liked me so much he wouldn't be interested in anyone else? That

his crush on me would somehow make him invisible to all other girls?

I did expect all of those things, but I realize they're ridiculous.

Wednesday, November 2

"She's bold," I said to Tris. "You have to give her that. Not everyone would be brave enough to make out with a freshman at the first dance of the year."

"That's exactly why she did it!" he said, shivering. It was lunchtime, and cold, and we'd snuck outside to talk without stopping to grab our coats from our lockers.

"What do you mean?"

"I bet she knew people would make fun of her for dating a freshman, and she wanted to control the narrative. So she broke the story herself, like, 'Yeah, I'm dating this guy and I'm excited about it and you should all be jealous.'"

"It worked," I said.

A crow flew overhead, cawing. I shivered.

"Have you seen Grady?" Tris asked.

"No. I'm taking insane detours to avoid his locker. I've been late to three classes already."

"So you're not going to tell him how you feel?"

"What, that I like him? No. No way. I already tried stealing Mac from Sienna, and it turned into a Dumpster fire."

Tris nodded and rubbed his arms.

"Plus," I said, "I don't like him anymore."

Tris gave me a look like *yeah, right.*

"Seriously," I said. "How could I like someone who makes out with *Reese?*"

I could tell he didn't believe me. I don't believe me either, but I want to.

Thursday, November 3

I NEVER WANT TO SEE OR SPEAK TO GRADY EVER AGAIN.

I was mid-detour, racing through the B wing, when I crashed into him as he came out of the bathroom. It was like a scene from a rom-com, if rom-coms were about bumbling, angry teenagers betraying each other.

"Hey!" he said, and grabbed my arms to steady me, or himself.

"Hi."

"I haven't seen you in a while," he said. He was watching me carefully.

"I saw you at the dance," I said. "From across the room." I tried to sound unemotional, but it must not have worked, because he got a pitying expression on his face, which made me furious.

"I don't care that you're with Reese," I said.

"OK."

"I'm a little confused about it, though. Remember all those times at the pool when we agreed she's the worst?"

It seemed somehow embarrassing that I'd brought up the pool, like I was referring to a magical realm we'd both agreed to pretend doesn't exist.

"She's actually really nice," he said defensively.

I laughed to show him how ridiculous I found this statement.

"She is," he said. "It just takes a while to get to know her." He started rumpling his hair, making it stand on end, which he always does when he's stressed out.

"'A while' as in 15 minutes of eating each other's faces in public?"

"Are you *mad* about that?"

We were raising our voices, but it didn't matter. The next class had started, and the halls had cleared out around us.

"Of course I'm not mad," I said. "Make out with whoever you want."

"Thanks, I will," he said. "It's none of your business."

"I'm aware of that."

"I don't think you are," he said. "Or you wouldn't be standing here criticizing my girlfriend like a stalker."

"Oh, *I'm* a stalker?" I said, but I was thinking, *Girlfriend? GIRLFRIEND?!*

"Chloe, I feel bad saying this, but I don't like you anymore."

I could feel angry tears forming in my eyes. I managed to choke out a "Yeah, obviously"; then I had to turn and walk away as fast as I could to escape before I started sobbing.

I'm so upset. I'm so mad. I'm so embarrassed. How did this happen? I didn't even like Grady a month ago.

Friday, November 4

Woke up with a fever, like the heroine of an old-fashioned novel who worries herself into a decline. Dad took my temperature, said "No school, kiddo," and brought me a ginger ale and my laptop before he left for work.

I spent half the day sleeping and half the day worrying about the Thanksgiving Day football game. I'm sure Grady and Reese will go, because everyone does, and I'll probably be forced to have some hideously awkward interaction with them. And some of the ex-seniors will come. Like Roy. Or maybe Mac. (Not Josh, because he's going away with his family for the holiday, so Hannah doesn't have to freak out.) I barely survived the Halloween dance, and now there's this new huge event to feel sick about for a month. It's exhausting.

Saturday, November 5

Slept for 13 hours last night and woke up feeling weak but clear-headed.

You know what, it's a good thing Grady showed his true colors before I got involved with him. "Stalker"? HA. He's the one who followed me around like a baby duckling for months. And all this pretending to like Reese is disgusting. Just admit you're with her because you want to get in her pants. What do they even talk about—her hair? Her clothes? Her latest scheme for torturing Noelle?

Doesn't he remember how we talked about real stuff at the pool? Doesn't he realize it's rare to find someone you feel so comfortable around? No, he doesn't, and that's why I'm not going to spend one more instant thinking about him.

Sunday, November 6

Tris showed up unannounced in the middle of dinner. Dad went to the kitchen to get him some food.

"I texted you," Tris said.

"I didn't see," I said. "You're panting!"

"I rode my bike over."

He looked upset, and I was about to ask him if he was OK when Dad came back, carrying a bowl full of pasta.

We talked about normal stuff while we ate: teachers, classes, how Tristan's brother is doing at college. By the time Tris and I finished washing the dishes and went up to my room, he had calmed down. He sat on my bed and said, "I have a bad feeling about Roy."

I sat next to him. "Did something happen?"

"A lot of little things. He takes forever to text me back. He sounds polite when we talk. I don't know. . . . He's being generally weird. I was sitting in my room before I came over and suddenly I felt sure he's cheating on me. It was like a premonition. Or, no, like a sixth sense."

"OK," I said. "I guess it's *possible* he is."

Tris turned pale.

"But I doubt it," I said quickly.

"You do? Why?" He was looking at me like I was about to reveal a great truth.

"There are so many other explanations. Maybe he's genuinely busy at school and it's hard to be in touch all the time. Or maybe you're paranoid, because you never get to see him and you don't know what he's doing, so you're hearing things in his voice that aren't there. Or maybe things do feel strange to both of you because of the long distance, but everything will go right back to normal when he comes home. You'll see him over Thanksgiving, right?"

"Yeah. He's coming home in time for the game, and then we'll have the weekend."

"So there you go."

Tris flopped backward onto my bed and sighed. "I'm dreading the game, to be honest."

"Oh God, I know."

"I wish it were illegal for college kids to come to it. They're done with high school. Can't they stay away from us?"

"Except for Roy, of course."

"Well, yeah. But even him. I want to see him for the first time on our own, not in a crowd of thousands of people."

"We could skip the game," I said.

Tris laughed bitterly but didn't even bother to respond otherwise. And why would he? It was a ridiculous suggestion. Yes, technically we could skip the game, but only in the sense that Elizabeth Bennet technically could have skipped the Netherfield ball.

Monday, November 7

Dear Chloe,

I've spoken with your father, who is intent on shielding you from the divorce process entirely. In theory, I agree with him, but I also want to

respect you as an intelligent being who likely
craves knowledge, even at the cost of psychic
pain. As I told him, if you ask me questions
about what's happening, I can't promise I won't
answer them. That said, *are* there any questions
you'd like to ask me?

—Mom

I want to reply, because of course I want to find out
if they've started mediation, and what the mediator looks
like, and how long the divorce is going to take. But at the
same time, I don't want to know at all. Also, I refuse to
fall for this clickbait in email form.

Tuesday, November 8

Reese came up to me between classes and put her hand
on my arm. "Chloe, I'm so happy we're running into each
other," she said, staring into my eyes. She was wearing a
soft white sweater, ripped skinny jeans, and suede booties.

"Hey, Reese," I said.

"Listen, I have to say something to you. I am so, so
sorry if Grady and I hurt you."

"Oh! Oh. No—"

"I know how hard it must be to see him with

someone else. This summer, I was totally secretly in love with him, but sometimes I wondered if he had a little crush on *you*! Thank goodness I was wrong." She narrowed her eyes at me like a hypnotist. So this was going to be the official version of events: Grady never liked me. I had an unrequited crush on him. Great. Fine. Whatever. I wasn't brave enough to put up a fight. Besides, what would be the point? She could tell people we actually go to school in a giant aquarium and breathe through invisible gills, and everyone would believe her, because she's Reese. She decides what's true and what's not.

She squeezed my arm. "Anyway, you must hate me for stealing him out from under your nose. You do, don't you? Admit it!" She got out her dimples and aimed them at me. Her eyes were so sparkly. Her skin was so poreless. She could turn everyone in the class against me with a snap of her fingers.

"Of course I don't hate you," I said.

"I'm so glad," she said. "We'll hang out at the Thanksgiving Day game, right?"

"Totally!"

She hugged me, and I hugged her back tightly. I was a mouse in a hawk's talons, adoring the hawk because it hadn't pierced my neck yet.

Miss Murphy and I bumped into each other after school, and she said, "How about that ride home?" I couldn't come up with an excuse fast enough, so I accepted.

Plenty of people noticed us walking together in the hall, but it's not unusual to walk with a teacher. I don't *think* anyone saw us in the faculty parking lot. I speed-walked over to her blue Jeep Wrangler to minimize the time spent out in the open with her.

"I like your car," I said, once we were inside it.

"I do too," she said. "I've wanted a Jeep since I was a kid. When I moved back to take care of my mom, I finally bought one for myself. It was kind of a consolation prize for leaving the city." She put on her right blinker and pulled onto Fielding Street.

"Do you miss New York?"

"Not really. I'd lived there for so long that it had stopped thrilling me. When you first get there, you go to Times Square on purpose, and it's like, *Lights, crowds, life!* Then 15 years pass and Times Square becomes this place you'd do anything to avoid. Booking a Broadway show, you're overjoyed and then you think, *Oh God, but I'll have to commute through Times Square.*" She glanced at me and said, "Don't listen to me. You want to move there, right?"

I nodded.

"Do it. You'll love it. You'll live in some amazing dump in Ridgewood, and you'll eat the best food of your life, and you'll get rush tickets and go to rooftop parties and see famous authors read for free. OK, I do miss it."

The thing about Miss Murphy is, she's calm all the time, even in situations that would make most people tense, like driving around with their married boyfriend's daughter. Her voice is steady. She sounds interested and amused. She flips her visor up and down with a flourish. I was twitchy with nerves when I got in the car, but her calm was catching. By the time we pulled into my driveway, I felt almost normal.

"Thanks for the ride," I said. I paused with my hand on the door handle because I was sure she was going to stop me and insist on having a big talk.

"Sure thing," she said, and smiled. I waited for another second, but all she said was, "See you tomorrow."

Thursday, November 10

Tris invited me over after school, which was perfect, because I didn't have to avoid Miss Murphy or accept another ride from her. We spent most of the afternoon debating which outfit he should wear to the game. When I suggested his cable-knit fisherman sweater, he said, "Why would I want to look like a dad?" Then he winced and said, "Sorry. Sorry. I didn't mean to be rude."

"Don't worry about it," I said.

"I know it doesn't matter what I wear," he said.

"Of course it does! You have to feel cute, or you won't feel confident."

He tried on every sweater he owns, but nothing satisfied him. I know the feeling. The problem is, sweaters don't help. The only thing that would help is the total certainty that the person you love loves you back.

Friday, November 11

Noelle's spending Thanksgiving with her mom at the Ace Hotel in Palm Springs. She'll be floating in a pool on an inflatable raft while I shiver in the stands, trying to pretend my heart isn't breaking while I watch Grady and Reese fawn all over each other.

Saturday, November 12

Dad came downstairs after lunch smelling like aftershave, wearing a new shirt. I looked up from my phone and asked him why he looked so fancy.

"I'm meeting Miss Murphy for coffee," he said, pretending to be nonchalant.

"Oh, cool. Have a good time," I said, pretending

right back at him. We stared at each other for a few seconds, and then he said, "I'll be home in time for dinner," and headed out.

I am a rock. I am an island.

Sunday, November 13

"Do you guys talk about me on your dates?" I asked Dad at breakfast.

"We do, actually," he said. "I hear you wrote an excellent paper on Emily Dickinson."

"Don't try to butter me up," I said.

But secretly I'm so excited Miss Murphy liked my paper enough to tell my father about it.

Monday, November 14

Miss Murphy came toward me after school today, said "Ride?" and turned an imaginary steering wheel. Nadine Wallach was passing by, and she looked at us with interest. "Hey, Chloe!"

"Hi!" I called. After she was around the corner, I said, "It was fun the other day, but . . ."

Miss Murphy waited.

"It's just that if other kids, like, see us together . . . I don't want them to think I'm getting special treatment, or whatever." I'd been staring down at the barf-colored tile during this speech, and when I glanced up to look at her face, I saw that I'd hurt her feelings, but she was trying not to show it.

"Right! Of course." She laughed. "I should have thought of that. I like to think I'm not a clueless old person, but of course I am. Anyway. I understand completely."

"Sorry if I—"

"No, no, there's nothing to be sorry about. Really."

I had no idea how to end the conversation. Maybe we'd stand there silently until the janitors came around and turned the lights off.

She cleared her throat. "If you're worried about your dad and me being spotted—we never go out in town. We always drive—none of the students here will ever know anything about my dating life, is what I mean to say."

She was blushing. I felt bad for her, and for myself.

"Have I tortured you enough for one afternoon?" she said, and laughed. "I'll see you tomorrow, kiddo."

Tuesday, November 15

I had to focus my entire attention on not being awkward in English class today, whereas Miss Murphy was being effortlessly normal. Maybe I'll learn how to do that when I'm 35 (which is how old Miss Murphy is, which I found out via a three-second Google search, which means she's 15 years younger than my dad, which is *revolting*).

Wednesday, November 16

Grady and Reese were full-on making out by the auditorium today. Isn't there some kind of ordinance against French kissing on school grounds?

Thursday, November 17

Klaxon! Klaxon! Klaxon! I'm texting with Mac!!!!!!!

> *You pumped to see me*
> *in a week?*

> *You're coming home?? Don't*
> *you have a game?*

> *Not until Saturday.*
> *Coming home Thursday*
> *leaving Friday morning*

> *And you'll have time for me?*

> *Of course dummy*

> *Yayayay*

Nothing since then. Should I text again proposing a specific plan, or would that be annoying? He probably wants to be spontaneous and see where the visit takes him, right? Fine by me. He's busy playing college football and being a big man on campus. I'm busy taking Snickers for walks and carefully rewriting tweets for an hour to make sure they sound casual and breezy. I can work with his schedule.

Friday, November 18

Seeing Mac is a terrible idea. Why do I keep forgetting this? He has a girlfriend. He's not interested in me. He treated me like garbage six months ago. I have to somehow stop my heart from racing whenever I see a text from him. My heart is an idiot!

Saturday, November 19

Dearest Chloe,

As Thanksgiving approaches, I want to tell you how grateful I am for your existence. Although we're apart right now, I am connected to you always and ever thankful that you are my daughter.

Love,
Mom

I'm sure this is beautiful writing, and it would make most daughters cry, but most daughters don't have my mom. Connected to me always? More like totally unaware of what's going in in my life.

Sunday, November 20

Dad came into the kitchen as I was eating peanut butter pretzels and said, "I heard Miss Murphy gave you a lift the other day."

"Yep," I said.

He was giving me an eager, hopeful look, and it made me want to hurt his feelings. I know he's dying for me to become best friends with Miss Murphy, or, at the very least, to say something nice about her. It's not even unreasonable, but it still makes me furious. I don't want him to force her on me. I don't want *her* to force herself on me. I want them both to leave me alone. I have one (awful) mother, and I don't need another one.

Dad lingered for a minute, but I refused to look at him. After he left, I felt terrible.

Monday, November 21

Would it be a bad idea to text Mac to see if he's going to the game? It's not that I care either way. It's that I want to know so I can prepare myself emotionally for either possibility.

Tuesday, November 22

I regained sanity and did not text Mac. Good gravy! "Prepare myself emotionally"? There should be no emotional preparations necessary. Mac is my jerky non-ex-boyfriend. He is not part of my life now, and he never will be. End of discussion!

Wednesday, November 23

Half day, which I didn't even enjoy, because no classes in the afternoon meant more time to sit around panicking about tomorrow.

As I was biking past the fields, I saw Grady walking back from the clearing with his friend Elliott. They were talking and laughing, and Grady was gesturing with his hands. He has good posture. He carries himself like he's somebody. Which he is, of course.

Thursday, November 24

This was like a fairy tale Thanksgiving. Not the kind that ends in a wedding—the kind with three visitors who look beautiful but are actually wizened crones.

The football game started at 10 a.m., which meant I had to get up at the crack of dawn to cute-ify myself. Hannah and Tristan and I met in the parking lot at 9:50 so we could walk to the field together. It was freezing, and we were all bundled up. It made me happy to see

Tris's and Hannah's familiar old hats from last year. I'd forgotten all about them, and now here they were, back again, pom-poms and all.

We bought hot chocolate and went to our usual spot at the north end of the bleachers. Hannah looked around cheerfully. Her phone chimed, and she said, "Sorry, I have to text with my aunt for a second." Tris stared at the field with his eyes unfocused.

"Roy thought he might be a little late," he said, which he'd already told me at least three times.

"I'm sure he'll come soon," I said, and then I noticed Grady and Reese arriving. She was wearing a white coat with fur trim, a pink knit cap with a white fur puff on top, and mirrored sunglasses with white rims. He had on a fleece jacket, a down vest, and a purple-and-teal knit cap that was either accidentally or intentionally '90s chic.

"Reese looks like a sexy marshmallow," Tris said.

"In a good way?" I asked. It was so nice of him to take an interest in my concerns when most people would have been too focused on seeing their boyfriend for the first time in months to pay attention to anything but themselves.

"Marshmallows should never be sexy," he said firmly. And then we stopped talking, because Reese turned, scanned the bleachers, spotted us, and waved enthusiastically.

"Did she hear us?" I said, trying not to move my lips.

"Impossible," Tris said, as Reese said something to Grady, who looked up at us briefly and nodded. Then Reese started climbing the stairs, stopping along the way to dole out hugs and dimples to her many admirers.

"Hannah," I said, elbowing her in the ribs. She emerged from her phone. "I think Reese is coming over." For some reason it seemed important that all three of us be completely alert for this strange event. I was right: Reese made a beeline for us and said, "Hey, cuties! Why are you hiding way up here? You know everyone else is down by the field, right?"

We smiled sycophantically. By "everyone else," she meant the tiny innermost circle of popular kids. She must have known we would never sit next to them uninvited.

Reese pointed a white mitten at Hannah and addressed me and Tris. "Are you aware that this girl is a field hockey star?" We nodded, still smiling. "Her first year and she's crushing it."

"Tris and I aren't, like, sports experts," I said.

"But we can tell she's good," Tris said. It felt like he and I were Hannah's lame parents, dazzled and scared by her confident new friend.

"She's a natural athlete," Reese said. She sat on the bleacher below us, next to Hannah's feet, and said, "Seriously, Hannah, where have you been all my life? I have no idea why we're not BFFs. We have everything in common. Plus you're soooo adorable, and you probably don't even realize it. You could be, like, hot." She stood up and held out her mitten to Hannah. "Come with me for two seconds? I want to introduce you to some people."

"Of course!" Hannah squealed. She took Reese's hand and called "Be right back!" to us over her shoulder as she followed Reese down the stairs.

"What is even happening?" Tris whispered.

"Is Reese stealing her from us?" I whispered back.

"It doesn't count as stealing when Hannah's falling all over herself to be stolen."

"We'd be exactly the same way," I said. "Do you hear yourself talking to Reese?"

"Do you hear *yourself*?"

"Yes! That's what I'm saying! Everyone talks crap about her, but no one's brave enough to be rude to her face. *Tris and I aren't sports experts*," I said in a simpering voice.

"*We can tell she's good*," Tris said in a singsong.

We looked at each other and shook our heads in mutual disgust.

"That BFF speech!" I said. "She insulted Hannah, like, four times, and me at least once, but I didn't even realize it while it was happening, because she was smiling the whole time."

"That part when she told Hannah she could be hot?" Tris shook his head. "So mean."

Down near the field, Reese was showing off Hannah to her friends.

"Do you think Hannah knows that Reese turns on people?" Tris said.

I shook my head. "She refuses to see any flaws in anyone, unless the anyone is me."

Tris was still staring at Reese, so I saw him first: Roy, threading his way through the crowd.

"He's here," I said, grabbing Tristan's arm.

"Oh my God," Tris said, and neither of us spoke again until Roy reached us, jogging the last few steps.

"Hey!" he said, and Tris stood up and threw his arms around him.

"Whoa, hi!" Roy said, hugging him back. They pulled apart and looked at each other, and I thought someone might say something romantic, but Roy only said, "I'm starving. Come with me to get some fries?" which actually might have been romantic, since it was an excuse to walk off alone together. Tris looked at me to make sure I didn't mind, and I looked at him back to tell him of course he should go.

Don't pull out your phone, I told myself as I sat alone on the bleacher. *There's no reason to feel awkward. No one cares that you're by yourself, doing nothing. No one even notices. And you're not doing nothing. You're watching a game. Just sit here enjoying the cold air and the sound of grunting football players.*

Reese had her arm around Hannah and was whispering something in her ear. Grady was on Reese's other side talking to Lianna. Mark and Dylan were there—two of Reese's male counterparts. It had to annoy them that Reese was dating some freshman, and not a member of their group. And didn't it bother Grady, sitting there while these body-sprayed bros pretended he didn't exist?

Grady must have felt me staring, because he glanced over his shoulder and we made eye contact. I immediately whipped out my phone and typed in my password at lightning speed.

I'm the only one left, I thought, staring into Snapchat without seeing it. *Reese came for Hannah. Roy came for Tris.* And then, like I'd willed him into existence, I heard Mac say, "Is this seat taken?"

I looked up. "Your HAIR!" I said.

He grinned at me and rubbed his hand over his head, which was buzzed. He looked like a marine. "My mom hates it," he said.

"Can I touch it?"

"Gimme a hug first."

I stood up, and he swept me off my feet and buried his face in my neck.

"That Choe smell!" he said, setting me down. "I missed it!"

"What do I smell like?" I said, horrified, and still reeling from the hug.

"Yourself. It's nice. Calm down," he said, and bent so I could reach his hair. He's so much taller than Grady. He's so much bigger than Grady. My hand looked tiny on his head.

"It feels like velvet," I said.

"I know," he said. "I look bangable, right?"

"I forgot how cocky you are," I said, and he laughed. He always thinks I'm funny, even when I'm not, and it's so hard to resist.

He sat down, and I sat next to him. He scooched over until we were pressed up against each other. "You missed Big Mac. Admit it."

"I missed you. But I'm mad at you."

"For what? Tell me, so I can apologize."

It was my chance to explain how miserable he'd made me last year. Finally, I could tell him exactly what I thought of him.

"It doesn't matter," I said. "Forget it."

Wonderful. So brave. So eloquent. I'm an inspiration to wronged women everywhere.

"So what's going on with you?" he said. "Who's your boyfriend?"

"I don't have one," I said.

He held his fist out. "Single and ready to mingle? Me too."

"What do you mean?" I said, giving him a bump.

"Sienna and I broke up."

"WHAT? Did you dump her?"

"We dumped each other about a week into classes. You'll see when you get to college. It's like, what would you rather do, fight constantly over FaceTime, take long bus trips, and get laid once a month, or not do that?"

"Do you have a new girlfriend?" I said.

He laughed. "Yeah, like, five of 'em."

"Oh."

"Come on, you don't want to go out with some old perv like me. You've got a lot going on here."

"Sure I do," I said.

"Aw, cheer up, cutie." He put his arm around me and jostled my shoulder. "You can be one of my girlfriends if you want."

"Stop," I said, and pretended to try to push him away, but he wouldn't be pushed. He kept his arm around my shoulder while we talked about college and his mom and how much the football team sucks now that Mac's class is gone. At one point Reese glanced up at us and then said something to Grady, who turned around and looked at me. I acted like I didn't notice him. I wish I could say I wasn't excited that he saw me snuggling with a college guy who's twice his size, but there's no point in lying to your own diary.

Eventually Mac left to find his friends, and I texted Hannah and Tris, *I'm exhausted have to go*, which was true, and after Dad and I had the loneliest Thanksgiving dinner of our lives, I crawled into bed with Snickers at 9 p.m. and lay awake for hours thinking about all the things I'm grateful for. My health. Dad's health. Our beautiful, creaky old house that generations of New England families have lived in. Fancy food, clean water, heat, air-conditioning. No one bombing us, no one oppressing us, no one taking away our civil rights. Dad's job in a city that's not underwater yet. The jobs I'll probably have in the future. My good school, where people pay attention to my performance and care about the grades I get. The 14 years I had with my mother, which is less than some people get, but more than other people do. I know I was born on third base.

Friday, November 25

Roy went out to lunch with his parents, so Tris stopped by to say hi. As soon as we were alone in my room, I said, "Did you have fun at the game?"

"Yeah. I almost couldn't look at Roy, I was so excited to see him."

"I know the feeling. You're hanging out with him tonight, right?"

"Oh, actually, I have to text him about what we're doing."

I waited until he'd sent the text and was messing around on the internet to say, "Mac and Sienna broke up."

"Really?"

Tris didn't even look up from his phone. I smacked it out of his hand (which sounds more dramatic than it was, since we were sitting side by side on my bed and it landed on my pillow).

"Chloe! You made me like AJ Singh's status by accident!"

"Your fault. You shouldn't have been stalking AJ Singh."

"If I unlike it, will he get a notification? We're not even friends!"

"I'm telling you something important about Mac!"

This time he threw his phone down. "No, you're not."

"How can it not be important that he and Sienna broke up?"

"Because it doesn't change anything. He's not going to magically turn into your boyfriend."

"I know that! I don't want him to be my boyfriend. Obviously. He's dating, like, five girls at school. He's a player and he's not nice and I don't like him at all anymore."

Tris looked at me with his eyes narrowed. "OK," he said finally.

I checked my phone every few minutes after Tris left, but not because I was hoping to hear from Mac, just because I was bored.

Saturday, November 26

It's almost midnight. I'm not disappointed. It's fine. It's more than fine—it's better this way.

Sunday, November 27

No texts from anyone. Nothing from Mac (obviously). Nothing from Hannah (unusual, but maybe she has lots of church stuff today or something). Nothing from Tris (unprecedented, and I'm almost worried).

Monday, November 28

Oh my God. Roy dumped Tris. No time to write.

Tuesday, November 29

We had to talk yesterday, but of course we were in class, so Tris texted me the whole story, hiding his phone under his desk. I tried to just listen and not interrupt him too much.

I'm so embarrassed

I was so hopeful and excited
to see Roy. Ugh ugh ugh

I had a bad feeling so why didn't
I hold back a little? Instead of
jumping all over him

> *Don't be embarrassed.*
> *Of course you were*
> *hoping for the best*

> *He seemed fine at the game*

He wasn't

He was barely talking to me

On his phone the whole time

But I was like he hates football,
maybe he just doesn't want to
be here

We hung out with his parents
that night and being with them
made everything seem normal

Like it was last summer

And they were so happy
to see me

It makes me want to cry
thinking about them

I'll probably never see them
again and they love me

Like more than my
dad loves me

                    Maybe you can still see them

Yeah right

                    So tell me what happened

So that was Thursday

Friday obviously you and I hung out
and Roy and I had plans at night
but he texted me to say he wasn't
feeling well and had to cancel

And I was kind of like oh no
but also telling myself maybe he
really was sick

Then Saturday we went out for
pizza and it was awful. He was
so grouchy and contradicting
everything I said

He was bragging about how
amazing new york is and
saying oh small-town life is
so dull, I don't know how
you can stand it, everyone
here is so provincial and
ignorant

I don't know why that made me
so mad because I agree

But it's like I'm still trapped
here and I have to make the
best of it

He was trying to make me feel
terrible about my life

So I got quiet and he was like
why aren't you talking, I don't
want to interview you

                        Ew rude

I know

I wanted to fix the day because
I had this countdown clock
in my head

We only had 24 hours until
he left and I couldn't stand
it that we were having such a
bad time

I knew I was going to obsess
about how awful the weekend
was until Christmas

So I forced myself to stop being
mad and suggested we go to
his house because I knew his
parents were out

When we got there I started
making out with him

He was just lying
there, not even touching
me back

So I tried to give him
a hand job

But he stopped me

He was like, sorry, I'm in
a bad mood today, being
back here is bumming me
out, I'm not up for messing
around

And I was like you've been
weird all weekend, what's
wrong

And he was like nothing
nothing I swear it's nothing
to do with you

And I started crying a
little so then he was nice to
me and we kissed for real
and I left thinking ok maybe
everything's fine

Then Sunday he came to my
house first thing in the morning

And it was awkward again

And I was like listen if you want
to break up just tell me

I don't want you to stay
with me because you
feel obligated

I said do you want to be
with me?

And he was like I'm not sure

Oh no

Where were you?

In my living room, so we were
whispering

My mom and dad were in the
next room and I know they
heard everything

Roy had showered and was
wearing his going back to NY
clothes

These black skinny jeans with
rips. I've never seen them before

And I was wearing my PJs and
looked like a toddler

I'm sure you looked cute

What did he say?

That long distance is hard

That he wants to enjoy college
without feeling guilty about not
calling me enough

That it's frustrating to feel
tethered to this town when
all he wants to do is get away
from it

My heart was breaking but it
was so confusing

Because he was being way nicer
to me during this conversation
than he'd been all weekend

And so I was like, so you're
dumping me?

It was humiliating to ask but I
had to know for sure if we were
just talking about it or if it was
happening

And he said I'm so sorry

We both cried

But I think he was forcing
himself

He said we'll always be friends,
all that stuff

And then he left and I didn't eat
for the rest of the day

You don't think I forced him to
dump me do you?

If I'd never said anything would
we still be together?

                    You didn't force him to
                    dump you!

                    It sounds like he came home
                    meaning to break up but
                    was too scared to do it

I still love him

I want him to be happy

If he's not happy being
with me, I don't want him
to be with me

*Well I'm more worried
about you*

Did you eat anything today?

Not yet

Meet me at my locker

The bell was ringing, so I met Tris and forced him to eat my emergency Pop-Tart—I keep one in my backpack at all times.

Tris is way sweeter, funnier, more interesting, and better in every way than Roy, but he doesn't believe me. How can he be so right about my love life and so wrong about his own?

Wednesday, November 30

Tris told me he started crying at the dinner table last night and asked to be excused, and his father told him to "shape up" and "quit acting like a girl." When Tris was telling me about it, he said "At least he didn't say anything awful about me and Roy" in a hopeful voice. I wanted to shout about what a bad person his dad is, but he was trying to look on the bright side, so of course I didn't.

Thursday, December 1

Is it weird that I still listen to Raffi's Christmas album even though I'm almost old enough to drive?

Friday, December 2

Tris came over for dinner. When he walked in, Dad said, "Hey, buddy," and Tris started crying. Dad gave him a hug and said, "Chloe told me. It's tough. There are no two ways about it."

When Tris felt better, we ordered pizza, and Dad had a beer and talked to us.

"'Puppy love' is such a stupid phrase," he said. "There was this girl, Jenny, in high school—man, I was crazy about her. We dated for about two months, but I loved her so much. Far more than I've loved most of my adult girlfriends, including women I've dated for years and years."

"Dad!!" I groaned. Why is he constantly forcing me to think about his sex life?

"No, go on," Tris said.

"I was catatonic when she dumped me. I must have lost 10 pounds."

"How long did it take you to get over her?" Tris asked, staring at my father like he was gazing into a crystal ball.

"You know, not long, because I met someone else fast. That's one good thing about dating in your youth:

you can feel reasonably certain you'll find love again. The older you get, the less certain you feel."

I couldn't even speak, I was so uncomfortable.

As soon as Tris and I were alone, I apologized. "I'm sorry my dad was saying all that stuff about the divorce and Miss Murphy."

Tris gave me an odd look. "He didn't say anything about the divorce or Miss Murphy. Anyway, don't apologize for him. He's the best."

He is, but he still embarrasses the dickens out of me.

Saturday, December 3

Hey Hannah banana. Want to come over?

I'm sorry, I'm just seeing this!
I was over at Reese's.

At her HOUSE?

Yes. Why?

OMG. What is her house even like?

I don't know. It's nice.

What's her bedroom like?
Does she have a canopy and
a pink duvet?

It's just normal.

Hannah, specificity is
the soul of narrative.
That's a quote from my
favorite podcast, which I
was listening to today
instead of hanging out
with you

Aw. I miss you! We should
definitely hang out after school
one day this week.

I've read this exchange 10 times, and I can't tell if she's lying to me, then irritated with me, then avoiding me and faking niceness, or if she's being genuinely sweet through the whole thing, like she usually is.

Sunday, December 4

During breakfast, Dad told me he's planning to ask Miss Murphy over for dinner on Friday night, if that sounds good to me. My Froot Loops were turning to ashes in my mouth, but I said sure.

Monday, December 5
I feel sad about how not-sad I feel about Mom. When I first found out about the divorce, I couldn't go five minutes without thinking about it. Now I can make it at least a day, sometimes two, before it pops into my mind. It's not that I want to be depressed about it. But maybe I do. If Mom were living two towns over and I had to stay with her half the week and watch her and Dad talking or not talking or whatever they would be doing while they handed me off, the whole thing would feel more real.

And why hasn't she emailed me? I don't care that I haven't responded to her in weeks. She promised to keep writing to me no matter what.

Tuesday, December 6
Noelle wants to take a driver's ed course that meets twice a week during lunch—mostly classes, but also some driving practice, once we get our learner's permits—and she wants me to take it with her. She didn't ask me what I thought. She just announced that we were doing it. Bossy, confident, in charge: these are the qualities of a popular person. It's no wonder I've been nearly invisible for the duration of my school career.

Wednesday, December 7

Tris looks thin and exhausted. Roy unfollowed him everywhere, which is gratuitously mean. The dumpee should be the one to unfollow, never the dumper.

Thursday, December 8

I've seen Reese and Hannah together in the halls four times this week. Hannah always waves to me and calls, "Hi, Chloe!" but she doesn't break away from Reese to come see me. There's nothing technically wrong with it, but it still feels like it's against all the laws of friendship.

Friday, December 9

Miss Murphy is coming over in 16 minutes, or possibly more if she's running late. I have butterflies, but I can't tell if they're butterflies of excitement or fear.

Saturday, December 10

I'm being a baby. Nothing so serious happened. There's no reason to be catatonic with sadness.

Miss Murphy came over wearing skinny jeans and a fuzzy sweater, neither of which she wears to class. I guess she has a whole weekend wardrobe, which makes sense, although I'd never thought of it before. Of course teachers don't want to sit around wearing blazers on Saturdays.

She had a Manhattan with Dad, and I had a Shirley Temple, because who cares if they're supposed to be for six-year-olds? They're delicious. We stood around the island and talked. Well, Dad and Miss Murphy did. I was so distracted by the overwhelming weirdness of seeing Miss Murphy in my kitchen that I couldn't speak, other than to answer their questions.

Dad seemed nervous. Miss Murphy seemed fine.

Dinner was pork tenderloin with salad and roasted sweet potatoes. Miss Murphy had brought a small carrot cake for dessert, which Mom would have hated, because she can't stand walnuts. I only ate two bites, even though it was excellent. I couldn't betray Mom by eating a whole piece.

On my way back from the bathroom, I saw Dad and Miss Murphy standing in the kitchen, and stopped to spy on them for a minute before they noticed me. Dad must have said something funny, because Miss Murphy was laughing. "I'll be sure to tell him that," she said. I had no idea what they were talking about, but it didn't matter. The point was that their voices had changed. They sounded more real than the voices they use to talk to me. And they were looking at each other with crinkled, happy eyes. *They're in love*, I thought.

After Miss Murphy left and the dishes were done, I went upstairs intending to cry, but I couldn't. Instead I lay on my bed watching the moon sit in the branches outside my window, and felt nothing.

Sunday, December 11

I'd been feeling sorry for Mom, what with all the carrot-cake-eating and eye-crinkling going on around here, but then I checked my email.

> Chloe,
>
> I have a favor to ask of you. Would you please take photos of my china, the contents of the bookshelf closest to the window in the living room, the upholstered bench in the foyer, the Le Creuset collection, and the blankets on the top shelf of the linen closet, and email them to me? I may think of more items I need photographed, in which case I'll email again. Yours in haste,
>
> —Mom

She thinks if she refuses to acknowledge that I'm ignoring her, I'll stop. And she thinks I'm going to help her steal the Le Creuset stuff from Dad, when that's what he uses to make short ribs and casseroles for me. FAT CHANCE, VERONICA.

Monday, December 12

Tris and I are a real barrel of laughs. Lunch today was 23 minutes of therapy, but with two patients and no therapist.

Tuesday, December 13

PSAT scores came out today. I did so well on reading. I did so well on writing. I did so, so horribly on math that my heart almost jumped out of my body when I saw the number.

Wednesday, December 14

Text from Hannah.

> *What are you doing on*
> *Friday night?*

> *Nothing how come?*

> *Would you like to go to the*
> *Bowline with me and Reese?*

> *Uhhhhhhh*

> *Please, Chloe? I think you and*
> *she would really like each other.*

You're both important to me,
and I want you to be friends.

                    OK OK fine

Great! I'm so happy!

                    I'm not promising anything

All I ask is that you give
her a chance.

                    Yep OK

I know I shouldn't be so grumpy, but come on! She can't expect me to be excited about hanging out with the girl who stole my almost-boyfriend and is in the process of stealing my actual best friend.

Thursday, December 15
I nearly bumped into Grady today because we were both looking at our phones while turning a corner. His eyes flickered, and I could tell he was considering walking away without saying anything, but then he said, "Hey."

"Hey. How's everything?"

"Pretty good."

"How's Bear?"

"Fine. Really into Winnie-the-Pooh these days."

"That makes sense." Blank look from Grady. "Because of his name. Bear . . . Winnie-the-Pooh is a bear . . . you know?" KILL ME.

"Oh, yeah, right," he said finally.

"I guess I'm hanging out with your girlfriend tomorrow."

"Yeah, she mentioned that."

"OK, well . . ."

"Yeah. See ya."

"See ya."

Neither of us smiled once during the entire conversation. If "conversation" is even the right word.

Friday, December 16

How can Hannah stand her? How? How? How???

Mrs. Egan and Hannah picked me up at quarter of seven and we drove to the Bowline, one of the few nice restaurants in our town, if by "nice" you mean "painted beige and full of dark-brown wood like something out of a 1990s home makeover show."

I can't wait to get my license. I wouldn't mind walking for hours at a time if I lived in New York, but here there are no sidewalks, plus older high school kids beep at you as they drive by to rub in the fact that you're walking. Sure, you can ride your bike around, if you don't mind carrying your helmet into restaurants and almost getting hit by cars when it's dark and you're on some ancient narrow New England road that used to be a cow path. So you're basically stuck in your house unless you can force an adult to give you a ride somewhere, and then you have to deal with them sighing like they're doing you this huge favor. And there's nothing more humiliating than being dropped off by someone's mom, who yells "Put on your hats, girls; it's freezing!" as you walk away as fast as you can in a failed attempt to pretend you didn't just get dropped off by someone's mom.

I was wearing a striped sweater I thought looked pretty cute, but as soon as I saw Reese, I realized I looked like someone's dorky nephew. She had on gray leather pants with ankle zippers and a sheer white shirt over a black bra with crisscrossing straps. All the pervy dads in the place stared at her when she ran over to us, squealing, to say hi.

Reese and Hannah sat on one side of the booth, and I sat on the other, which I told myself was a coincidence and not a symbol. I ordered nachos. Hannah ordered a salad with grilled chicken. Reese ordered a burger with onion rings and had two bites. She and Hannah talked about field hockey for a long time, which made me feel stupid and left out, because I didn't understand anything they were saying (what is "tipping an aerial"?!) and obviously had nothing to add. Finally Reese was like, "Ugh,

Hannah, do you even realize how boring we're being? Chloe has no idea what we're talking about. Anyway, there are way more important things to discuss. Now, listen, Chloe, we have to set Hannah up with someone. She's a total catch—it's insane that she doesn't have a boyfriend."

"She had a boyfriend last year," I said. "Maybe she hasn't mentioned him."

"You mean Josh?" she said, killing my attempt to prove that I know Hannah better than she does. "She can do so much better than that kid."

"I agree," I said.

She leaned over the table and lowered her voice. "You know who I was thinking? Zach Chen."

Hannah and I looked at each other.

"What?" said Reese. "Tell me!"

"No, it's nothing," Hannah said. "I used to have a crush on him, that's all."

Reese smacked the table. "I'm, like, a mind reader! I swear we're psychically connected. What color am I thinking of?" She stared at Hannah, and Hannah stared back intently.

"Purple?" Hannah said.

"YES!" shrieked Reese, and they grabbed each other's hands and gasped.

"That was amazing!" Hannah said. Was she serious? Nothing could be less amazing than guessing Reese's favorite color. Didn't she remember the time in sixth grade when Reese's mom took her to Prime Cuts to get purple highlights and we all died of jealousy?

"Zach loves me," Reese said. "I'll hook it up."

"Oh, don't say anything to him!" Hannah was writhing with discomfort. "The thing is, I think something almost happened with us a few months ago, but then he found out . . . he found out about me and Josh—you know—and he wasn't interested anymore."

"Oh, your V-card?" Reese said. So Hannah had told her. I shouldn't have felt betrayed—Hannah's allowed to tell anyone anything she wants—but I did, a little.

Reese waved her hand in the air to swat away Hannah's worry. "I'll tell him you made that up to try to impress him."

"But—" I started. They both looked at me like they were wondering why I was talking. "But Hannah shouldn't have to lie. Who cares about her—her V-card?"

"Zach does, obviously," Reese said. She turned back to Hannah. "You'll see. We'll be double-dating in a month." Then she looked at me again and put her hand over her mouth. "Sorry," she said, laughing. "I forgot." What did she forget? That her boyfriend is my ex-friend? That I'm a spinster who will never get to go on a double date? That Hannah was my friend first, and that if anyone should be stage-managing her love life, it's me?

We spent the rest of the night talking about Zach:

how dreamy he is, what an amazing musician he is, how sexy his man bun is, etc. Eventually Reese got out her phone, and she and Hannah sat with their heads almost touching, looking at pictures of him together. I got out my phone too and jumped around from place to place, texting with Noelle, distracting myself. Thank God I *have* a phone and didn't have to sit there trying not to look unhappy while they didn't talk to me.

Saturday, December 17

Woke up to a text from Hannah.

Last night was fun!

> Yeah

Didn't you think?

> Yep good times

I can tell you don't mean it.

> It was fine Han

I'd rather you be honest with me.

What do you want me to say?

*That you guys ignored me
for most of the night?*

*That she obviously doesn't
like me?*

Oh, Chloe, I'm so sorry
you feel that way.

*I don't FEEL any way.
I'm just stating facts*

I definitely did not think
I was ignoring you.

Well you were

This was humiliating! I felt like a pouting toddler.

And I know Reese likes
you a lot

She texted me how adorable
and sweet you are

*Hannah do you hear how
condescending she is?
"Adorable and sweet"*

I'm not a shih tzu

She didn't mean it that way

Is this about Grady?

Is WHAT about Grady

This attitude toward Reese?

*!!! I'm not the one with the
attitude!*

Whatever it doesn't matter

It does matter to me.

Then neither of us typed. I could feel her looking
at her phone, and I was looking at mine, but eventually
I put it down and went to get breakfast. I hope she was
still staring into her screen, waiting to see if I was mad,
while I ate my cereal.

Sunday, December 18

Dad and I decorated the house for Christmas today. I've never felt less festive in my entire life. All I can think about is my fight with Hannah.

After the tree was up, I took Snickers for a long walk. It was cold and damp, and I could see my breath in the air, and Snickers's. Most people in our neighborhood wrap their railings in lights, or put a candle in each window, or hang a wreath on the door. I'm not sure why it makes me feel so lonely, walking along in the late-afternoon darkness, seeing these nice houses lit up and people moving around inside. It makes me think about how everyone has their own little lives and their own worries and fears and problems, and how brave and sad it is that people bother to put up lights and try to be cheerful.

Monday, December 19

Noelle turned 16 today. Thalia Rosen and I were taping streamers to her locker first thing in the morning, before homeroom, when Reese and Grady and Hannah came by, giggling and whispering with each other. Hannah said hi to me. Reese and Grady didn't. I could feel Reese eyeing us, though. Good! She tried to cast Noelle into outer darkness, and she failed. At least two people still like her enough to try to make her birthday happy. Three people, actually. I was forgetting her mom, who took her to the DMV to get her permit right after school.

Tuesday, December 20

I'm shaken up. We had our first driver's ed class today. The teacher is Mr. Tansel, who intimidates me because he rarely smiles. He wears horn-rimmed glasses, he's short and compact, he has rumpled white hair, and in general he looks like a staring owl. Most teachers yell at everyone to be quiet, but he waited at the front of the classroom, observing us impassively until we all shut up of our own accord. Then he said, "Is anyone here afraid of flying?"

Maybe 30% of the kids raised their hands.

He crossed his arms. "Who here can tell me the likelihood of dying in a plane crash?"

"One in a million?" Noelle said.

"One in 11 million," Mr. Tansel said. "And the likelihood of dying in a car crash?"

"High," someone said.

"Very high. One in 5,000. Think about that for a moment. If you're looking at lifelong risk, one in 120 Americans dies while driving."

He was talking in a calm, chatty voice, which made what he was saying scarier.

Putting his hands in his pockets, he said, "Now, it's very unlikely that you'll die as a teenager. Less than 1% of all Americans who die in a year are 19 or under. But if you do die young, it'll probably be in a car. Accidental injury accounts for almost half of all teen deaths, and of those, almost three quarters are caused by motor vehicle accidents. Now, what's your guess—would you say car fatalities are increasing or decreasing?"

"Increasing," said Griffin Gonzalez, who was sitting in the front row.

"Correct," said Mr. Tansel. "In fact, we haven't seen an annual percentage increase like this in more than 50 years. What could account for this spike?" He picked up an imaginary phone and mimed texting. Then he dropped his hands and looked at us. "It's possible that the robotics PhDs will perfect automated cars in your lifetimes. Until then, I'd urge you to take this class seriously."

All those images I see of someone running down Dad—it's not my diseased brain torturing me. It's a rational fear. Someone could kill him. *I* could kill him. Or I could kill Bear, or someone like Bear.

Wednesday, December 21

Dad went out with Miss Murphy tonight, which I know because he told me where he was going before he left. I asked if he wanted to have her over to our house again, and he said maybe at some point.

"Did I embarrass you last time?" I asked.

"Not at all. Did I embarrass you?"

"Nope," I said.

He was at the hall closet, looking through the basket of gloves and scarves. "I thought the atmosphere was a little strained."

"Maybe a little," I said.

He found the scarf he wanted and put it around his neck. "I know this is difficult, Chloe. I appreciate the effort you're making."

After he left, I did all the empty-house stuff I normally do: ate some brown sugar with a spoon, danced to hip-hop in my undies while checking out my moves in the mirror, etc. It was fun for an hour, and then it got lonely.

Dad never stays out all night. Where do he and Miss Murphy have sex? Do they go to hotels for a few hours? Do they do it in the car? Or, like, on a park bench somewhere??

I don't want to think about these things, but I can't help it.

Thursday, December 22

Half day at school. Tris and Hannah and I went to the mall, which we'd been planning to do today since before

Thanksgiving, so it seemed too awkward to cancel it, even though I wanted to. For once I was relieved to see Mrs. Egan, who never stops talking and is oblivious to bad vibes. She dropped us right in front of an entrance and said "You guys go on in. I'm sure I'll find a parking spot eventually" in such a genuinely sunny voice, even though the mall was a total horror show and she definitely wasn't going to find a spot without driving around for at least half an hour, that for a second I realized it really is generous of grown-ups to chauffeur kids around constantly when of course they'd rather be clicking on their phones like everyone else. And then Mrs. Egan said "Are you picking up something for your mom, Chloe?" in a syrupy voice, and I snapped out of it. "Thanks for the ride!" I called, ignoring her question and slamming the door shut.

I thought Hannah and I were making a big effort and being normal and happy with each other, so I was surprised when she went to the bathroom and Tris said, "What is *wrong* with you guys?"

"Are we being weird?"

"I feel like I'm in a movie about two robots programmed to act like perfect teenagers. Are you in a fight?"

"I'm still mad about the Bowline," I said. I'd already spent about four hours telling him every detail of what happened, so he didn't need the backstory. "It's one thing to ignore me, but she can't even admit she did it. I don't think she even *knows* she did it."

"No, thanks," Tris said loudly. "I'm not in the mood for Auntie Anne's." I briefly wondered if he was having a stroke, and then I turned around and saw Hannah right behind me. She smiled, but maybe the smile looked a tiny bit forced? Oh, please, please, please let her not have overheard me.

Friday, December 23

Dad dragged me to the grocery store, which I was actually happy about, because I love seeing everyone bustling around, getting ready for the holiday. After we'd picked up the food, Dad suggested stopping at Starbucks, which was a Christmas miracle, because whenever I ask to go there, he's like, "We can make perfectly good coffee at home," which is missing the entire point.

We'd ordered our drinks when I heard someone squealing, "Chloe Snow!" and turned to see Reese heading toward us, pulling Hannah along with her. Hannah, who normally looks like she just stepped off a Swiss alp— no makeup, pink cheeks, long braid—was almost unrecognizable. She must have cut 10 inches off her hair, which was now in a razor-sharp lob, and she was wearing dark eye shadow and liquid liner so perfectly applied, she looked like the end result of a YouTube tutorial.

"Is this your dad?" Reese asked. "Hi. I'm Reese!" She shook his hand with enthusiasm.

"Nice to meet you, Reese," he said.

"Chloe, how amazing does Hannah look?" Reese said. Then she held her hand to her mouth, like she was telling me a secret, and said, in a stage whisper, "She's all ready for her big date tonight."

"You have a date?" I asked Hannah. Even though things were awkward with us, it was embarrassing that she hadn't told me.

"I'm going to the movies with Zach. Reese set it up." She cupped her fingers around the back of her head and said, "Do you like my haircut?"

"You look great," I said, because she did. She looked beautiful, and sexy, and grown-up. And her whole face was sparkling, which was the worst part of all. Reese clearly makes her so much happier than I do.

"Reese seems sweet," Dad said when we got back in the car.

I snorted and said, "Yeah, sweet like a snake!" which doesn't make sense but also makes perfect sense.

Saturday, December 24

As usual, Dad and I watched *Meet Me in St. Louis*, but this year, in a fun new twist, I started ugly-crying two seconds into "Have Yourself a Merry Little Christmas." I wonder if the holidays will ever make me happy again, or if they'll always remind me of the old days that are lost forever, when I still believed in Santa and my parents were together.

Sunday, December 25

Hannah called in the afternoon to wish me a merry Christmas, and of course I asked her how her date was.

"It was amazing," she said. "He put his arm around me when the movie started, and then he kissed me, and we basically didn't stop making out until the credits."

"Wow!" I said, and I put all my acting ability into sounding delighted. And why do I have to act? I should be genuinely happy for her.

"I know you're not crazy about her, but Reese was so nice to set me up with him."

"You set yourself up with him," I said. "Remember the day he came over and chopped vegetables? He's always liked you."

"Yes, but I messed it up."

"You didn't," I said.

"I did, but at least Reese fixed it."

"What do you mean?"

"She did what she said she would. She told him I

really am a virgin, I just fibbed and said I wasn't, to try to impress him."

"'FIBBED'?"

"Like you said, my past is none of his business," she said. I didn't have a comeback, but it still seems wrong to me. Why should she be ashamed of herself, or have to lie? She shouldn't!

I went downstairs in a horrendous mood and found Dad sitting on the couch, still in his pajamas, resting his feet on Snickers and reading the newspaper on his iPad.

"Don't you want to see Miss Murphy today?" I said. My tone was fine, but it was hiding the fury in my heart.

He looked up at me. "Christmas is for family," he said, and there was a tiny dash of nobility in his voice that made me so furious I turned and stormed back up to my room without saying another word. I considered refusing to come downstairs for dinner, but I didn't want to miss the steaks, so in the end I settled for sulking and speaking only in monosyllables while eating as fast as I could, which of course I feel guilty about now, because (1) I ruined Christmas and (2) if I keep acting like this, Dad definitely won't want to hang out with me instead of Miss Murphy.

Monday, December 26

I just realized Mom didn't email or call yesterday. God, I HATE her.

Tuesday, December 27

We're not even halfway through it, and already I'm completely over winter break. There's only so much coziness, chocolate, and caroling a person can take before she starts longing for broccoli and exercise.

Wednesday, December 28

I took Snickers for a run!!!! He stared up at me in amazement the entire time. I don't think he realized I'm physically capable of moving my legs faster than strolling speed.

Thursday, December 29

Rode my bike over to Tristan's, which was probably dangerous, since it was sleeting, but I had to get out of my house. Dad is still martyring around feeling pleased with himself for not seeing Miss Murphy, and I can't take it. Tris was down in the dumps the whole time and finally admitted he was sure Roy was going to call him during the break. "But he hasn't, and he probably won't," Tris said, and quickly looked at me to see if I'd say, "There's still time—he might!" but I couldn't bring myself to lie.

Friday, December 30

I can't believe it, but Dad has agreed to let me sleep over at Tristan's house on New Year's Eve for the first time ever! It's another Christmas miracle!

Saturday, December 31

Oh my God. Oh my freaking God. I caught Dad and Miss Murphy having a sleepover. Can't write; Tris is downstairs waiting for me.

Sunday, January 1

What happened was, Tris and I were sitting on his couch eating cheese and drinking sparkling cider, gossiping about Hannah and Zach, who are now officially together, according to Zach's Instagram, and I was feeling so happy and carefree, and then suddenly I jumped up and ran to the bathroom without saying a word to Tris, and sure enough, I'd gotten my period and ruined my favorite undies, the green plaid ones, and probably also my favorite jeans, although those jeans can take a licking. They are survivors.

It turned out Mrs. Flynn had no tampons or pads or anything, which she seemed sad about, and which I guess means she already went through menopause?! So now I know something about her I should not know, thanks to my stupid period. She was so sympathetic and offered to drive me home to grab some stuff. Tris came to keep us company. I was terrified I was going to bleed through the giant wad of Kleenex I was using as a makeshift pad and wreck the Flynns' Toyota Highlander seats, but instead I just wrecked the sweatpants I'd borrowed from Tris.

I ran inside while Mrs. Flynn idled in the driveway, and there in the kitchen were Miss Murphy and Dad!!!!!!!! She was leaning over the island, resting her elbows on it, wearing comfy pants and one of Dad's T-shirts. He was sitting across from her. They both had a glass of water in front of them, and their hair was messed up, and most of the kitchen lights were off, and in short, I'm completely positive they had JUST finished having sex.

They looked up at me with round, frozen eyes, like they were lions hunched over a kill and I was an explorer who had burst out of the shrubs unexpectedly.

"Uh, hi," I said.

"Hi," they both said.

"I came home," I said stupidly, and then stood there staring at them.

"Marian was—" Dad started, but Miss Murphy cut him off to say, "I was on my way out."

This was so obviously a lie, when her feet were bare and I could currently see her nipples through Dad's shirt, that I didn't dignify it with a response.

I ran upstairs, took a five-second shower, threw my clothes in cold water to soak, got dressed, grabbed an entire box of super-plus tampons, wrote in my diary for two seconds because I had to get it down on paper to keep my head from exploding, and ran downstairs again. Dad was on his own in the kitchen.

"Where's Miss Murphy?" I asked.

"She had to take off."

"Dad! Are you seriously . . ." I stopped. I couldn't go on. I couldn't make myself say, "Are you seriously pretending she was just stopping by, and that you weren't using my sleepover as your big chance to have your own sleepover?"

"I have to go," I said. "Mrs. Flynn is waiting for me."

"Hang on," Dad said, but I hurried toward the door, calling, "Happy New Year's Eve, bye, sorry, bye!" and fled to the driveway.

When we got back to his house, Tris and I talked so hard about what had happened that we missed midnight by more than an hour.

Monday, January 2

This morning was strange. To put it mildly.

I came downstairs wearing Mom's striped bathrobe, feeling like a full-body migraine. I hadn't even had time to say hi to Dad when the doorbell rang. Dad and I looked at each other like, *What the . . . ?* and he got up to see who it was. And then, in the front hall, I heard Miss Murphy's voice! Why is she haunting my life? I couldn't hear the conversation, because she and Dad were whispering. Then I heard Dad going upstairs and Miss Murphy walking toward the kitchen.

"Chloe, I'm sorry to burst in on you like this, but I wanted to catch you before school."

I've never wanted to escape to Narnia more desperately. My period was murdering me. It felt like a bowling ball made of fire was bearing down on my vagina. My face was unwashed and my teeth were unbrushed. In the kitchen was this woman who is trying so hard to be nice to me and whom I used to adore and now desperately want to at least like and feel normal around but who only makes me stiff with discomfort. I needed snow and a lamppost and a faun, and the closest thing I could think of was the freezer, so I went to it, opened it up, and stared at the old Creamsicles. Then I rested my forearm inside the freezer, rested my head on my forearm, and let the cold air wash over my head.

"Chloe, are you crying?" Miss Murphy said.

Help me, C. S. Lewis, I thought, and his name alone gave me strength.

"No," I said, pulling my head out of the freezer and shutting the door.

"Well, good," she said. "Listen, Chloe, I want to apologize for what happened on New Year's Eve. That's not the way I wanted to—"

"It's fine," I said. "I don't care if you sleep over. I mean, you and Dad are . . . whatever. And you're adults. So obviously you're going to—anyway, I'd rather you stay here, instead of at a . . . wherever else."

"OK."

"Because I don't want to sleep here by myself."

It seemed like she might try to hug me, so I crossed my arms over my bathrobe to ward her off.

"Can I ask you something?" I said. It's not often you have honest conversations in this life, and I wanted to seize the moment.

"Sure," she said.

"Doesn't it gross you out that Dad is 15 years older than you?"

She laughed. "14."

"What?"

"My birthday is January first."

"Happy birthday! Wait, your birthday is New Year's Day? That's awful."

"How come?"

"Have you ever even had a birthday party that wasn't also a New Year's Eve party?"

"Sure, when I was a kid, before anyone started caring about New Year's Eve. And childhood is the only time your birthday matters, anyway. If you still want a fuss when you're in your thirties, there's something wrong with you."

I was enjoying this conversation, which was the first normal one we'd had in a while, but not enough to forget that Miss Murphy had come over at 6:40 a.m. to apologize because I'd caught her and Dad five minutes after they finished having sex in my parents' bed.

It's not even the sleepover that annoys me. It's the sneaking around. And it's the fact that Dad and Miss Murphy are forcing me to sound like someone's mom. ("Kids, I'm disappointed you felt the need to lie to me.") I don't want to be the mom, irritated with two teenagers for being idiots. I want to be the idiot teenager.

"To answer your question," Miss Murphy said, "I actually like the age difference. He knows a lot of good bands I've never heard of."

"Don't play our version of Trivial Pursuit with him," I said. "He's like an encyclopedia of '80s facts."

A silence fell. Snickers wandered into the kitchen and looked at Miss Murphy curiously.

"This was anticlimactic," Miss Murphy said. "I thought you might throw a cereal bowl at my head. I was even prepared to give you some inside info to compensate for messing up so royally on Saturday."

"Really?" I said.

She lowered her voice. "You want to know what the musical's going to be?"

I widened my eyes. "Of course."

"*South Pacific*."

"Oh my God. Can I text Tris?"

"No way. Don't tell a soul until Friday."

She finally left. I was half an hour late to school because there's no room in my getting-ready schedule for impromptu conversations with my married dad's girlfriend.

Tuesday, January 3

I told Tris everything about Miss Murphy's visit except for the *South Pacific* part. I don't think I've ever kept a secret from him before, and it's making me feel like a criminal.

Wednesday, January 4

I told Tris! I had to. He screamed a little and everyone in the hall around us turned to look. After school we spent the afternoon downloading and watching the movie, streaming the 2008 Broadway revival cast recording, Googling "south pacific audition scenes," and trying to find the script online.

Obviously Tris is going to be Lieutenant Cable and I'm going to be Nellie. This couldn't be more perfect! Nellie is excitable. I'm excitable. Nellie is optimistic. So am I. Nellie is spunky. I'm pretty freaking spunky.

There's also an upsetting aspect of the character: Nellie is a racist. She repents at the end, but still, it's shocking. The point of the musical is that Nellie's racism is disgusting and that you can be a cute, fun girl everyone considers so nice and still have this snake coiled in your heart. And furthermore, the point is that racism isn't something you're born with. You learn it from your parents, and you have to recognize it in yourself and force yourself to change, and turn your back on your family if they have a problem with that. And if you don't, your soul is going to die the way Lieutenant Cable literally dies in the show. It's terrible that all of this is still so relevant today, 70 years after it was written, but it is.

Thursday, January 5
Practiced "Honey Bun" after school today until I lost my voice. This is going to be SO FUN. I wish I didn't have to wait until the end of the month to audition.

Friday, January 6
All the theater geeks were freaking out today after they'd found out what the musical is, and I was dying to tell them I knew first, but I controlled myself. Tris and I did give each other a lot of meaningful looks, however.

Saturday, January 7

Text from Mac!

> *Hey whats that word that*
> *means grumpy but with a cat*

> *A cat??*

> *Oh cantankerous*

> *Thanks kid. Need some vocab*
> *words for a paper. Wish you*
> *were here to write it for me lol*

I sent him a smiling cat in response, and he sent me a cat with heart eyes!!!!!!!!!

Sunday, January 8

I don't think Juliet would have been so impressed if Romeo sent her a cat with heart eyes. Why are my standards this low? And why do I care what emoji Mac is sending me anyway??????

Monday, January 9

I went over to Noelle's after school. Her mother's traveling for work, and it felt strange to be in the house alone, knowing it would get dark and no one would come home. We'd been watching TV for a while when Noelle stood up, turned it off with the remote, and said, "This is boring. Want to go for a drive? Mom left the Volvo."

I stared at her. "We can't. You have to be with an adult before you get your license."

"Oh my God." She rolled her eyes. "Would you relax? We're not going to drag race. I'm a good driver—I've already practiced a ton of times with my mom."

I was shocked that she would suggest taking the car out without a grown-up. Of course I didn't say so, because I didn't want to sound like a child. But I couldn't stop myself from asking, "What if someone sees us? Like a cop?"

"We'll take turns being the adult. Here . . ." She pulled me into the kitchen, opened a drawer, and got out a pair of sunglasses and a baseball cap with MARTHA'S VINEYARD stitched on the front in white thread. "These are my mother's. Put them on."

It's hard to resist a direct order. Or it is for me, anyway. I put on the cap and glasses and followed Noelle outside.

It started out fine. Noelle drove around the neighborhood for a while, slowly and carefully. She accelerated too fast a few times by accident, and once she slammed on the brakes, but overall, she's a good driver. Eventually she pulled into a cul-de-sac, put the car in park, and said, "OK, your turn." She hopped out and came around to the passenger side without waiting for me to respond. Opening my door, she reached in, took the cap and sunglasses off of me, and put them on herself. "Move it, toots," she said. I thought about refusing, but I didn't want to get into a big thing.

By the time I was in the driver's seat with my seat belt on and my hands on the wheel, my heart was racing, I was sweating all over, and there was something wrong with my vision. I could still see, but it was like someone had dropped gray gauze over my head. Everything looked darker.

"Are you OK?" Noelle said. I'd never heard her sound so concerned, and it made me feel worse. I pictured putting the car in drive and then losing control and smashing into a tree. Or what if an evil urge overtook me and I swerved into oncoming traffic? What if I swerved into *Dad's car*?

"I can't drive," I managed to say.

"Yeah, no kidding," Noelle said. "You sound like you just ran a marathon. Should we go to the hospital?"

I got out of the car and leaned against the roof, resting my head on my hands and closing my eyes. After a few minutes, I felt better. Noelle had gotten out and was standing next to the passenger seat, staring at me.

"I'm fine," I said.

We didn't say much on the ride home. Noelle almost took the side mirror off pulling into the garage, but other than that, nothing scary happened.

"So, that was weird back there," Noelle said while we were waiting for my dad to pick me up, and I said, "Yeah, it was," but was it? Why is it weird to be scared of driving? You *should* be scared! You're very, very likely to die while doing it! You wouldn't mess around with a loaded gun, so why would you intentionally operate a car?

Tuesday, January 10

Mr. Tansel went over basic rules of the road today. He showed us a PowerPoint that included plenty of cheesy clip art, which I think he intended to be funny, though you can never tell with him.

I don't mind learning about four-way stops and the two-second rule. If we could sit in the classroom just talking about driving forever, I'd be fine.

Wednesday, January 11

I biked past the junior parking lot today. Literally half of the kids driving cars were also on their phones, including Zach, who was scrolling while waiting to turn left. And there was Hannah in the passenger seat, smiling like she wasn't in danger. I tried to stop looking, because I was getting so upset, but I couldn't.

Thursday, January 12

If I move to Manhattan, I won't need a license! I'll take the subway everywhere. It's actually cooler not to drive these days.

Friday, January 13

I told Noelle I'm going to drop driver's ed, and she said, "Are you serious? Why?"

"I want to go to college in New York, so I won't need to drive. And when I'm here, I'll bike."

"Is this because you freaked out in the car the other day?"

I didn't say anything.

"You can't ride your bike in the snow," she said. "What's going to happen when you're 40 years old, bringing your kids home to visit your dad for the holidays?"

"He can pick us up at the train station," I said. "Also, I'll probably never have kids, because the way things are going, I'll be a virgin forever."

We were walking through the front lobby, past the administrative office. I looked inside at the grown-ups sitting at their desks, staring at their computers. They'd all driven to school that day. They were lucky to be alive.

"You know what, you're right," she said. "You could ride your bike for the rest of your life. You don't need a license. But you should get one anyway."

I started to groan, but she cut me off. "It's a rite of passage. It'll make you feel more free. You'll be able to rely on yourself to get places. And you can help other people! You'll give me a ride home when I get drunk at a party. You can, like, give your dad a ride to the hospital if he has a heart attack."

"Noelle!"

"I'm just saying. It's safer to have one. It's part of being an adult. Come on, you can't drop the class. Don't be a baby."

We were outside now, watching other kids climb onto bright-yellow buses. Tris would never tell me not to be a baby. Hannah wouldn't either. Noelle's mean to me sometimes. Or maybe it's more fair to say she's so straightforward, it hurts. But it feels good, too.

I know she's right. I do want to drive. I have to force myself to do it somehow. At least my birthday's not until May. I have a few more months to get over this phobia.

Saturday, January 14
Email from Mom.

> Dear Chloe,
>
> I'm writing to apologize for failing to be in touch on Christmas. I admit I was angry and wanted

to punish you with silence, the way you have
punished me. It is difficult, writing into a void,
and I am losing heart.

To give you the full picture, I must tell you I've
been forced to take a job at the yoga studio.
I make change for customers, I restock the
juice bar, and I do a weekly deep cleaning. It's
humbling work, but it's a necessity for me, as my
financial future is, to put it lightly, unclear, and I
can't rely forever on the kind of support I've come
to expect (and indeed, in my view, to deserve)
from your father. Given my new duties, I have very
little time in which to continue querying, much
less work on a new project, so you can imagine
how soul-starved and desolate I'm feeling and you
will, I hope, forgive my recent petulance.

—Mom

Mom is deep cleaning a yoga studio?!?!? I don't
think I ever even saw her wiping down the kitchen
counter! She considers all menial labor demeaning and
anti-feminist.

I'm kind of impressed. And I feel bad for never
responding to her. But the longer my email strike goes on,

the more impossible it seems to call off. How would I end it after keeping it up for so long? What would I even say?

Sunday, January 15

You know what, she can eff right off. She's the one who left, and now here I am motherless, Hannah-less, and loveless, and the person who should be helping me has no clue what's going on. And why should Dad subsidize her while she works on her tan and pretends to write a novel? Keep swabbing those yoga mats, Veronica! See if I care!

Monday, January 16

Martin Luther King Jr. Day. I have to stop being so self-obsessed. I'm wasting my entire life fixating on myself when I could be fighting for social justice. As soon as I'm done getting ready for this audition, I'm going to focus on not being such a despicable waste of DNA.

Tuesday, January 17

Tris came over and we ran lines and practiced our songs for hours. I didn't even think about looking at my phone the entire time, which hardly ever happens, and which feels so good, like I'm getting a short break from being a cyborg.

We invited Hannah, but she said she had plans,

which was a relief. She was in the chorus last year, and Tris and I both had leads, and if we were all getting ready for auditions together, I'd spend the whole time thinking, *Does she think I'm showing off? I'm not going to half-ass it to avoid hurting her feelings. Is that a diva-ish thing to think? But I'm not being a diva. I just want to do my best.* Etc., etc. When it's me and Tristan alone, I can belt it out and not worry.

Wednesday, January 18

These are Nellie's songs, in descending order of how excited I am to sing them.

* "Honey Bun": I'll be pretending to be Nellie pretending to be a bro, and I'll get to sing about a pretty girl while wearing a comfortable sailor uniform. Also, the melody of this one really lets me show off.

* "I'm Gonna Wash That Man Right Outa My Hair": Breakup anthem! Truly the "Single Ladies" of its day. I'll think about Mac while I'm performing and amaze everyone with my acting chops.

* "I'm in Love with a Wonderful Guy": This is the one that gives me chills every time I listen to it. But that's because when Kelli O'Hara

sings, you can hear the joy in her voice. I'm
pretty good, but I'm no Kelli O'Hara.
* "A Cockeyed Optimist": Nellie knows it would
be cooler to be jaded, but she can't help
looking on the bright side all the time. I think
I'm like this. Or I want to be.
* "Twin Soliloquies": I'm worried Miss Murphy
will cast Rob Newell as Emile, because he's
the bassiest bass in school, and I cannot stand
Rob. He's a nerd, which, great, everyone wants
to be a nerd these days, but he's a mean one.
He loathes everyone at our school for not
caring about veganism as much as he does, and
he's never not rolling his eyes. I can't imagine
faking chemistry with him.
* "Some Enchanted Evening (Reprise)": See
above, plus it's a reprise, so everyone's like, "We
already heard this one; move on already."

Thursday, January 19

Hannah found me between classes today, which felt
unusual, and that's so depressing. At first she pretended
she wanted to catch up with me, but after a few minutes of small talk she said, "By the way, have you heard
Grady's going to audition for the musical?"

"No," I said.

"And so is Reese," she said.

"*What?* Really?"

"They thought it would be a fun thing to do together."

"But Grady doesn't like old music," I said.

"Well, Reese really wants him to do it with her."

I tried not to ask, but then I couldn't stop myself. "How's her voice?"

"It's good!" Hannah said, but that doesn't mean anything. She can't perceive talent clearly through the fog of her own niceness.

Something occurred to me. "Are you telling me this because you didn't want me to freak out when I saw them at auditions?"

She looked uncomfortable. "I wanted you to know, that's all."

Our friendship may be struggling, but at least she's still looking out for me.

Friday, January 20

I saw Grady standing by the traffic circle, one foot on his skateboard, one hand on his head. He's always messing with his hair or scratching his abs or putting his palm on his chest while he makes a point. It's like he wants to make everyone think about touching him.

Saturday, January 21

I spent the entire night scrolling through Reese's accounts in the hopes of finding a video of her singing, which of course I didn't. She must suck, right? She can't be popular *and* be a musical-theater phenom.

Only nine days until auditions.

Sunday, January 22

Tris and I were watching TV at his house and I said, "I'm going to get a Diet Coke. Want anything?" and he yawned and said no, he was good, but could I grab the blanket on my way back? I said the striped one or the blue one? and he said the striped one.

Sometimes I feel like we're married, and it's so nice.

It's going to be terrible when one of us gets a boyfriend.

Monday, January 23

Exactly one week until auditions. Tris and I have started texting each other a palm tree emoji every night before bed, for good luck. But we won't need good luck; we have great voices.

I've been trying to convince Noelle to try out, but every time I bring up the topic, she rolls her eyes and says something like, "Theater is not cool, Chloe. I'm sorry." Today I made another attempt while we were walking across the field to get to the clearing so she could have a cigarette. I reminded her Reese is trying out, and she's the most popular person in our grade, so by the transitive property, theater is cool.

"Nope," Noelle said. "It doesn't work like that. Reese is slumming. She's descending to the level of the musical. It doesn't rise up to meet her."

"You are the biggest snob I've ever met in my life," I said.

She shrugged, smiled, and put on her sunglasses.

"Also mean," I said. "I'm a music theater dork, remember?"

"'Dork' being the operative word," she said.

I pulled her hair a little, and she laughed and pulled mine back.

I wish Noelle wouldn't smoke, but it's actually nice having a reason to sit outside on a log on a freezing, snowy day. She wanted me to give her the latest gossip on Hannah and Zach, but I couldn't, really, because I'm hardly even friends with Hannah now. I know she and Zach are together, but that doesn't mean anything; the whole school knows that. All the interesting little details about their relationship—I don't hear those from her. Reese does, I guess.

Tuesday, January 24

Mr. Tansel showed us a Werner Herzog documentary about texting and driving. I wanted to watch it, but a few minutes in, I started shaking and sweating. I asked Mr. Tansel for a hall pass, whispering so I wouldn't distract the other kids, and he whispered back, "Can't it wait, Ms. Snow?" On the TV screen a bald guy who'd caused an accident while looking at his phone was talking about getting out of his car and seeing bodies lying in a ditch. He was struggling not to cry, and I got choked up and left the class without waiting for the hall pass. I thought I might get in trouble, but after I'd walked around for a few minutes and pulled myself together, I went back in, and Mr. Tansel only said, "Everything all right?" He is a good man. He's not trying to scare us. He wants to keep us safe and alive.

After class Noelle looped her arm through mine and said, "That's not going to happen to you."

"I'd rather die myself than kill someone else," I said.

"Stop! Shut up," she said. "Don't even let the thought into your head. I'm going to remind you we had this conversation when we're both 95."

I wish I could extract some of Noelle's strength with a syringe and shoot it into my heart.

Wednesday, January 25

After school I walked past the art room, which I've never been inside, because I've never taken art as an elective. The sun was shining through the windows. There were canvases and watercolors and sketchbooks everywhere, but no people except for Mrs. Kingsley, the teacher, who was washing out jars in a utility sink and humming, and Grady, who was sitting on a stool in front of an easel, working on a painting. I think it was a self-portrait, and I think it was set at the pool! It showed a guy with dark hair wearing a gray suit, floating on his back in turquoise water. It was interesting to see Grady handling his palette and brush so expertly. He looked as natural with them as I probably do with my phone. As I stood there, he tipped his head back and groaned. "Mrs. K., can you come look at this?" he said. "I think the foreshortening is all messed up." He sounded like himself, not like the cold robot he's been to me since our fight. I wanted to keep watching and listening, but I made myself hurry away.

Thursday, January 26

Apparently Miss Murphy is coming over for dinner tomorrow. I keep bracing myself for the big sleepover, now that I gave them the official go-ahead, but it hasn't happened yet. I wish they'd do it and get it over with.

Friday, January 27

Dinner would have been fun, but my fear of driving kind of ruined it. Miss Murphy brought sushi, and we were eating at the dining room table when she told us about almost getting into a fender bender on the way over, which made my heart start racing. Then Dad told a story I'd never heard before. Apparently when I was five and he was driving me to a playdate, speeding along Route 2, I managed to get out of my car seat, then stood in the foot well behind him and put my hands over his eyes. "I don't see what the big deal is," Miss Murphy said. "You weren't on the rotary, right?" Dad laughed, but I thought I was going to pass out. The room was getting dim and kind of flickering. I almost killed Dad and myself in a car when I was five. What if it's fore-shadowing? What if it's like *Final Destination*, and death is waiting for me and will get me as soon as I start driving? It sounds like I'm joking around when I write down these questions, but I'm not. I'm scared.

I couldn't finish my food, which I think Dad and Miss Murphy interpreted as evidence that I was having a bad time. I wanted to make up for my lack of appe-tite with vivacious conversation, but I couldn't, because I was so distracted by thoughts of an alternate past in which my five-year-old self kept her hands over Dad's eyes for a second longer, Dad crashed into the guardrail, and we both died.

Saturday, January 28
I asked Dad if he'd consider biking to work, and he said he's not up for a two-hour ride in both directions.

"Why do you ask? Do I look like I'm on the verge of a heart attack or something?"

"Driving is so dangerous," I said.

He shrugged. "It's one of the risks we live with. Also, I'm an excellent driver. I survived the great Route 2 disaster of 2006, right?"

He seemed so unconcerned that I feel better. A little better, anyway.

Sunday, January 29

Auditions are tomorrow. I'm not nervous; I'm really not. I'm just excited. I can't wait to make everyone sick with jealousy when they hear me sing "Honey Bun." I can't wait to go to rehearsals every day and complain about how exhausted and busy I am. I can't wait to play Nellie and knock the audience's socks off.

Monday, January 30

Reese sabotaged me. I don't know if I even did well enough to get called back. Too upset to write. More tomorrow.

Tuesday, January 31

I showed up feeling so good. Maybe that was the whole problem. Maybe this is my punishment for being conceited.

Tris and I were sitting in the third row, chatting casually, feeling superior to the terrified freshmen around us. I imagined they were sneaking glances at me and whispering, "That's Chloe Snow. She got the lead last year. She's a shoo-in for Nellie. And see that guy next to her? That's Tristan Flynn. He was Rolf. His voice is amazing."

Hannah was on my right, and next to her was Reese, who was making a big display of her ignorance. "Wait, what do I write under 'Previous Experience'? Do my hip-hop classes count? Ugh, I'm so nervous. You guys have to promise not to make fun of me when I sing."

We were all in group A, and Grady was in group B, so I didn't get to see his acting, just his singing (which was fine) and his dancing (which was pretty cute, I have to admit. He was seriously messing up the choreography, but he was grinning the whole way through. He never gets embarrassed and he always looks like he's having fun. Except when he's talking to or looking at me, that is). My scene went well, even though I was paired with Rob, just like I predicted. I learned the choreography pretty easily, and Nellie doesn't have to dance that much anyway. And then we were halfway through our group's vocal auditions, and Miss Murphy called out, "OK, let me have Nadine next, and then Chloe, followed by Izzy," and I finally felt jittery, knowing I was about to go up onstage and destroy "Honey Bun." And then, while Nadine was singing, Reese leaned over Hannah, gripped my arm, and whispered, "Don't worry."

"What, about Nadine?" I whispered. "I'm not."

She smiled. "No, about everyone else."

A voice in my head said, *Don't ask her what she means*, and I knew the voice was right, but I couldn't help it. "What do you mean?"

"Well, the fact that Miss Murphy is your dad's girl-friend . . . Everyone's saying it doesn't matter how your audition goes. People think Miss Murphy and your dad were probably going out last year, too, and that's why you got the lead as a freshman. Grady said you're not even that great of a singer. And I was like, 'Grady, you can be such a jerk!' Seriously, Chloe, you have to just block out the haters."

She was staring into my eyes, looking completely sin-cere and kind. She's such a good actress, better than I'll ever be. She'd bided her time and knifed me right at the most effective moment, and she looked like an angel doing it. Hannah was nodding and looking sympathetic, as if Reese were actually trying to help me. How does she not see the truth about her?

"Chloe, you're up," Miss Murphy called briskly. I glanced at Tris, and he looked at me like, *Ignore her. You can do it.*

I walked up to the stage thinking, *You can do it. You can do it.*

The accompanist played the opening bars of "Honey Bun."

I looked down at the kids looking up at me and thought, *They all know. They're sitting there resenting me for getting special favors. I have to show them I deserve the lead. This is my one chance to prove it.*

I opened my mouth and sang, "My doll is as dainty as a sparrow," and it came out small and wobbling. You could hear tears around the edges of my voice. For a minute I thought I would have to stop, but after I got through the preamble and launched into the main part of the song, the swagger of it carried me along, and by the last few bars, I sounded like myself.

"That was a train wreck," I whispered to Tris as soon as I got back to my seat.

"It wasn't," he said, and he sounded convincing, but of course he did. He's not only my best friend, he's also a wonderful actor.

This girl named Izzy Briggs sang right after I did. She's a kooky, energetic clarinet player who didn't audition last year and who turns out to have a voice like a happy bell. Fantastic. Well, I'll get her during callbacks. If I'm called back at all, that is.

Wednesday, February 1

Not that it matters, but I can't believe Grady said I'm not a good singer. I can't *believe* it. Was he annoyed by me all those times I sang to him at work? I thought that guy was my friend for real. Did he ever even like me?

Thursday, February 2

Told Noelle I'm worried I won't get called back, and she said, "Does that mean you won't be in the show, or whatever?" without looking up from Instagram. Then she handed me her phone and said, "Look at those slides. Do you think I could pull them off, or would they make my legs look stumpy?" She couldn't be less interested in my theater problems, and it's a relief. Most kids are barely aware the musical exists! I need to stop acting like the fate of the nation depends on the outcome of these auditions. Who even cares if I get called back or not?

Friday, February 3

I GOT CALLED BACK. RELIEF. JOY.

Also terror, because now I have to make up for my subpar performance on Monday and prove to the world and Miss Murphy that last year wasn't a fluke.

Tris got called back! Hannah didn't. But Reese did.

REESE. If she's cast as Nellie, I'm going to have to transfer to a high school in Antarctica.

Saturday, February 4

As usual, I revealed my flawed soul to Tris, and as usual, he didn't judge me.

> Am I terrible for being happy
> Hannah didn't get called back?
>
> I should want the best for her,
> but I'm too mad to be nice

Don't be mad, she's like
a cult victim

> Is she though? What if she
> knows Reese is awful and
> doesn't care because she
> wants to be popular so bad?

This is Hannah we're talking
about remember?

> Yeah OK I guess she would
> never do that

Maybe Tris is right, but at some point being clueless is the same thing as being evil.

Sunday, February 5

Callbacks are tomorrow. I'm so nervous, but that's OK: I can channel my fear into energy. Getting parts isn't just about singing and acting. It's also about psychological fortitude. I have to be able to take everything in stride: Reese trying to get in my head, a less-than-wonderful first audition, the pressure of living up to my previous success. Last year I didn't have to hide my stress under a performance of happiness, because I wasn't stressed. I was a freshman with nothing to prove. This year is different. This year I do have something to prove. So I'll prove it. It's a new and bigger acting challenge, and I'm up for it.

Monday, February 6

It went well, I think. I belted out "A Cockeyed Optimist." I didn't embarrass myself doing the choreography. I'm pretty sure I hid my revulsion toward Rob during "Some Enchanted Evening." I might have been a touch over-the-top doing the drunk scene, but I got laughs. It wasn't like last year, when my mind emptied out and I felt like I was actually a rebellious nun and Josh was actually my handsome but rude boss; I was thinking hard the whole time. Thinking about showing Reese she can't get to me, about proving to Grady that my voice is amazing, about letting everyone know I deserve the lead, about redeeming my crap performance at the first auditions. I felt tense. Did it show? I don't *think* it did. The more worried I felt, the more I tried to project sunshine and lollipops.

Izzy was good. Really good. I can't tell if she's acting or just being herself, but she comes across as simultaneously daffy and sincere in a very Nellie-ish way. And when she finished reading with Rob, Tris whispered to me, "Are they going out?" which unfortunately I know for a fact they are not, because I saw Rob and Gloria Lingley holding hands a week ago, so what Tris was really noticing was their convincing onstage chemistry, dammit.

Tuesday, February 7

The cast list is going up tomorrow. My callback performance might not have been the greatest, but I *am* perfect for the part, and Miss Murphy knows that.

I need to get through the next few hours, and then everything will be fine. Once I have the lead and everyone sees how great I am as Nellie, they'll forget all about my lame auditions.

Reese rushed up to me today and said, "Are you OK? I'm so sorry."

"What do you mean?" I said. Her eyes flickered, and for one second you could see the glee behind her performance of concern.

"Didn't you see? The cast list is up. You're an ensign. Bessie, I think?"

Bessie? Who in God's name was that?

"I'm an ensign too!" said Reese. "Dinah Murphy. It's not a huge part, but I'm happy with it. I have a bunch of lines. I guess you could say I'm the lead ensign!"

"What about Tris?" I said.

"You are so sweet, thinking of him instead of yourself. He's Lieutenant Cable. Izzy's Nellie, which totally makes sense. She's amazing, right? Hannah's in the chorus. So is Grady."

"Great," I said. My lips felt numb.

"So you're going to do the show? You'll take the part?"

"I don't know yet," I said. *You told me about this two seconds ago, you scheming monster.*

She gave me a hug. Her cheek was cool and her hair felt clean. "You're being so strong," she said into my ear. "It must suck to be the lead one year and a chorus girl the next."

I was still trying to come up with a response when she pulled away and left, giving me a sad wave while making a pouty face.

Thursday, February 9

Miss Murphy was normal in class today, but I couldn't look at her. I know it's not 100% rational, but I'm furious. Fine, so Izzy was better than me at callbacks. Doesn't my experience count for anything? Doesn't the fact that the director is *dating my dad* count for anything?

There's no way I can take this little nothing part. It would be too humiliating, hanging out with the kids who can't really sing, being a peasant after I was the queen. On the other hand, I'll never see Tris again unless I do the show. Or Hannah, or the other kids.

On top of everything else, it's Carnation Day tomorrow. Like I need another reason to be depressed! At least I can count on Hannah and Tris for a few pink carnations.

Friday, February 10

I can hardly even enjoy it, because I'm so upset about the musical, but something nice happened today: I got 55 carnations, 25 white and 25 red (I counted) from a mystery person, plus 10 pink (five from Tris and five from Hannah). Everyone stared at me in homeroom, and then everyone continued staring at me all day long, because

I couldn't fit the flowers in my locker and wound up carrying them from class to class, which made me feel ridiculous but which I also loved, because of course everyone said, "Wow, who are those from?" and "Is that a school record?" Reese rushed up to me between classes and said, "Everyone's talking about your flowers! Can I see? Amazing! You didn't send them to yourself, did you? Just kidding!" I have a feeling they're from Dad, but I'm going to tell myself I really do have a secret admirer. It made the day exciting; every time I passed a cute guy in the hall, I thought, *Was it you?* The whole thing was almost enough to make me forget about the show for minutes at a time.

Saturday, February 11

I've decided: I'm going to turn down the part. It'll be awful, sitting at home while all my friends are at rehearsals, but better that than watching everyone pity me or revel in my downfall.

Sunday, February 12

Miss Murphy stopped by today. She must have warned Dad beforehand that she wanted to talk to me alone, because when I heard her Jeep pull into the driveway and yelled up to him that she was here, he yelled, "Be right down!" and then never showed up.

After I opened the door for her, I said hello curtly, then turned on my heel, walked to the kitchen, and pretended to be absorbed in my homework. She followed me, set her bag on the island, took off her jacket and hung it over the back of a chair, and sat down to watch me. After a few minutes I couldn't take the awkwardness and looked up at her. She looked back at me steadily.

"Do you want some water or something?" I asked in a rude voice.

"I don't blame you for being upset," she said.

"I'm not *upset*," I said.

"OK."

I had planned to speak to her as little as possible for the rest of my life, but I found myself saying, "It's so unfair. I would be the perfect Nellie. I feel like I *am* her."

"I agree," she said, nodding.

"Wait, what?"

"You're right. That part is made for you."

"Then why am I Bessie-What's-Her-Butt?"

She cocked her head. "Why do you think you are?"

It was so annoying that she was in English-teacher mode. I said, "I know Izzy was better than me at the audition. And at callbacks."

She opened her hands like, *There you go.*

"But you know me!" I said. "You know I would have been amazing!"

"It can't work that way," she said. "I have to cast shows based on what I see at auditions."

"Reese got to me," I said miserably. "She messed with my head. She told me everyone knows about you and Dad."

Miss Murphy looked alarmed. "Chloe, I'm so sorry to hear that."

I felt a little beam of hope shoot through my body. "If you'd known, would you have given me the part?" Maybe it wasn't too late!

She looked down and made a triangle with her thumbs and index fingers. "No." The beam of hope clicked off. "I wish Reese hadn't done that to you, and I feel awful that I was the cause of your distress, but knowing what got to you is irrelevant, in a way. The only relevant event is your audition."

"Was I that terrible?" I said.

"You weren't terrible at all."

"But Izzy was better," I said. She didn't respond, but she gave me a sympathetic look.

"It was so easy last year," I said. "I just did my best. I wasn't thinking. This time, I could feel myself thinking. And then I was acting on top of the thinking." My auditions last year were like a pure mountain waterfall. This year they were like a polluted river people push old cars into.

She laughed. "Welcome to being an actor. Forget

singing, dancing, line reading—getting out of your own head is the real challenge."

"I was trying to, so hard, but I couldn't," I said.

She squeezed my hand. "You'll figure it out. This isn't your last shot."

I didn't squeeze her back. I wasn't mad at her, exactly, but I didn't want to sit around holding hands with her either.

"So what do you think?" she said. "Will you take the part?"

"*Bessie,*" I said. "Not even a featured role."

"That's the way the cookie crumbled this year," she said. Sometimes she reminds me of Noelle.

"Yeah, OK, fine," I said.

She stood up and put her jacket on with a flourish. "Excellent!"

So that's that. Months of humiliation to look forward to.

It hurts to say it, but I know I have no reason to be angry. Miss Murphy couldn't give me the lead. It's my fault, not hers. Izzy was better—Izzy was great—and Miss Murphy did the right thing, casting her.

Monday, February 13

We had our first rehearsal today. Miss Murphy started out by saying the show has its heart in the right place

and was extremely progressive for its day. In fact, legisla-
tors in some states were so outraged about Rodgers and
Hammerstein's defense of interracial marriage that they
tried to ban the show unless they removed "You've Got to
Be Carefully Taught." (R&H refused to take it out.) But,
she said, although the show wants to be about the evils of
racism, it's also itself racist. All the point-of-view characters are white. Bloody Mary can come across as a carica-
ture, Liat is presented as exotic, sensual, submissive—all
these offensive stereotypes about Asian women—and
Bali Hai, the island, is supposed to be a spiritual balm
for the souls of overly rational Westerners, which is more
exoticism. She said it's important to her to present Bloody
Mary and Liat as real, three-dimensional people, and to
bring them forward in the production. She said every
member of the cast is responsible for analyzing the script
and noting any problematic elements we find, so we can
address them. And she wants to have a panel discussion
before the last weekend of shows to talk about the musical's achievements and failures.

Tuesday, February 14

That wasn't the worst Valentine's Day I've ever had! Tris
came over after school, and we ate cheap chocolate from
a heart-shaped box, watched *Titanic*, and cried. Then we
looked at our phones to find out why Rose didn't just share

her raft with Jack, then we checked out pictures of young Leonardo DiCaprio, and then we read a history of his friendship with Kate Winslet. (He walked her down the aisle at her latest wedding!) And then, because we had our phones out and it was so tempting and so easy, we stalked Mac and Roy and found a picture of Mac at a party, shirtless, wearing a football helmet and sunglasses, and a picture of Roy kissing a cute guy who looks like Tris. I got out a step stool and put our phones on top of a kitchen cabinet, to make them annoyingly difficult to reach, but it turned out to be pointless, because Tris's mom arrived to pick him up and I had to get his phone back down immediately.

As soon as Tris left, Hannah texted me.

Happy Valentine's Day!

> *Same to you! Are you and Zach doing something fun?*

He's taking me out to dinner tonight.

> *Cool have fun!*

If someone stole my phone and read this exchange, they wouldn't think anything of it. Only I know how fake and uncomfortable my side of it is. Those exclamation points! The TWO "funs"! Ugh.

Wednesday, February 15

I never should have taken this tiny part. I go to rehearsal and Hannah talks to me for two seconds before running over to Reese. Tris comes to hang out with me whenever he can, which is not too much, because he's a lead, so Miss Murphy needs him all the time. Grady and I are constantly waiting in the same section of the auditorium but not looking at each other. Every time I see the side of his face by accident, I hear Reese saying, "Grady said you're not even that great of a singer." Miss Kijek rehearses our songs with us, and I can sing my heart out or not try at all and she doesn't notice either way, which makes sense, because I'm one voice in a giant chorus. It's nothing like last year, when Miss Murphy's eyes were on me three hours a day. I used to feel like it was too much pressure, especially when she yelled at me, but now I'd give anything to hear her say, "Chloe, project!" or "Chloe, that's not your mark!" or "Chloe, more energy! More intensity! More sparkle!"

Thursday, February 16

Noelle's going to Maryland to visit her dad for the break, and she came over to say goodbye after school. When I asked her if she was excited for her trip, she said, "I'm dreading it. I'll have to sit in his house all day by myself while he's at work, then sit in restaurants with him at night while he checks his phone every two seconds. He holds it under the table, like I won't notice that way."

It was the first time she's ever talked about her parents for real.

"What's he like, your dad?" I asked.

"I just told you. Impatient. Rich. Not interested in me. Whatever. It's only a week. I can stand anything for a week."

Before she left, I hugged her for as long as I could, until I could sense her gearing up to say something like, "Chloe, get OFF!"

I have to stop fretting about the musical thing. Really, it couldn't matter less.

Friday, February 17
Uhhhhhhhh, texts from Mac.

Hey kid

I'm off on Monday

*Coming home to see
some of my boys*

You should come to the
bowline for drinks

I stared at my phone for a full minute, squeezing it like a stress ball. What does he mean, come for drinks? Does he remember I'm still barely out of my tweens? Finally I wrote

Sounds fun
I'll try to make it

I think that was sufficiently devil-may-care, right?

Saturday, February 18

Hannah and Zach are going to the Bowline too—according to Zach, alums always meet there for drinks on Presidents' Day, and I guess the cool high school upperclassmen get to go too. Hannah said she and Zach can pick me up. I've spent half of high school so far sitting in the backseat like a child while Hannah and her serious boyfriend sit in the front like my parents. I'm grateful for the ride and everything, but it's still humiliating.

Sunday, February 19

Lying here wide awake at 2 a.m. because I'm so nervous about seeing my ex-whatever, and also because I'm nervous that I'll look sick and unattractive tomorrow due to lack of sleep.

Monday, February 20

It's the middle of the night but I have to write!

First of all, when I heard a beep and ran out to the driveway, I saw Zach and Hannah in the front . . . and Reese and Grady in the back. Of course! Duh! Why didn't I assume they'd be there? The light over the garage door was illuminating their faces, and I thought, *Yeah, naturally they're together. Two beautiful people with the kind of cheekbones normal humans need plastic surgery to attain. It's so obvious, it's boring.* I got in the backseat and it smelled like going out: shampoo and perfume and aftershave and gum and hair product. Everyone said hi loudly and enthusiastically, including me, and off we went. I pressed my knees hard into the door so I wouldn't risk touching Reese.

When we got to the Bowline, Reese was in the middle of telling Hannah about this flat iron she wants to buy, and the two of them went ahead with Zach, leaving me and Grady to walk next to each other. Knowing I was about to see Mac gave me confidence. Who was Grady compared to Mac? Some freshman nobody. And yet he had the nerve to talk crap about me!

I wondered if we'd ignore each other, like we've been

doing at rehearsals, but then he said, "I like being in the musical so far." He didn't sound like his summer self— not even close—but he was being decently friendly.

"Oh," I said, making my voice cold.

"It's kind of embarrassing, though. Just bursting into song."

I'd been planning to give him only one-word answers, but I couldn't. "All the singers in the bands you like just burst into song."

"They're not pretending to have normal conversations one second and singing the next."

I wanted to ask him what he thought patter was, but I was too angry to keep being polite.

"I know what you said about me, Grady," I said.

"What are you talking about?"

But we'd gotten to the door of the Bowline, so I shook my head and yanked it open without responding.

The bar area was crammed with current and former seniors and a few underclassmen, and everyone seemed to be drinking, even though I know for a fact most of the kids there were under 21. The music was loud, and people were shouting over it, and yelling whenever anyone new came in, and the adults who were there trying to have a nice dinner looked annoyed. I saw a few of them complaining to their waiters and I wanted to make everyone around me shut up, because I was embarrassed to be part of this big group of unruly teenagers, who were now spilling out of the bar area and into the eating area.

But then Zach handed me a beer, and after I had a few sips, I decided the sad old people currently glaring at us should lighten up and stop being jealous of our youth and beauty.

Mac wasn't there yet, and Grady had gone off to stand in a corner with Reese, not that I wanted to hang out with them, so I stood around talking to Zach and Hannah, and I learned something: she's nervous around him. She gazes at him adoringly when he talks, she rushes to laugh whenever he makes a joke, and she uses this high, breathy voice around him. I'm not judging her! I used to talk like a living doll around Mac. And of course I understand why she can't relax: Zach is a babe, and not an under-the-radar babe. Everyone at our school knows he's this handsome guitar-playing guy. But something else I learned tonight is that he's REALLY BORING! He's the kind of person who doesn't ask any questions whatsoever, so you have to do all the question asking, and when you do, he drones on and on about this new limited-edition Telecaster something something rosewood neck (???), never noticing his audience doesn't care at all about his topic of conversation. And why would he notice? Girls like Hannah do nothing but gaze adoringly at him!

When he left for a minute to say hi to some people, I whispered to Hannah, "How's it going with him?" and she whispered back, "Great!"

I said, "Did you end up telling him the truth about . . . ?" and her face closed a little, and she said, "No, I didn't."

So their relationship is founded on a lie. He still thinks she's a virgin. How depressing.

"Doesn't he deserve to know?" I said. "If the roles were reversed, you'd want to know the actual history of someone you were about to have sex with, wouldn't you?"

"Chloe, shut up," she whispered angrily. "We're not going to have sex, OK? Not that I wanted to discuss it with you right now."

"Sorry, Han," I said. And I was sorry. I didn't mean to make her uncomfortable.

I wasn't sure what to say next, and neither was she, I think. She got out her phone, and I glanced at the door, which I'd been doing since we arrived. Glance, glance, glance, every three minutes. Whenever it opened, I felt sick with excitement, but it was never Mac. I was starting to think he might not show up, and although that made me sick too, it was also kind of a relief. And then I glanced, and the door opened, and it was him. Everyone in the bar screamed for him, and he came in like a celebrity, clapping guys on the back and leaning down to hug girls, but he kept moving, and then he saw me and called "CHLOE SNOW!" so loudly that I could feel the grown-ups eating dinner seething with anger. He pushed through the crowd, came right to me, and picked me up off my feet. His face was still cold from being outside, and his breath smelled like alcohol.

He said hi to Hannah and Zach, and then he took my hand and led me to a corner. I could feel everyone watching us.

"Look at you!" he said. "You look older since Thanksgiving!" He was slurring a little.

"Do I?" I said. "I can't tell. I'm too close to myself."

He laughed. "God, I miss you! Why don't you call me? Why haven't you visited me yet?" He put his hands on my hips. "I messed up with you, Chloe. I know that."

He was saying all the things I wanted him to say after he dumped me last spring. I should have been ecstatic, but I wasn't. He was too drunk, and it was too unexpected, and too public. Everyone was sneaking glances at us.

"Is Sienna coming tonight, do you know?" I asked.

"Sienna! I have no idea where she is. Man, why didn't you make me dump her? It's your fault you weren't my girlfriend last year. You know that, right?"

He was leaning over me, looking into my eyes, and then he was kissing me, and I was kissing him back, and we were really making out, and he was pulling me close to his chest, and it was so disappointing, it was so, so disappointing, because I didn't feel anything. The last time we kissed, my whole body turned into a star, burning with light. And my mind was the space around it, dark and huge and quiet. I thought that was a chemical reaction I had to him! I didn't realize it could change! I wasn't turned on tonight, not even a little bit. I tasted the familiar flavor of his mouth, under the booze. I smelled his skin. I felt his arms around me. All the right parts, but my body didn't light up, and I was thinking a million miles a minute. I couldn't stop wondering how many people were watching us and whether they thought that we were being disgusting or that I was being slutty.

I pulled away from him and said, "I'll be right back," and he said, "Don't take too long."

I pushed through the crowd, not knowing what to do, and my eyes went right to Grady, who was staring at me with a somber look on his face. Reese, too. (Not the somber look, just the staring.) Well, good! Great. Now they know I have other fish to fry. The farther I went, the less I could think of something to do that would be a plausible reason for running away from Mac, but I kept going, sometimes scooching people out of the way with my hands to make a space, and finally I was at the door, and then, before really deciding what to do, I'd opened it. I looked back, wondering if Mac would notice I was leaving, but he was talking and laughing with the bartender.

I didn't have a plan. I barely know Zach, and we hadn't been at the restaurant for that long, so I didn't want to ask him for a ride. Dad was out with Miss Murphy, plus I'd lied to him and told him I was going to Hannah's for the night. I could go back to the house and pretend I'd gotten a lift from Mrs. Egan, but I couldn't ask him to pick me up at a bar. It was pitch-black out, and cold, but not snowing. And at least I had my coat with me. I headed for home, walking as close to the guardrail as I could get, and hoping I wouldn't be smashed by a car. It took me 45 minutes, and my house has never felt warmer than it did when I made it inside.

Tuesday, February 21
Mac texted me at 2 a.m.

> *What happened to you?*
> *Keeping me guessing huh? lol*
> *its working*
>
> *See you next time right?*

I haven't written back yet.

If I'd gotten the star feeling again last night, I would be a mess today. I would be telling myself, *He wants*

you to visit! He wishes you'd been his girlfriend last year!
He's right—it's your fault everything went wrong! and
feeling sick with nerves while I drafted a text to him.
But because I didn't get the star feeling, I'm fine. My
mind is unclouded. I'm thinking rationally. Mac said
all that stuff partly because he does like me when he's
with me, but mostly because he was drunk, and also
because he probably wants to have sex with me when
he's home.

And that would have been so nice! I would have lost
my virginity to the guy I was so obsessed with for a year!
I guess we could still have sex, but if I'm not deranged
with lust for him anymore, what's the point? Please, let
me be deranged with lust again.

Wednesday, February 22
Another text from Mac! This is unprecedented.

> *Did you like your carnations*
> *btw?*

So he was my secret admirer! I want to time travel to
last year and tell my younger self about this. She would
expire from joy.

Maybe I was having an off night on Monday. Maybe

the next time I see Mac all the old feelings will come back. I probably shouldn't hope for that. I know it's better not to be drowning in a sea of stress and love, but I miss drowning.

Thursday, February 23

Tris and I quickly debriefed about Mac, then moved on, because Roy was home for one night before going away for a long weekend with his parents, and Tris was going to hang out with him, so we had to discuss what he was going to do if Roy was distant, or on his phone the whole time, or wanting to hook up, etc., etc. I wish Tris had refused to see that cheating piece of crap, but I didn't say anything. It would be too ridiculous coming from me, a person who spent a year in love with a cheating piece of crap and who is currently, and masochistically, trying to talk herself back into loving him.

I texted Tris at midnight, and he wrote back right away.

> *Tell me what happened*
> *when you get home*

We went out for coffee
and he talked about
himself the entire time

He lost his virginity to that guy
he was kissing on instagram

!!!!!!!!

But he said it like it was
no big deal

"We're just really good friends"

He acts like nothing is a
big deal

He was pretending to be so
bored by the bar scene in
new york

I was like you've lived
there for 10 minutes

Did you say that?

No of course not

I nodded and said yeah
totally to whatever he said

#coward

#normalhuman

Also something happened

I feel weird texting about it

This sounds exciting

The three dots that mean "I'm typing" kept appearing and disappearing, and finally he texted:

I gave him a BJ

WHAT? WOW

Before he was annoying
or after?

After

I know, it makes no sense

He was being so awful and so
braggy about being this jaded

new yorker that I wanted to
FORCE him to stop it and be
nice to me

Also I was intimidated
because he's had sex now
and I don't want him to think
I'm a child

Yeah I get that

So what was it like?!?

Physically difficult!

My jaw hurt

Oh my god

I wonder if I can do some
face workouts to prepare

In case I ever get any action

Anyway did it make him
realize he misses you?

I don't know, but he was in a
way better mood afterward

So was I actually

It cleared the air!

                    And now you've lost your
                    BJ virginity

                    Congratulations!

Thank you!

                    Wait

                    Did he give you one back???

No

I don't know why but it
didn't seem like the right
moment

It didn't seem like the right moment because Roy is
a selfish POS, but of course I didn't say that.

Friday, February 24

Miss Murphy and Dad are here as I write this. I'm hiding in my room.

Dad came into the kitchen quietly this morning, so right away I knew something was up. Usually he's all business, marching around in his suit, putting his laptop into his briefcase, eating toast with one hand while loading the dishwasher with the other.

Today he slowly got a coffee cup out of the cabinet, then looked at me and said, "I was wondering if it would be OK . . . Marian and I are going to the movies tonight, and I thought . . ." He trailed off, and I panicked.

"I do *not* want to go to the movies with you guys, if that's what you're suggesting," I said.

"Oh, no, that's not what I . . . I was thinking it might be a good night for her to stay here."

"Like a sleepover?"

He nodded.

"Sure. Whatever."

"Was that a disgusted 'whatever' or an accepting 'whatever'?"

"Dad, it's fine. I told you that ages ago."

"You told Miss Murphy."

"But I knew she'd tell you, and clearly she did."

It felt like we were in a fight, even though I was trying to be nice.

They got home half an hour ago, and I felt too awkward to go downstairs, so I snuck over to my door and shut it as quietly as possible. I haven't brushed my teeth or washed my face yet, but I'm going to go to bed anyway. I don't want to venture out to the hallway and risk seeing them.

Saturday, February 25

Awkward. Awkward. So horribly awkward.

Normally on weekend mornings I wear my most disgusting pants, the orange ones with the sagging elastic and the big rip on the right knee, plus a giant sweatshirt and no bra. But today I brushed my hair and my teeth and put on jeans and a bra (a sports bra, but still). My heart was pounding like crazy as I walked downstairs. When I got to the kitchen, Dad and Miss Murphy were there drinking coffee and looking at their phones. Miss Murphy was wearing jeans too, and we both looked ridiculous, because wearing anything but comfy stuff on Saturday morning is absurd.

Dad asked if we wanted French toast, and Miss Murphy and I said sure. We all had a normal conversation; they told me about the terrible Thai place they tried after the movies last night, and I told them about the rumor that Nadine Wallach's Canadian boyfriend is actually a stock photo model she steals pictures of from the internet and then posts on Instagram. But the whole time I was thinking, *Miss Murphy slept over last night,*

Miss Murphy slept in my mother's bed, this is so strange, we're all sitting here talking politely and pretending everything is normal, but nothing is normal.

Sunday, February 26

Noelle's back! I rode my bike over to her house. Her mom opened the door wearing silky pants, a gray T-shirt, and lots of thin gold rings on her fingers, and holding a glass of white wine. You can tell she was popular in high school and then turned into the kind of adult who works out three times a week and spends a lot of money on good haircuts and expensive skin creams.

"Keep your coat on, Chloe," Noelle said, running down the stairs two at a time.

"Nice manners, Noelle," her mom said. "Ever heard of saying 'hello, how are you'?" For a second, I missed my mom so much I got a cramp.

Noelle said hi, gave me a one-armed hug, and got her jacket out of the front hall closet. "I had an idea," she said. "You should sit in the driver's seat. Just sit there. You don't have to turn the car on or anything."

"I'm not even going to ask what this is about," Noelle's mom said. "Please don't total my car, Chloe."

"She's too scared to drive an inch, Mother," Noelle said. "That's the whole point."

Mrs. Phelps was already walking away from us

down the hall, pretending to cover her ears.

We sat in the Volvo in the garage, me in the driver's seat, Noelle in the passenger seat. I was crawling out of my skin, but I forced myself to take deep breaths and stay where I was. *You are going to learn to drive*, I told myself. *You don't have to let your fear control you. You can do this.* I managed to put my hands on the steering wheel, then yanked them off and said, "How was it, seeing your dad?"

"Terrible," Noelle said. "He has a girlfriend. Put your hands back on the wheel."

"In a second," I said. "What's she like?"

"Mid-twenties, veneers, big blowout like some kind of debutante. I don't know what beauty pageant he found her at, but she's really something."

She was making a big effort to sound detached and amused, but I could tell she was upset.

"That sounds awful," I said. "I'm sure it won't last."

I told her about my mother's much-younger boyfriend, and that seemed to make her feel better. I also touched the wheel again, briefly, because Noelle said I had to or she wouldn't let me back into her house. Maybe I sort of made a little progress? It was a thoughtful idea of hers, anyway.

Monday, February 27

People aren't staring at me during rehearsal as much, probably because I haven't burst into tears or tried to punch Izzy. They wondered if I was going to act like I'm better than them, or create a bunch of drama, but I haven't, and I'm not, so they're losing interest. It should make me feel better that I'm not being watched all the time, but it makes me feel worse. It's like I'm gradually becoming invisible. And Grady ignored me today. Not that we've been speaking to each other at rehearsal, but sometimes I can feel his eyes on me, or sense he's paying attention when I'm talking. Today he acted like I wasn't there. Once I got close enough to him to sneak a look at his notebook. He was drawing an unsmiling girl sitting on a beach chair underneath a palm tree. Reese, I'm pretty sure. He uses a thick black pencil and draws fast and confidently.

Tuesday, February 28

Grady and I sat right next to each other during "Honey Bun." We'd been refusing to acknowledge each other for two hours straight when I couldn't take it anymore and whispered, "My legs are completely asleep."

He nodded his head minimally to show me he'd heard me.

Fine, I thought. *I tried.*

A few minutes later, when Miss Murphy was busy criticizing Elliott for looking inhibited and nervous, Grady said, "Did you have fun at the Bowline?"

"Not really," I said. We were both whispering, which made our conversation seem exciting.

"How's Mac?" he asked. He didn't say "How's *Mac*?"; he put equal weight on both words, which is how I knew he was making conversation, not being rude. I could have responded, "No idea," or "Fine, I guess," or something else that would show there's nothing going on with us, but I didn't want to give him the satisfaction of knowing I'm still single when he's basically married, so I said, "He's good."

"Good."

A silence fell. Well, we were silent. Miss Murphy was still talking. Grady looked pained, probably because Elliott's his friend and he was currently cowering and turning pale as Miss Murphy accused him of lacking energy.

"How's Reese?" I asked.

"Good."

Good, good, good, good, good. Great. Wonderful. Perfect.

We didn't talk again, even when the scene ended and everyone got up and it was awkward not to say goodbye.

Wednesday, March 1

Tris hasn't heard from Roy yet, and he's freaking out. The blow job has his hopes up that they'll get back together, which seems like wishful thinking to me, but what the hell do I know?

Thursday, March 2

Zach came to pick up Hannah from rehearsal today. He had his hair pulled back and was wearing a half-zip sweater and black jeans. He looked confident and grown-up, especially when Hannah went over to him and he kissed her on the mouth like it was no big deal. Grady and Reese walked up too, and the four of them stood together talking and laughing. Meanwhile, Tris was onstage with his arms around Olivia, gazing into her eyes and singing about springtime. I finished putting my stuff in my backpack and headed out to meet Dad. I had to pass Hannah, Zach, Grady, and Reese on my way out. Reese was saying, "My cousin gave me her ID. Everyone says we look like twins, even though she's 25." Hannah interrupted her to call, "Good night, Chloe!" I said goodbye without looking over, and hurried outside. Dad wasn't there yet, so I stood by the curb, feeling the chilly air on my skin, telling myself, *There's no reason to feel sorry for yourself. You're a straight, white, upper-middle-class person with no actual problems.* But my problems do feel real to me, even if they shouldn't.

Friday, March 3

The only thing worse than going to rehearsal and being an anonymous chorus member is not even having rehearsal in the first place, because you're an anonymous chorus member and it's not like you have a bunch of scenes and songs to learn.

Saturday, March 4

Hannah texted saying she feels like she hasn't seen me in forever and can I sleep over tonight? I considered pretending to have plans with Tris, but then I realized he'd already posted a picture of himself at the movies with some of the *South Pacific* sailors, so that lie was out as an option, and in the end I said I could go. Now I'm sitting here procrastinating while Dad waits downstairs to give me a ride. I used to sleep over at Hannah's house once a week! Mrs. Egan bought a pillow for me so I wouldn't have to carry mine back and forth! How did things get this bad?

Sunday, March 5

Well, that didn't go too well. Mrs. Egan made dinner, and I could tell from the vibes around the table that she and Mr. Egan know something's off with me and Hannah.

"I'm so glad you're here!" Mrs. Egan said. "We've all missed you."

"I'm happy to be here," I said, like I was a celebrity and Mrs. Egan was a late-night host.

After dinner Hannah and I went up to her room. I

felt nervous, wondering what we were going to do. What did we ever do? Look at our phones together, talk about boys, make up dance routines. It was always easy. We were just hanging out; we weren't trying to fill the time. But last night Hannah sat on her bed and I sat on her desk chair, and I thought, *How are we going to get through all the hours until bedtime?*

"So how *are* you?" Hannah asked.

"I'm good! How are you?"

"Good!"

Is this what my life was now? A series of vacuous conversations centering around the word "good"?

"It's hard to find time to get together, right?" Hannah said. "I guess we're both really busy."

"Yeah, I guess."

"*South Pacific* and school and everything."

A little piñata of anger burst in my chest. "Well, and Zach and Reese."

She smiled. "Them too."

"How's everything with you and Zach?"

"So great. I think I might love him. He's so talented, but he's not conceited about it. And he's chivalrous. He holds doors for me and pays for me when we go out. And he already asked me to junior prom!"

"Wow, it's early for that."

"I know! I'm so excited. My mom's taking me dress

shopping soon. What about you? Do you like anyone right now?"

"Nope."

"I saw you and Grady talking at rehearsal the other day."

I narrowed my eyes at her. "Did Reese tell you to invite me over?"

"What? No, she didn't."

"Did she see me and Grady talking and get mad? Are you supposed to find out if I still like him?"

"Chloe! Listen to yourself!"

"Sorry, I just don't see why else you'd want me to sleep over."

"Because you're my best friend?"

I snorted. "We haven't talked in weeks."

"I have a lot going on right now, but that doesn't mean anything's changed with us."

I shook my head. "Hannah, you know things have changed. Look at you—your hair looks amazing and you're wearing full eye makeup. Your boyfriend is the guy everyone wants to date and your new best friend is a mean girl."

Hannah pressed her hand into her pillow. "Is it possible you're jealous?" She said it kindly.

"Yeah, right. I'm dying for Reese to like me."

"She *does* like you."

"She doesn't, Hannah. You're too nice to realize she doesn't like anyone. She doesn't like you! She likes playing games with people and being the one in control."

Hannah was shaking her head. "You think you have everyone all figured out. You don't know Reese at all, and you don't know Zach, and I'm very sorry you didn't get the lead and you don't have a boyfriend, but that's no excuse for being mean to me when I haven't done anything wrong. I'm allowed to have a boyfriend! I'm allowed to make new friends!"

"I'm aware of that," I said. We sat there in silence for a while, not looking at each other. Eventually I said, "Maybe I should go." I thought she'd ask me to stay, but she said, "If that's what you want," so I went downstairs and asked Mrs. Egan if she'd mind giving me a ride home. She tried to get the story out of me in the car. I said I had a stomachache and wanted to sleep in my own bed, and she didn't press me.

Monday, March 6

The thing is, of COURSE I'm jealous. I'm so jealous I can hardly function! I wish Reese had adopted *me* and shown *me* what to wear and how to do my makeup. I wish I had a cute, fun boyfriend. But that doesn't mean Reese isn't the worst. And maybe I was mean to Hannah on Saturday, but she was mean to me, too. She was meaner.

Tuesday, March 7

Great, now Grady AND Hannah are avoiding me at rehearsal. I wish that there were an island for misfit teenagers and that I could move there.

Wednesday, March 8

Reese came up to me and Tris at lunch today and said, "Chloe, I heard about the fight. I'm so sorry." She winced and then pouted.

"Yeah, thanks," I said. How much had Hannah told her? She couldn't have mentioned the rude things I'd said about Reese, right, or Reese wouldn't be standing here?

"Hannah's really upset. She's so sweet. She can't stand drama. That's just her personality."

I nodded instead of saying what I wanted to, which was, *YOU don't get to explain my best friend since kindergarten to ME!*

She tipped her head to one side. "Do you want me to talk to Hannah for you?"

"Uh, that's OK," I said.

"I'm a really good counselor," Reese said. "Last year Noelle and Nevaeh got in a huge thing, and I stepped in and helped."

I bet you did, I thought.

"I can talk to Hannah myself, thanks," I said, and for

one second Reese's control faltered and I saw her irritation. She's not used to anyone crossing her, even in something small. But she recovered instantly and said, "Good luck working it out," which might have sounded sarcastic if she hadn't been using her cherry-pie voice.

Tris and I widened our eyes as she walked away, and sat there in silence until she was back at her table. Then Tris said, "Poor Noelle and Nevaeh," and we analyzed the conversation as fast as we could until lunch ended.

Thursday, March 9

Tris seemed distracted and out of it at rehearsal. Miss Murphy even asked him if he was feeling well. We went to the vending machine together during the break, and he told me he broke down and texted Roy last night, and Roy hasn't texted him back yet.

"What did you write?" I asked.

He handed me his phone.

Hey is everything ok?

I haven't heard from you since
you know what . . .

I probably shouldn't say this but
I miss you

"This is not that bad," I said.

"It's SO BAD. The BJ reference, oh God. And why would I tell him I miss him? I guess I thought he'd have to say he misses me, too. I never imagined he'd ignore me!"

"Maybe he lost his phone," I said.

"Chloe, seriously."

I looked at him, and he stared into the glowing red face of the vending machine. "I can't stop thinking about it. I can't handle being onstage because I'm so far from my phone. All I want to do is check it every 10 seconds. I keep looking at it to make sure I didn't turn the volume off by accident."

"I'm sorry," I said, which is the worst response possible when someone is upset, but I didn't know what else to say. There isn't anything you *can* say when someone's waiting for a text back. It's like Tris let go of his trapeze and he's falling through the air, waiting for Roy to catch him, but Roy is outside the circus tent making out with the lion tamer.

Friday, March 10

Roy posted more pictures with that Tris look-alike, which I haven't mentioned to Tris, even though I'm SURE Tris has seen the same pictures. If he doesn't want to discuss them, I'm certainly not going to bring them up.

Saturday, March 11

Did you see those pictures?

Yes :(

What do I do?

Definitely don't text him again

Yeah

OK

I know I shouldn't

DON'T

I think all you can do is wait
for time to pass

In a year you'll be like I can't
believe I was ever into him

A YEAR?????

Maybe a few months?

Love sux

It's better to have loved
and lost etc

Yeah right

The sadder but wiser girl for me

I guess

Want to come over and
watch a movie?

Yes

If my mom can drive me

I have to get my license

We can't depend on our
parents for every little thing

Yes obviously

You'll get over this fear

I have confidence in you

         Thanks

         I hope you're right

I am

*If I'm ever sad after I get my
license remind me we used
to have to ride our bikes
everywhere*

*Or wait for our moms to get
off FB and give us rides*

         At least you have a mom

You have one!

         Sorta

Sunday, March 12

Miss Murphy brought lunch over today. After we finished and she was getting ready to leave, I asked Dad if he could drive me to CVS.

"I can take you," Miss Murphy said. I thanked her, and we got in the Jeep. After I'd finished picking up my stuff (shampoo, nail files, tampons), she asked if I wanted to get a coffee, and I said yes, please. She bought me a latte, and we wound up sitting in Starbucks for almost an hour, sometimes looking at our phones but mostly talking. I asked to see pictures of her apartment in New York, and she said she wasn't sure she had any, but then she found some taken at a birthday party. The photos showed a small place with a hardwood floor, a pale couch, a view of another apartment building across the street, and an orange cat. Most of them included a handsome guy with curly dark hair. I was brave enough to ask who he was, and she said her ex-boyfriend. I felt jealous on Dad's behalf, which is 100% insane for several reasons. But then she said, "Cute, right? But he was awful," so that was OK.

Monday, March 13

If someone had told me last year that I would hardly remember what it was like when my mom lived here, I wouldn't have believed them.

Tuesday, March 14

Everyone had to pair up with a friend for in-car instruction back when our driver's ed class started, and Noelle and I picked each other. The idea is the non-driving student learns something from the ride, because she's watching her friend drive and hearing Mr. Tansel's feedback. Noelle had her first session today after school. She did well: Mr. Tansel never used the brake on his side, and most of his corrections were about not being overconfident. "Full and complete stop, Ms. Phelps, not just a pause." "Did you check your side mirror, or only the rearview?" "Give the Honda Fit more room. You're bearing down."

I don't feel nervous at all when someone else is driving. It's not that I think Noelle or my dad or whoever could never get into an accident. I know they could. That's why I'd rather we all biked or walked everywhere. But if someone else is at the wheel and causes a death, at least it wouldn't be my fault. It's the responsibility that scares me. I don't want the power to take someone's life, or my own.

Wednesday, March 15

Tris and I were sitting on FaceTime while doing our homework after rehearsal, which we do a lot. Sometimes 20 minutes go by without either of us speaking, but it's still nice to hear him turning pages and coughing occasionally.

"I'm going to go to bed," I said finally. "I'm pooped."

"OK. Oh, wait. I wanted to ask you something. Do you think Elliott is cute?"

"Elliott from *South Pacific?* Grady's friend?"

"Yeah."

"Yeah, very. Why?"

"He asked me to hang out on Friday."

"WHAT? Like a date? How did you not tell me about this earlier? We've been sitting here doing geometry for an hour!"

"I don't know. I feel very meh about him."

"What are you going to do, pine away for Roy for the next three years?"

"No. Yeah, maybe."

"Elliott seems really nice."

"You can tell Miss Murphy regrets casting him in that part. He always looks embarrassed during 'Honey Bun.'"

"He's wearing a bra made of coconut shells! Or he'll have to starting at dress rehearsal, anyway."

"Plus, he's a freshman. So unappealing."

"You realize we had this exact conversation about Mac and Grady in the fall, right?"

"That was different."

"How was it different?"

That stumped him.

"I guess I could go out with Elliott and see if we have fun," he said. He sounded horribly depressed.

"You know I want you to be single forever so we can always be life partners," I said. "But I still think you should definitely go out with Elliott."

"He asked me to go bowling. Isn't that lame?"

"What? No! Bowling is fun!"

"OK, OK, OK, I'll go."

I burst into applause, which at least made him smile.

Thursday, March 16

I checked out Elliott more carefully at rehearsal. He was wearing skinny black jeans, a teal T-shirt, and glasses with out-of-date wire frames, but who cares? Tris can help him pick out new ones. He has a shy way about him—he ducks his head and looks up with nervous eyes—but I think it's endearing.

I don't care if Tris disappears into a new relationship and never has time to hang out with me. Anything would be better than watching him gaze into his phone like Roy's suddenly going to appear on the screen and say, "I made a terrible mistake!"

Friday, March 17

How's it going????? Text me when he goes to the bathroom

It's ok

The bowling balls hurt my fingers

Oh boy

Well they do

Are you having any good conversations?

Yeah he's interesting

He's really into books

He's a librarian on some site?

I don't know

You would like him

OK he's coming back gotta go

He sounds like he's having a terrible time, but at least he got off his phone when Elliott came back. That's something.

Saturday, March 18

Miss Murphy is sleeping over tonight. She just called up, "Chloe, we're ordering. Do you want chicken or shrimp?" and I called back, "Shrimp, please." For some reason that exchange makes me sad. It's so mother-and-daughter-esque.

Sunday, March 19
Miss Murphy and I both wore comfy pants this morning. And I didn't wear a bra!

Monday, March 20
When I asked Tris about the date in person, he said "It was fun" in the same way you'd say Easter lunch at your great-aunt's was fun. Elliott was darting glances at Tris during rehearsal, and I saw Tris through his eyes: a handsome, preppy guy with the voice of an angel. I didn't see Tris darting any glances at Elliott, unfortunately.

Tuesday, March 21
Hannah and I aren't in a fight, exactly, but we also aren't talking or texting. Today Miss Murphy sent her downstairs to get me and a few other chorus kids, and she looked at a spot just above my head while she talked to me instead of making eye contact.

Wednesday, March 22
Hannah, Zach, Grady, and Reese left rehearsal together today, talking loudly and laughing together. Reese pushed

Zach and said, "Zach, shut up, seriously!" and Zach said, "What? Reese's Pieces is a cute nickname!" and then they walked through the door and their voices died away.

Thursday, March 23

Last year I loved going to rehearsal because it was an escape from my life. This year there's no escape from anything.

Friday, March 24

Tris and I were halfway through *All About Eve* when he said, "This is so much better than going skating with Elliott."

I paused the movie, because it's sacrilege to drown out Bette Davis.

"Did he invite you skating?" I said.

Tris nodded.

"And you turned him down to sit on the couch with me and fight over who's hogging the blanket?"

"Yep."

I looked at him and then unpaused the movie.

Tris paused it again. "Don't you want to lecture me?"

"No. It's none of my business."

"Oh. OK." He sounded disappointed.

"If you don't like him, you don't like him."

"I don't *think* I like him."

We looked at the TV, which was frozen on Marilyn

Monroe sitting on a staircase, laughing, wearing a strap-less dress.

"He suggests grown-up things," I said. "Real dates. He seems mature."

"Mature for his age."

"I'm happy you're hanging out with me tonight, by the way," I said. "That's not what I'm saying."

"I know that," he said.

Saturday, March 25

Noelle invited me and Thalia out for dinner tonight. I thought we'd go somewhere close by, but we went all the way to Harvard Square—and Noelle drove. Her mom sat in the front seat and screamed with laughter most of the way, like it was all a hilarious joke and none of us were in life-threatening danger. She cracked up when Noelle accelerated onto Route 2, when she passed a car on the left, and when she successfully got around the rotary.

"Mom, stop!" Noelle said. "You're distracting me."

"I'm sorry," Mrs. Phelps said, still laughing. "I can't get over you driving."

"Thanks a lot!"

"No, you're doing great. It's blowing my mind, that's all."

Noelle rolled her eyes. She doesn't realize how lucky she is that her mom is nice, and encouraging, and doesn't bite her head off about every little thing. And how lucky she is to be brave enough to drive on a highway, something I'm scared I'll never be able to do.

Sunday, March 26

Dad finally gave me some divorce news tonight at dinner. First he asked a bunch of vague questions about how I'm doing, am I missing Mom, is there anything worrying me (I said fine, no, nothing much [except for everything, but I didn't mention that]). Then he said the talks with the mediator aren't going as smoothly as he'd hoped, and it looks like the divorce is going to take longer than planned. I asked him what he and Mom are fighting about, but he wouldn't tell me, and I could tell from his tone of voice that pestering him wouldn't get me anywhere. He asked me how I feel about the timeline changing, and I said I feel fine. But I don't feel fine. I hate being in limbo. It's not that I think they'll get back together, or that I even *want* them to get back together, but until they get divorced, it feels like there's a chance they'll work it out. I don't want to have any hope. I want my hope to die so I can move on.

Monday, March 27

I guess it's also possible the divorce will make everything worse than before, and I'll reread yesterday's entry and feel nostalgic for the time I was so naive, I actually wanted my parents to split up.

Tuesday, March 28

It was beautiful today, warm and sunny, and we were all trapped in a windowless auditorium, and I didn't mind at all. What's wrong with me that I'd rather sit inside listening to Rob's terrible French accent than be outside frolicking in the sun?

Wednesday, March 29

Every time I walk by the art studio, I hope to spot Grady in there. I don't know why, but for some reason it's comforting to see him working on a painting or hunching over a sketch pad. Usually the studio is empty, but today I passed by after school and there he was, with a pencil behind his ear and another one in his hand, looking at a toy train on the table in front of him and then back down at his paper. Mrs. Kingsley stopped behind him and said, "Such an improvement in your value range," and he smiled like she'd told him he'd won the lottery. His hair wasn't sticking up too much, so I could tell he was in a calm mood.

Thursday, March 30

I was sitting in my favorite spot in the auditorium—back of the house, stage left, next to the aisle—doing my history homework, when I looked up and saw Grady standing in front of me.

"Hey," he said. He whispered it, actually, because

Izzy and Rob were mid-scene, and Miss Murphy gets irate if anyone distracts the actors.

He sat next to me. "So, you know Elliott, right?"

"Of course," I said.

"And you know he and Tris have been hanging out?"

"I heard something like that."

"I was wondering if Tris is into him."

"Did Elliott ask you to ask me?"

"No," Grady said, while nodding his head yes.

"I honestly don't know," I said. "The thing is, Tris isn't over his ex-boyfriend."

A little look passed over Grady's face, and immediately I wanted to take back what I said, since it sounded like a reference to Mac. We both faced the stage, where Izzy was crying while telling Rob she couldn't see him anymore.

"I don't think Elliott should give up," I said. "There's still hope."

"OK. Thanks."

Grady gave me a half wave and then left, probably to report back to Elliott.

Friday, March 31

It goes without saying that I told Tris every detail of my conversation with Grady.

"What is this, fifth grade?" Tris said. "It's like playing

telephone." But I could tell he was happy Elliott is so into him he's getting Grady to talk to me. Plus, it's fun to be the center of attention once in a while, with everyone whispering to each other and speculating about how you feel and what might happen. Not that I would know what that's like.

Saturday, April 1

I ran out of toothpaste, and when I went into Dad's bathroom to steal some of his, I noticed a small navy-and-white-striped bag sitting on the counter. I didn't go through it, exactly, but it was unzipped, so I could see a container of dental floss, a bottle of concealer, a tub of lip balm, and a few other items that obviously belong to Miss Murphy.

Dad was out at the package store. I went downstairs and found Miss Murphy mincing garlic and listening to NPR on her phone.

"Is it ever annoying, having to sleep here?" I said.

She paused her app. "Not at all. Why? Would you rather I don't?"

"No. I don't care. I mean, it used to seem weird, but it doesn't anymore."

"Thank God. I love my mother, but it's good for us to have a break from each other occasionally. She likes her night nurse better than me, anyway."

"What's it like, living with your mom?"

"Oh, it's terrible. *She's* not terrible; she's stubborn and difficult, but also brilliant and funny. But caring for someone with cancer is hard, obviously. And I don't recommend moving back into your childhood bedroom if you can possibly avoid it."

"Does it still look like it did when you were in high school?"

She laughed. "No. My mother turned it into a guest room as soon as I left."

"Does your father live there too?"

She started mincing again. "My parents divorced when I was in high school. He moved out west and started a new family. I don't see him much anymore."

"Oh," I said. I could tell she was waiting for me to ask her more, and I wanted to, but then Dad walked in carrying a brown paper bag and a bouquet of daffodils. It was the first time in ages I can remember being disappointed when he interrupted me and Miss Murphy, instead of relieved.

Sunday, April 2

I slept in and then shuffled downstairs in my orange pants and hoodie, and ate Cinnamon Toast Crunch while looking at my phone and ignoring Dad and Miss Murphy, who were talking about the Red Sox. Dad went for a run while I took a shower, and then Miss Murphy and I did the crossword while Dad paid bills. We had leftovers for lunch. I worked on my homework while Miss Murphy graded papers and Dad cleaned up the kitchen. It was a completely normal day, and it was so relaxing, and the whole time . . . I can hardly write this, I feel so guilty. . . . The whole time, I was thinking how glad I was Mom wasn't here. I do miss her, OK? I do. But she's impossible to live with. She can't stand to be contradicted, and she can't stand to be criticized. This morning Dad asked Miss Murphy, "Want me to turn the heat down under those eggs? Looks like they're cooking pretty fast," and all Miss Murphy said was, "Yeah, sure. I don't know what I'm doing with eggs." Mom might have said something like that, or she might have thrown the eggs into the sink in a fury. That's what's so scary about her: she's unpredictable. You never know what's going to set her off. I've spent my whole life tiptoeing around, trying not to make her mad. But there's nothing you can do or not do—she loses her temper for random reasons.

In a horrible way, it's exciting, living with someone like that. When she's happy, you feel the normal plea-sure of being with a happy person, plus this special, extra relief that you're not currently being screamed at, plus a nervousness that the good times won't last. When she's mad, you're scared and furious and pumping out adrenaline like crazy. Either way, it's not boring.

I wonder if Dad and Miss Murphy are in a honeymoon phase, or if they can keep this up. Do people live like this, laughing and being nice to each other and never hissing, "Don't you *dare* disrespect me like that *ever* again"?

Monday, April 3

Elliott and Tris talked at rehearsal today! I was too far away to hear what they were saying, but they were both smiling. Is it pathetic how excited I am that someone likes Tris? I don't want to be a romance vampire just because my own love life is a desolate wasteland.

Tuesday, April 4

Why do I do things I *know* will make me feel terrible, like read emails from my mother? Why don't I send her to spam?

Miss Murphy doesn't want us to look at our phones anywhere in the auditorium, which is a rule I normally follow. But today I was sitting in my usual spot, out of view, and I was finished with my homework, so I snuck a look at my email. I knew it was a mistake as soon as I saw the name "Veronica Snow" in my inbox, but I couldn't stop myself from reading more.

Chloe,

Another three months gone, and still no word
from you. It breaks my heart to know you've
turned away from me. You, the sweet baby I
carried inside my very body for nine months.
You, my co-conspirator, my confidante, my
closest friend. Your father tells me you're doing
splendidly, and how glad I am of that. I would
never wish for you to suffer in my absence. And
yet it does strike me as unnatural that you're
capable of thriving away from the sunshine of a
mother's love. I fear for you, Chloe. I fear you're
becoming someone I won't recognize, someone
you yourself won't recognize. Don't let yourself
grow cold, my sweet angel.

"Can I talk to you for one sec?" It was Grady, who'd
stopped in front of me and was whispering. "Elliott says
Tris isn't . . . What's wrong?"

I shook my head.

He sat down next to me. "Are you OK?"

He's the last person I would have picked to confide
in, but I wanted to talk about it, and he was there, and
asking.

I handed him my phone. "Read that."

He looked serious as he read. Suddenly I was dying to hear what he thought. Maybe he'd say, "This isn't so bad," and then I could stop being angry and sad. Maybe he'd say, "She's nuts," and then I could stop wondering who was crazy, Veronica or me. I cared about his opinion.

When he was finished reading, he said, "She moved to Mexico, right?"

"Yeah." I'd told him the basics of the story at the pool.

He handed the phone back to me. "She sounds like my dad."

"Really?"

"He's not mushy and fancy like that when he writes, but he does the same stuff to me. He's always trying to make me feel guilty for not seeing him more, but he's the one who moved to L.A."

"I hate the mush," I said. "I hate hearing about her being pregnant with me."

He didn't respond right away, and I wondered if he thought I was being mean. Then he said, "It's weird how annoying that stuff is. I feel like my parents still basically see a baby when they look at me. My mom's always like, 'You used to say "kee-pee-pee" instead of "computer."' I think she wishes I still said it like that."

"I know," I said. "I never knew myself as a baby, so I

don't even know what my mom's so nostalgic about. And it's like she's mad at me for taking away my baby self, even though the baby self is me! You know?"

He nodded, and we both got quiet to listen to Miss Murphy telling Izzy her cartwheels looked messy. For the first time, I felt almost glad not to be the lead. It was nice to be whispering with Grady in a comfortable seat while someone else got criticized in front of everyone.

"What does your dad do in L.A.?" I asked.

He shook his head. "Not much. He says he's a photographer, but he never works. I think he mostly plays around on his phone and feels sorry for himself."

"My mom's like that!" I said.

Grady started to say, "One time my dad . . . ," but then he broke off because Reese had come through the side doors. She smiled and waved, but I could tell she didn't like it that we were talking. Grady stood up, but before he left, he said, "Don't write back to her. Don't let her get to you." Then he went over to Reese, like a puppy obeying its master. Or, no, why am I being a jerk? Like a boyfriend walking over to see his girlfriend.

Wednesday, April 5

I should delete that email from Mom instead of reading and rereading it like I've been doing.

The problem with parents is, even when you know

intellectually that they're wrong, you can't make yourself *believe* that they're wrong. They get in your head. I keep hearing the word "unnatural." I'll be taking a shower or waking up or eating a piece of toast, and my brain shouts *Unnatural!* at me. It makes me feel like Frankenstein's monster. Like I'm a freak instead of a human girl. What if Mom's right? Is it weird that I'm doing OK even though she's not here? The only way I can get through the day is by shutting her out of my life and trying not to think about her. I want to turn myself into steel for this moment in time, and then go back to feeling everything in a few years. But maybe she's right. Maybe I'm making myself permanently cold and cruel. Maybe I'll never be able to undo it.

Thursday, April 6

No. No. No. No. I'm not cold and cruel! It might be a little heartless of me to give her the silent treatment, but it doesn't make me a monster. I'm still me.

Friday, April 7

As I was waiting by the door to the lobby today, Grady passed by and said, "Hey, how's it going?" but then Reese came running over and said, "Hi Chloe!" and then, to Grady, "Hi baby!" She was all over him the rest of the afternoon, rubbing his head, holding his hand, picking a piece of fluff off his shirt, jumping on his back so he had to give her a piggyback ride. At one point she was squealing and laughing and pretending to spur him with her heels, and Miss Murphy stopped rehearsal to bellow, "Hey, lovebirds, keep it down!" Reese pretended to be embarrassed, but you could tell she loved it.

Saturday, April 8

Tris is at the movies with Elliott. Miss Murphy and my dad went to dinner. Hannah's probably out with Zach. Noelle's over at Thalia's. I'm sure Grady and Reese are being attractive together somewhere, and they're probably not wearing pants. And here I sit, with only a flatulent Boston terrier for company, friendless and loveless, writing in my diary.

Sunday, April 9

Tris came over after lunch, and as soon as he walked into the house and saw Miss Murphy, he froze.

"Hey, Tris," she said, and waved. She was sitting on the couch with her feet up, wearing her glasses and doing something on her laptop.

As we walked upstairs, Tris whispered, "You didn't tell me she'd be here."

"I forgot that it's awkward," I whispered back. "I'm so used to her now."

When I asked, he said he'd had fun with Elliott at the movies, and this time he almost sounded like he meant it. But we'd only been talking about it for 20 minutes when he suggested doing homework, so I'm not feeling that optimistic. We used to be able to spend 20 minutes analyzing a single one of Roy's facial expressions.

Monday, April 10

A bunch of us were standing in the wings today, waiting to rehearse "Honey Bun." We'd been there for half an hour already, because Miss Murphy was working with Izzy first, and she wasn't happy with Izzy's impersonation of a nurse impersonating a sailor. "Again!" she shouted. "And make it more overtly stagy!" (I have no idea what that means. I think Miss Murphy thinks we're smarter than we are.)

Grady came to stand beside me and whispered, "How's it going?" I could barely hear him, and I knew why: Miss Murphy goes nuts if anyone talks in the wings. Already people were turning around to look at Grady with wide eyes, like *Do you have a death wish?*

"Fine," I whispered.

"Did you . . . ?" He moved his thumbs like he was writing on a phone.

I assumed he was asking me if I emailed my mom back, so I shook my head no.

He gave me a thumbs-up.

I gave him an A-OK.

He touched the tips of his fingers to his thumbs and put the circles over his eyes like glasses.

I pretended to ask for the check.

He mimed eating a banana.

I acted like I was crashing cymbals together, and then he started laughing, and so did I. We were doubled over, trying not to make any noise, and everyone else in the wings was glaring at us.

"WHO IS THAT?" Miss Murphy hollered from the audience. "DO NOT MAKE ME COME BACK THERE." That made it worse, and I snorted.

"Sorry, Miss Murphy!" I called.

"Chloe, absolutely no talking in the wings. If I have to ask you again, you're out of here for the day. Is that clear?"

"It's clear!"

I was glad she yelled at me. The other kids would hate me if she didn't.

Tuesday, April 11

Grady and I were just goofing around. Right?

I'm NOT going to do what I did last year. No flirting with someone else's boyfriend. It only leads to disaster.

Wednesday, April 12

I'm panicking.

> Chloe,
>
> If you and your father think you can railroad me
> like this, think again. Yes, I moved to Mexico.
> Yes, I privileged writing over baking cookies, or
> whatever it is your father thinks a wife should do.
> Yes, I practiced self-care. Yes, I broke free of the
> constraints placed upon modern women. That does
> not mean I should or will relinquish my rights as a
> mother. I am not letting go of you without a fight.

What is she talking about??? I have to find Dad right this minute.

Thursday, April 13

I got it out of him. She wants shared custody. She wants me to live with her in Mexico for at least half the year. That's why mediation failed. I'm too scared to write right now.

Friday, April 14

I don't want this. I don't want to leave Tris, or Dad, or Snickers, or even Miss Murphy. I don't want to miss a second of my horrible high school life.

Saturday, April 15

Dad swears no sane judge would grant her custody. He says she moved to another country by choice, leaving me with him, and any court would interpret that as an admission that he's a fit guardian. And that furthermore, judges like to keep children in place, if possible, to avoid disrupting their routines.

I'm trying to believe him, stop Googling, and calm down. He's an attorney. He knows about stuff like this. And he's *probably* not just trying to make me feel better.

Sunday, April 16

Last year, all I wanted was to move to Mexico. I was picturing reading novels on the beach and wandering around town wearing a straw fedora while the cute local guys whispered "Who is *that*?" to each other. But I never thought about what it would be like to live with Mom without Dad around. And I know why I never thought about it: because it would have ruined the fantasy. Mom doesn't want to be a parent, not for real. She doesn't make dinner. She doesn't care if I miss curfew. She doesn't sign my permission slips or notice my grades or buy my birthday presents or pretend my school events are fun or remember I need to get my teeth cleaned. I'm not saying she's supposed to do any of this stuff because she's a woman. It doesn't matter who takes care of the house and the kid(s). In our family, it's Dad, and that's fine and great. In some families, it's both parents, or a single parent, or a grandparent. I just want to live with someone, anyone, who cares about me, and that someone is not my mother.

Monday, April 17

Dear Mom,

I'm sorry I've been out of touch. To be honest, I was mad at you for leaving, and I didn't want to talk.

I'm writing now because I wanted to tell you, first of all, Dad and I aren't trying to railroad you. He almost never mentions the divorce to me. He did tell me the mediation wasn't going well, but he didn't say why. Until I got your email, I didn't realize there was a disagreement about custody.

I also wanted to tell you something. It's hard to say, but I have to say it. Basically, I want to live here full-time. I hope this doesn't hurt your feelings. It's not about loving Dad more than you, or anything like that. It's that I have my whole life here—school and everything—and I don't want to leave.

OK, well, I really am sorry I haven't emailed in so long. I'll be better about it now.

—Chloe

Tuesday, April 18
She hasn't written back yet. It's the second day of spring break and I've barely noticed. All I'm doing is staring at my inbox.

Wednesday, April 19
Still nothing. I guess this is a taste of my own medicine. I can't complain, since I did the exact same thing to her for so long. But it's still the worst.

Thursday, April 20
What if she's not writing back because she's gearing up for a court battle, and she doesn't want her emails to be seized as evidence? What if she wins and I have to live with her and Javi half the year?

Friday, April 21

I told Noelle what's going on, and she said nice stuff ("Seriously? That sucks," "I'm sure your dad will get custody," "Divorce is the worst") and also some stuff that was supposed to be nice, even if it made me flinch a little ("Wow, your mom sounds crazy"). But it was odd, because I confessed all these embarrassing, scary details, and I guess I assumed she would tell me about her parents' divorce in return. It's not that I'm dying to know about their divorce in a gossipy way. It's just that when one friend tells a secret, it's normal for the other friend to tell a secret too. It's like swearing a blood oath. You both have to cut yourselves.

Maybe she's more private than I am. Maybe she doesn't trust me yet. Maybe she doesn't mind being in awkward situations, because she's so cool and confident. Maybe she doesn't want to hear the truth about what's happening with my parents, so she's shutting down the conversation and hoping I'll get the hint.

It's weird that Grady and I aren't even friends, and we're so much more comfortable talking about this stuff than Noelle and I are.

Saturday, April 22

I rode my bike around today trying to memorize the town. Before now, I've never really thought about the stone walls colonial New Englanders built with their own hands. Imagine how long it must have taken! The walls are beautiful. They're works of art that connect us to our forebears. I can't leave them! And why have I never visited Emily Dickinson's house, or Louisa May Alcott's house? They're less than an hour away by car. I go to Walden Pond only to sit on the beach whining! What is wrong with me? I should be taking meditative walks around the lake and thinking about how lucky I am to have Dad. If I get to stay here, I swear I'll be different. I'll appreciate my town instead of constantly complaining about how boring it is. I'll look at things instead of racing by them on my bike while drowning out my own thoughts with a podcast. I won't be such a spoiled brat.

Sunday, April 23

Chloe,

I understand your point of view. Truly, I do. But as your mother, the woman who has cared for you since your first moments of life, I have my own opinions about what's healthy for you. I will and must navigate by my own stars. If you're angry with me for pursuing the course I know to be best,

well, I can accept your anger. I'll absorb it, like a
judo practitioner. As Clementine said in Bikram
class yesterday, I'll "meet rage with kindness."

All my love,
Mom

Mom,

I'm not angry. I just don't want to live with
you. Please don't treat me like a child. I'm old
enough to have my own opinions about what's
best for me.

—Chloe

Monday, April 24

Dad's birthday. Miss Murphy came over and made dinner (salmon), and afterward we sang to him and I brought
out a cake I'd baked (chocolate, from a mix). We didn't
talk about Mom or the divorce, but I could feel everyone
silently stressing out about it.

Tuesday, April 25

I raced out of rehearsal today, so I was the first person
at the bike rack, but I couldn't get my lock undone, and

everyone was streaming past watching me struggle. I was almost in tears when Grady came over and said, "Are you all right?"

"Yeah, I'm fine." I dropped the lock. I needed a break from it.

"OK."

I could tell he was about to leave, and I didn't want him to. "Wait. I was lying."

I told him about my mother, and the custody issue, and not wanting to move to Mexico. He nodded through the whole thing and winced at the right points, and when I was done, he said, "That's so messed up."

"What was it like when your parents got divorced?"

"They started out saying, 'Oh, it's going to be totally amicable. We'll split everything 50-50—the money, you, whatever.' And then they got into it and it turned into *Alien vs. Predator*. I was 10, but I was like my mom's best friend at the time, because she and Dad used to be so wrapped up in each other, they didn't have other friends. So she'd come home from seeing her lawyer and tell me every detail. They spent three weeks fighting about who was going to get this watercolor painting they'd bought at a yard sale. I remember her always saying, 'It's not the money; it's the principle.' She'd say that at least once a day."

"Did it upset you when she told you that stuff?"

"I always thought I wanted to hear it, because it made me feel like a grown-up to be in on the secret, but then afterward I hated that I knew. You're an only child, right?"

I nodded.

"Yeah, I was then too," he said. "It's the worst. No offense. You know what I mean. It's the worst when all the pressure is on you."

"I wish I had someone to roll my eyes with."

"Exactly. Like, someone you could turn to and whisper, 'They're insane,' when your parents are fighting."

We were still standing by the bike rack, shifting our weight from foot to foot. Most of the other kids had left, aside from a few who were waiting for rides.

"So they didn't fight about custody?" I asked.

"No, because my dad didn't want it."

I must have looked horrified, because Grady laughed and said, "Yeah, he's a dick. The thing is, I used to be on his side. He always said my mom was passive-aggressive and didn't appreciate him, and I thought he was right, but now I'm like, what was she supposed to be so appreciative about? The way he never really worked or took care of me?"

"He sounds like my mom," I said. "Maybe we should set them up."

Grady laughed, but suddenly it felt awkward, like I'd reminded us both of what happened last summer. And of the fact that we were having a serious conversation, the kind you have with a friend you trust, when we weren't supposed to be friends anymore.

"Is Reese waiting for you?" I said.

"No. Hannah's mom picked them up early. I guess I should go."

"You're walking?"

"Yeah."

"OK, well . . . It was nice to talk to you."

"I hope your mom writes back. Or I hope she doesn't, I guess."

"There are no good options," I said, and we laughed together, the sad laugh of two kids whose parents suck.

Wednesday, April 26

I couldn't wait to talk to Grady again today. All I want to do is spend hours hearing his thoughts on divorce. I found him in the back of the auditorium, waiting to be called onstage and drawing in his notebook, and I sat down right next to him, which seemed exciting and strange but also totally normal, like yesterday's conversation had canceled out all the months of hating each other.

He was sketching Izzy and Rob embracing on the stage, glancing up at them and then back down at his notebook.

"That's really good," I said.

"Thanks," he said. He didn't sound conceited, but he sounded like he's aware that he's an excellent artist.

"Can I ask you a question? How long does it take to feel normal after your parents get divorced?"

He stopped drawing. "I don't know if you ever feel normal. Especially when your parents start going out with new people."

"Is your dad remarried?"

"My dad, no. But obviously my mom is."

"Do you like your stepdad?"

"I try to like him. He always seems disgusted with me, though. But whatever. He has a job. He's good to my mom. He's Bear's dad."

"Is he nice to Bear?"

"Yeah, very."

"So he *can* be nice, just not to you."

Grady laughed a little. "I guess so."

We looked at each other, and I felt so sad for him, and he looked so brave, and his eyes were so beautiful, and I wanted to punch his stepfather in the face and then kiss Grady and kiss him and kiss him until he felt better.

I stood up. "I have to go."

"Oh. OK."

"Thanks for listening to me."

I was already walking away when he said, "Yeah, sure."

Thursday, April 27

I'm in love with Grady. Oh God.

Friday, April 28

I could tell him. We're in high school—it's not like I'm trying to break up someone's marriage. But no, no, I can't do this again! It doesn't matter that I loathe Reese. She's a person with feelings, and she loves Grady. Also, I'd only be humiliating myself. Grady is clearly crazy about her. They've been together for months now. They make out in the halls. They're never not holding hands. So, fine. I won't say anything, which is (a) the right thing to do and (b) the dignified thing to do.

Saturday, April 29

Tris texted.

> *What's going on with you*
> *and Grady?*

What nothing what do
you mean

Stop you know what
I mean

You guys have been
talking at rehearsal
all week

It's really bad

I think I like him

!!!

I do like him

!!!!!!!!!!!!!!!!!!!!!!!!!!!!!!!!!

Do not tell anyone

Of course not

But didn't you hate him
a week ago?

You and Elliott brought
us together

And he's still the easiest
person to talk to

Besides you obvi

I'm my real self around him

I'm my real self around Elliott
but because I don't care what
he thinks of me

You don't have to go out
with him you know

No I like *him*

He's growing on me

He's so into me I'm like what's
wrong with you?

Anyway what are you going
to do about Grady?

Nothing. You're the
only person I'm
telling

I can't be around him
anymore

I don't trust myself

If I keep talking to him
I'll try to kiss him or
something

I told you he was hot

I know

I told you you were making
a big mistake

I KNOW I KNOW

Very comforting, I'm sure! But Tris *did* try to tell me. He'd have to be a saint to resist saying "I told you so" now that I've finally seen the light.

Sunday, April 30

I woke up intending to get all my homework out of the way right after breakfast, and then I picked up my phone. Now it's dark outside and all I've done is memorize every pixel of every picture of Grady on the internet.

Monday, May 1

So to summarize, I turned down a gorgeous guy who makes me laugh, is easy to talk to, and was crazy about me because I wanted to sit around waiting for texts from a cheater who saw me as, at best, a booty call. What sense does that make? And why did it make total sense to me a few months ago?

Tuesday, May 2

It feels like it should be possible to go back to last summer and redo it. All those times we brushed against each other by accident during work—it was so annoying then, and now I would give anything to brush against Grady. We were half naked by a pool! We had literally hours every day to talk! I didn't appreciate any of it!

Wednesday, May 3

So far I've been avoiding Grady at rehearsal, which is easy enough to do if I hide in the girls' dressing room whenever I'm not onstage. But Hell Week starts this Sunday, and the whole cast will be together 24/7. Somehow I have to steer clear of Reese, Grady, Hannah, and whichever new enemies I make in the next four days.

I told Noelle about my realization, and she said I should definitely tell him how I feel. But I'm pretty sure she's mostly excited about the possibility of me messing up Reese's relationship, which is exactly what I don't want to do.

Thursday, May 4

I have this one selfie Grady and I took last summer. We're sitting on towels in the grass, our lips are blue from the rocket pops we just ate, and we're giving each other mustaches with our index fingers. Grady's raising one eyebrow, and I'm laughing so hard you can see my tonsils. I stare at this picture for hours every night, and stalk Grady online, and think about him as I'm falling asleep. Then I see him at rehearsal the next day and it's almost a shock. It's like I'm surprised to be reminded that he's real, this person I've been obsessing about in my mind for hours. And then usually, at some point, I see him and Reese hugging or something, and that's a shock too, because when I'm daydreaming about him, of course I don't think about her.

Friday, May 5

Dad asked how I'm doing, and for a second I thought he'd found this diary and was asking about Grady, but then he said, "You haven't heard from your mother again, have you?" and I said no, I haven't, which is true. I guess that's the upside of my fixation on Grady: I worry about Mom and Mexico all the time, but I'm simultaneously thinking about Grady, and that makes the Mom stuff less awful. I know I'm boy crazy, but I can't blame myself. Even when it's painful, thinking about guys is a way to stop thinking about my parents.

Saturday, May 6

I asked Dad if Miss Murphy was coming over for dinner, and when he said no, she was getting ready for Hell Week, I was a little disappointed. It's too quiet with just the two of us.

Sunday, May 7

Something's going on with Hannah. I saw her crying backstage, and when Miss Murphy gave notes, she said, "A few of the ensigns looked listless during 'Wash That Man.' That song will fail unless you bring actual happiness to it, OK?" which I think was a reference to Hannah, who was slumping around onstage all day with her eyes unfocused, like her dog died. Or maybe she was exhausted from the double run-through. It *is* soul-crushing to do two shows back to back.

Monday, May 8

Last year I didn't know how deeply boring the cue-to-cue rehearsal is. This year I was prepared. Not that it saved me from the boredom; I still had to stand around trying to meditate and breathe deeply while Oscar changed the gels or Leo ran out to fuss with Elliott's coconut bra. But at least I knew what was coming. Also, it was fun to see the freshmen arrive all excited for a new kind of rehearsal only to realize they were going to be trapped onstage for approximately nine hours while Leo screamed "Hold. I said HOLD!" from the wings.

Tuesday, May 9

Tris and I were sitting in front of the mirrors down-stairs when Hannah walked past, looking sick, and dis-appeared into the dressing room. At the beginning of the year, I would have gone after her, but today it felt like following her would be intrusive. Then, two min-utes later, Reese came down and ran into the dressing room, closing the door behind her.

"Something's up with Hannah and Zach," Tris whispered.

"No way," I whispered back.

He nodded. "I saw them fighting yesterday in the junior parking lot."

"Could you tell what about?"

"I heard him say 'What do you *want* from me?' But then they lowered their voices and I couldn't hear the rest. I had to keep walking. I didn't want to, like, stop and stare at them."

Ugh, poor Hannah. I hope she's OK. Would it be inappropriate to text her and say that?

I want to tell Noelle all about what happened today, but it feels like it would be disloyal to Hannah, which makes no sense, since Hannah and I are barely friends anymore.

Wednesday, May 10

Dress rehearsal. It went horribly, but Miss Murphy said, "Bad dress, good opening," and it sounded like she meant it.

Reese looks like a pinup girl in her red polka-dotted crop top. She and Hannah spent all the breaks together, talking with intense looks on their faces.

Grady walked past me at one point and looked at me

like he was considering stopping to talk, and it took all my strength to pretend to be engrossed in my science textbook, especially because he was wearing a white sailor hat and a fake anchor tattoo and I wanted to jump him.

Thursday, May 11

Day off before opening night. Last year at this time, I was getting ready to sing onstage, alone, in front of a thousand people, and I was too nervous to eat or concentrate on anything. This year I feel relaxed and a little bored. I'd give anything to feel sick with fear again.

Friday, May 12

Opening night is in the books! We had a good show. The guys got tons of laughs during "There Is Nothing Like a Dame," no one slipped on the shampoo during "I'm Gonna Wash That Man Right Outa My Hair," and Tris slayed with "You've Got to Be Carefully Taught"— I heard at least one person in the audience crying. Izzy was great, dammit. I guarantee not one person was thinking, *Chloe Snow would have done a better job.* But that's OK. I got to run around in my little high-waisted shorts and look cute, and I got to sing about being in love, and I had fun, actually.

Reese did not have fun. She sounded strangled trying to get her lines out, and you could see on her face that she was panicking. Downstairs after the show, I heard Hannah say, "Maybe you had stage fright? I'm sure you'll be fine tomorrow."

Reese was yanking off her fake eyelashes. She snapped, "How would you know? You've never had a speaking part in your life."

It was the first time I'd ever seen her drop her mask of sweetness, and I was shocked. So was Hannah. She reared back like Reese had slapped her. I don't know if they made up; I had to run to meet Dad and Miss Murphy, who were taking me and Noelle out to dinner with Tris and his family. POOR HANNAH again!

Saturday, May 13

During one of the many long stretches when I didn't have to be onstage, I was sitting downstairs eating Skittles, wearing my hoodie (it's freezing in the basement), and playing Would You Rather with Nadine. Hannah was sitting a few seats down, but we were pretending not to notice each other. I heard someone storming down the wooden stairs under the trapdoor and glanced up to see who was cruising for a bruising—Miss Murphy is always telling us to tiptoe on those stairs—and saw Reese. She raced right up to me and got in my face.

"What are *you* looking at?"

I wish I could say I came up with a snappy retort, but

I just stammered and turned red. I guess in theory it's good, this new version of Reese who's not pretending to be nice, but in reality it's terrifying.

"What'd you do?" Nadine asked me after Reese had disappeared into the dressing room.

"I have no idea!"

"Reese hates you, huh?"

"Thanks, Nadine. I already put that together."

"Just saying."

We tried to keep going with Would You Rather, but I couldn't concentrate.

We were heading back upstairs after intermission when Hannah stopped me and said, "Don't be mad at her. You were in the wrong place at the wrong time."

"You make her sound like a hurricane who destroyed my house. She's not a force of nature. She should be able to control herself."

"She messed up her lines again, that's all. I know she's still paranoid that you think you're better than her."

"What, like a better person?"

"No, at acting, singing . . ."

"That's not paranoia. I am better."

Hannah's face changed. "Chloe, you can be so conceited, you know that?"

"First of all, Reese is the one who came at me. How has this turned into a lecture on how awful I am?

Second of all, why are you defending her? I saw her yelling at you yesterday. Open your eyes, Hannah! You're on the wrong team!"

She refused to talk to me again, and we stomped upstairs in silence. My "Honey Bun" performance was abysmal, not that it matters, since I'm a random face in the crowd.

I know Hannah's mad at me, and I'm mad at her, too, but it still felt good to talk to her. I wish I could tell her what's in my heart: It's not that I'm conceited, although maybe I am. It's that I've known her for so long and I'm so comfortable with her that I can tell her the truth about what I think, even if the truth doesn't flatter me.

Sunday, May 14

I stood in the wings watching Tristan's performance today, and it gave me chills. He makes Lieutenant Cable this swaggering bro who becomes sensitive and thoughtful after he falls in love with Liat. And then, after he realizes that he's racist, and also that he's not strong enough to overcome his own racism, he hates himself. When he sings "You've Got to Be Carefully Taught," his voice shakes from anger. Tris is a different person when he's playing Cable. The way he walks, the way he moves his hands, his expressions—it's like watching someone who looks a lot like Tris but has nothing else in common with him.

He came offstage after his last scene and saw me. "Are you crying??" he whispered.

I nodded.

"I made you *cry*?" He jumped up and down with happiness.

He's probably going to get into Juilliard, and after he graduates, he'll star in Broadway shows while I wait tables. And I can take it. He deserves all of his imaginary future success.

Monday, May 15

This is the best part of the run. First weekend of shows behind you, only one rehearsal to worry about during the week, and a whole second weekend of shows to look forward to. Tris and I celebrated our day off by riding our bikes to Pop's for fries—and Elliott came!! He was extremely nervous and talked a lot, very fast. Tris kept interrupting him to explain to me what he meant, or to correct him. I pretended I had to go to the bathroom so I could sneak away and text Tris.

> *You're terrifying Elliott*
> *cut it out!*

He's embarrassing me!

No he's not calm down

I like him

Really?

Yes! Let him talk!

It was better when I went back to the table, but from the way Tris was staring back and forth between me and Elliott, I could tell he was dying to jump in. Right after I got home, Tris called me and said, "What do you think?"

"I told you, I like him!"

"But do you REALLY?"

"Tris, yes. Do *you* like him?"

"I still can't tell. Whenever we're together, I spend the entire time trying to figure it out. It's exhausting."

"Maybe he's not the guy for you, then."

"But when you say that, it makes me die inside a little."

We were quiet. I looked at Snickers, who was lying with his head on my pillow, mumbling in his sleep. "It's easier to be the Elliott in relationships," I said. "If you're in love with the other person, all you have to focus on is whether he loves you back."

"None of it's easy. It's all terrible," Tris said, and that's true too.

Tuesday, May 16

Today was the panel discussion. All the cast members who weren't on the panel themselves were required to go, and probably 60 parents and other people showed up for it. I was nervous. Our town is so painfully white it's like a snowman with marshmallows for buttons standing in front of a white house. And it's supposedly a pretty liberal place, but you never know these days. I was worried someone would ask an offensive question, or accuse us of being special snowflakes for holding the event in the first place. But after the panel discussion, when Miss Murphy opened the floor for questions, people asked stuff like, "How did you deal with the question of accents?" and "Did you consider cutting some of the more troubling lines?" One person asked Olivia what her experience has been like, being a person of color in a majority-white town, and she said, "It's been pretty hard, honestly." She talked about being treated as other, being marginalized, having to listen to jokes about her eyes from people who think they're making fun of racism by saying something racist, being put on the spot with questions like the one she was answering. It was hard to hear, because it made me realize I'm basically a human version of the show: the main cast of characters in my life is white, and I'm sure I'm racist in ways I don't even know about, and that's a sickening thought. Olivia is brave to say what she said, and brave to get up every day and come to school knowing she's going to be surrounded by a bunch of ignoramuses like me.

Wednesday, May 17

MAJOR DRAMZ. Zach dumped Hannah!!!!!!!!!!!! (Those are exclamation marks of shock, not excitement.) When I walked down the ramp to the basement, I saw Hannah clinging to Reese and sobbing and Reese patting her on the back with a sympathetic expression—but somehow, under the sympathy, you could see she was psyched to be co-starring in an interesting meltdown everyone would be talking about for days.

Tris was already at the mirrors, putting on foundation. I looked at his reflection and raised my eyebrows like, *What's up?* and he mouthed *Zach* back to me, and from that alone I guessed what had happened, because how could it be anything else? Then, in the girls' dressing room, Nadine asked me if Hannah's OK. I didn't want to admit she and I basically don't talk anymore, so I said, "She seems pretty upset," which sounded knowledgeable but was actually just a statement of fact based on what I'd observed two seconds earlier.

"I can't believe Zach broke up with her in a text. They went out for so long!"

In a text! That douche!! "I never liked him," I said.

"He's a fox, though," Nadine said thoughtfully. Girls

are ruthless. They'll try to steal your ex-boyfriend when he's only been your ex for two seconds!

I was upset on Hannah's behalf, and worried about her all night. We did a run-through, but added gags and jokes, which is the tradition between show weekends. Tris and Olivia switched parts for the duration of the rehearsal, and her rendition of "Younger Than Spring-time" was actually pretty great. The sailors performed an original song called "Our Costumes Are Pretty Lame" to the tune of "There Is Nothing Like a Dame," which is an inside joke that is only funny to the cast, because we all know about the sailors' hatred of their bell-bottom pants. And the chorus girls dumped water on Izzy during "I'm Gonna Wash That Man Right Outa My Hair," which I had argued against doing, since I was in Izzy's position last year and that would have made me furious, but she, unlike me, is a good sport and just laughed.

Poor Hannah looked shocked onstage and in the wings. I wonder what happened. I know Zach is a sexy musician, but he's also a boring mansplainer, and Hannah is so beautiful and nice—what's his problem?

Thursday, May 18

Tris got the scoop from Elliott, who got it from Grady, who got it from Reese. Apparently Zach thinks Hannah is great, but he "wasn't feeling it" anymore. God, I can't imagine anything worse! She didn't do anything wrong and nothing changed—except he suddenly stopped being attracted to her.

Friday, May 19

I do Tris's makeup before every show. Nothing dramatic, since Lieutenant Cable is a butch sailor, just a little definition of the features. It's truly a friendship rite of passage to sit four inches from someone's face, breathing onto his nose, feeling him breathe onto your chin, while putting light-brown eyeliner on his lids. Tris can't keep from twitching, because he isn't used to constantly poking himself in the eye with pencils. Today I finished doing his waterline, which is the part he hates the most, and then told him to close his eyes so I could do the top. He looked so innocent and trusting, sitting there with his eyes shut, smiling a little, presenting his face to me. I'm already dreading graduation. I don't ever want to grow apart from him.

Saturday, May 20

Being in the chorus is still humiliating, and I still hate it, and I still envy Izzy with every fiber of my being. But it *is* fun to have more time backstage with the other kids. Today we played Celebrity, and now my stomach muscles ache from laughing so hard. And our pre-show rituals are more fun now that I'm not a lead. When we stand in a circle holding hands and squeezing energy from palm to palm, I watch people more carefully, because I know them now, and I actually care about how their performances go. And when we all scream "BREAK A LEG, TIME TO FLY, MAKE 'EM LAUGH, MAKE 'EM CRY" before we go onstage, which has been an MH theater-kid tradition since the 1982 production of *Peter Pan*, they make eye contact with me and smile as they're screaming, which didn't happen last year.

Grady and I wound up next to each other for the hand-squeezing tonight, so I got to hold his hand guilt-free. It's big and solid and his fingers feel strong. I tried to send a message from my palm to his palm: *I'm so sorry I hurt your feelings last summer, and although I wish I could say I hope you'll love me again someday, I can't, because I want the best for you, and I see how happy you are with Reese.*

Reese still has terrible stage fright and sounds like a parched mouse when she's delivering her lines. Too bad, so sad. Noelle texted me, *Was she garbage again tonight?* and I texted back, *She sure was*, and she texted back the smiley poop. We would be mean girls if we weren't utterly powerless.

Sunday, May 21

Today was our last show—how is it over already?? After the curtain came down, everyone cheered and then hugged each other. Half the kids started sobbing immediately, and the other half joined in after we got down to the basement and started taking off our costumes for the last time. Someone opened nonalcoholic cider, and we stood around drinking it out of Dixie cups and sporadically bursting into tears. Of course it's ridiculous and melodramatic to be so upset about a show ending, but it's also not. We only get four shows like this in our whole lives, because let's be honest: aside from maybe Tristan, there are going to be way more HR reps than Broadway stars among us. We're only teenagers once, and we're right to be sad that it goes so fast and that soon we'll have to grow up and work in offices and accidentally marry the wrong people and then go through grueling, expensive divorces. This is one of the only times in our lives we'll feel like stars, and it's hard to let go of it.

Monday, May 22

I'm 16. It feels anticlimactic. 16 is one of those birthdays people care about, like 18 or 21 or 30 (grown-ups care about turning 30, right?). I'm not sure why 16 is special. Maybe it's that 15 sounds like a kid, and 16 sounds like a for-real teenager. Maybe it's that Hollywood and MTV have brainwashed us into believing that 16 is a milestone. Maybe it's that I would feel a little weird if I lost my virginity at age 15, but I wouldn't feel as weird if I lost it at 16 (am I slut-shaming myself?). Maybe I'm overthinking it, and it's that people—normal people, not me—get excited about it because it means they can finally drive.

My birthday was sheer glamour: classes all day, striking the set all afternoon. Hannah wished me a happy birthday, but she was too busy having serious conversations with Reese to pay much attention to me. I walked by them once and heard her say, "But I must have done *something*!" Reese said, "I'm sure you didn't, sweetie." I avoided Grady.

Dad's been asking me for weeks if I want a party, but I said all I wanted was for him to take me, Tris, and Noelle to Olive Garden, which I love unironically, and he said yes, even though he hates it. He also agreed not to complain about how inauthentic the food is the entire time. I was a little nervous, because it was only the second time Noelle and Tris and I have hung out. Tonight they were quiet at first, but then Noelle told Tris his shirt was cute and asked where he got it, and after that it was easy. I was having a great time until Dad turned to me and said, "So, should we head to the DMV after school tomorrow to get your permit? I can leave work early!" It's easy enough to refuse to drive around illegally with Noelle, but how am I going to get out of driving with Dad?

Tuesday, May 23

I was hoping the DMV would take forever, but we were in and out of there in less than half an hour. Dad asked me if I wanted to try driving home, and at first I said I did, which was true. I *wanted* to drive. I just couldn't. We were walking toward the car when I pictured getting in a crash and killing Dad, but not myself, and I heard myself saying, "Actually, maybe I should practice in our neighborhood first," which he seemed to think was reasonable.

When we got home, I distracted myself from my car phobia by calling Mrs. Franco to ask if I can be a lifeguard at the pool this summer. She said opening day is June 3, and I would have had to complete a training course by late March to be considered, but I'm welcome to work at the concession stand again. I accepted, hung up, and then realized how excruciatingly awkward it's going to be to hang out with Grady all day every day. How will I manage to pretend I don't like him for three months in a row? And oh God, Reese will be there too, preening and posing on the lifeguard chair. Great. This should be a real laugh riot.

Wednesday, May 24

The Senior Costume Contest is tomorrow. No matter what happens, it can't be as disastrous as last year's SCC. I would bet money no one will spray pee on me from a squirt gun, for example!

Thursday, May 25

GREAT SCOTT I THINK THERE'S SOMETHING GOING ON WITH REESE AND ZACH OMG OMG OMG

Friday, May 26

Tris and Noelle and I have been talking and texting about this nonstop and I still have no idea what to think.

What happened was, Tris and Elliott and I went to the gym for the costume contest, which is mandatory. I'm not sure why the administration thinks it's edifying for us to see a bunch of seniors, most of them drunk, running around dressed as memes, but whatever. We were sitting in the bleachers, watching in silent judgment instead of clapping and cheering, because we're theater kids like that, and then Grady came in late and sat next to Elliott. He leaned over him to push my knee and said, "Hey, happy belated birthday." The thing is, he wasn't flirting with me. He was just being nice, and that made me so sad. I desperately wanted him to be touching me because he secretly likes me, and I couldn't take the fact that he was bopping me on the knee like one friend bops another.

I muttered something about coming right back and then stepped over everyone and walked out through the double doors. The hallway was deserted except for Reese and Zach. She was leaning against the lockers, and he was next to her, running his index finger down the inside of her forearm—I *think*. I saw it for one second, and then they jumped apart and Reese said "Hey, Chloe" in a voice so warm it was like hot chocolate on a snowy day. She can't fool me with her fake niceness; she's even worse than I ever suspected.

Should I tell Hannah? No, right? It's not like I know for sure Reese and Zach are . . . doing whatever they're doing. Even if I did, I'm not Hannah's best friend anymore. I'm barely her friend, and that means I don't have a moral obligation to break it to her. Or am I making that argument because I want to avoid telling her something she'll hate hearing? The thing is, even if I did tattle, Hannah might think I'm making up stories to convince her Reese is awful.

And what about Grady?? How could anyone cheat on sweet, wonderful Grady with snoozy, beautiful Zach? If Reese dumps him, he'll be single. But I can't even hope for that. I can't hope for Grady and Hannah to wind up brokenhearted.

Saturday, May 27

I was sitting on the deck in the late afternoon with Miss Murphy and Dad. They were eating chips and salsa, and I was furiously texting Tris, and when Miss Murphy said, "What's going on? Anything interesting?" I spilled the beans and asked them if they thought I have to tell Hannah. It was a little awkward asking them for advice about turning in a cheating couple, since they were/are a cheating couple themselves, but Miss Murphy was so interested in the gossip that it overrode the weirdness.

"What do people think about Reese?" she said.

"You don't know?" I said. I was surprised. Miss Murphy seems omniscient.

"Not at all," she said. "The pecking order is invisible to me. I try to guess, but I can't read the signals."

"She's the most popular girl in our class," I said. "No one can stand her, but everyone wants to be her friend."

"Got it." Miss Murphy was nodding. "We had a Reese in our class. Heather Mason."

"Ours was Karen de Vries," Dad said.

Neither of them thought I should tell Hannah. Dad said I don't have enough evidence, and Miss Murphy said sometimes you're forced to interfere in other people's relationships for one reason or another, but this isn't one of those times.

Then we ordered food and watched *Real Housewives*. It's nice being able to outvote Dad again.

Sunday, May 28

This morning I called downstairs, "I can't find my hair dryer," and Miss Murphy called up, "Sorry. I borrowed it. Look in your dad's bathroom," and I checked and had started to say, "It's not there. Did you—" when Dad bellowed, "Stop yelling between floors, both of you." We're half pretending to be a real family, half being one.

Monday, May 29

I had the day off from school for Memorial Day. Dad came down in the morning wearing his swim trunks and a T-shirt and said, "Want to go to the beach?" I gulped down the rest of my breakfast and ran upstairs to get ready. We were walking to the car when he said, "How about you drive us to Dunkin' Donuts?"

I got as far as turning the key in the ignition and putting my hand on the gearshift before I started shaking and getting dizzy.

"I can't," I said.

"Yank it to the right a little before you pull down."

"No, I mean I can't drive."

"What? How come?"

"I don't know. I'm scared."

"Really?"

"I hate even sitting here. I'm having trouble seeing—it's like everything's getting dark."

He looked alarmed. "You can't drive like that."

"I know!"

"Are you sick?"

"No. I don't know. I don't think so."

"Do you need some water?"

I took the bottle he offered me and had a sip.

"It's not better," I said after a minute.

"Let's switch places," he said, and I was so relieved, I tried to jump out of the driver's seat without undoing my seat belt.

We stayed at the beach all day, and he didn't even ask if I wanted to try driving home.

Tuesday, May 30
Texted Noelle.

> *How do you make yourself*
> *do stuff that scares you?*

Like what?

> *I don't know . . . what*
> *scares you?*

I can't think of anything

Of course she can't! Really I should be asking her, how can I be more like you in every way?

Wednesday, May 31

I'm still wincing about what happened at lunch.

The cafeteria felt empty without the seniors (their last day was Friday). Tris and Noelle and I spread out at what used to be the varsity lacrosse players' table and talked about how nuts it is that we're going to be juniors next year. Reese was sitting one table over, alone, playing on her phone. She pretended not to see us, or maybe she actually didn't. We'd finished eating and were about to leave when Hannah came up to Reese's table, pale and shaking.

"I know about you and Zach," she said.

Reese made her screen dark. I could see her thinking as she looked down at it. When she looked up, her expression was warm and concerned.

"Oh, sweetie," she said. "I didn't want you to find out this way."

Hannah stayed standing and burst into tears. "All those conversations we had—I told you everything. I asked you for advice. I went to you for help, and the whole time you were the one hurting me."

"Hannah . . ."

"You made him dump me, didn't you?" she said. She was having a hard time getting the words out. People at the immediate tables were staring, including me and Tris.

Reese pressed a hand over her heart. "Hannah, of course not. It was a total coincidence. After you guys broke up, I texted him to see if he was OK, and it kind of progressed from there."

She's lying! I shrieked at Hannah in my head.

Hannah said, "I don't believe you. All that stuff he told me about not feeling it anymore—I didn't understand how everything could change so fast, but now I do. You guys were already hooking up."

"I would never," Reese said.

Hannah pulled herself together enough to laugh bitterly. "But you did."

Reese reached up and squeezed Hannah's forearm. "Han, don't you think you're being a tiny bit immature about this? It's high school. It's not like either of us is going to marry Zach."

Hannah looked down at her, and I wondered if she was about to fall for this BS. Then she said, "Youth is no excuse for bad behavior." Her old catchphrase! She's still Hannah under that perfect smoky eye and cool lob.

Reese said, "Hannah, no offense, but you sound

like someone's mom." Then she stood and picked up her phone and her books. The cafeteria was quiet. Some people were pretending not to notice the argument, some people were openly watching, but everyone was paying attention. I wanted Hannah to scream obscenities at Reese, or throw the nearest Snapple in her face, but instead she said quietly, "Reese, you are not a nice person."

Thursday, June 1

Everyone's saying Reese destroyed Grady by breaking up with him. Elliott told Tris that Grady didn't even know what was going on until last night, when Elliott couldn't take it anymore and texted him saying he needed to call Reese ASAP. She and Zach were officially going out before she even had the courtesy to dump Grady! Humiliation on top of heartbreak. Someone said Zach gave Reese a ride home and they made out in the junior parking lot for 15 minutes and he put his hand up her shirt right there in front of everyone (which sounds made up, but who knows?). Someone said Grady punched a locker. And someone else said he was crying in biology.

Noelle keeps texting me, *Reese, you are not a nice person,* followed by the applause emoji, or fireworks, or the yellow face with X-ed out eyes. I texted back, *Youth is no excuse for bad behavior,* and Noelle texted back, *SLAY,* and then I almost felt bad for Reese and that's saying something.

I spent all day today wondering how soon I could make my move and whether it would be gross to confess my feelings to Grady less than 24 hours after he got dumped. As an opening gambit, I texted him saying, *Are you OK?* and waited by my phone, literally sick to my stomach, for him to text back. When he finally did, 40 minutes later, he said, *Yeah*—no period. He's either mad or devastated. Either way, he's not interested in me. And it makes sense. Where do you go after dating the most popular girl in the grade above yours? You don't stoop back down to me.

Friday, June 2

Tomorrow's opening day at the pool, which is bizarre, since classes won't be over until the 19th (the college-age kids cover the 9 a.m. to 3 p.m. shifts until then, and they act like they're doing us a giant favor). I don't like the over-lap. School should end on Memorial Day so we can start basking in summer, glorious summer, without being dis-tracted by finals and other pesky academic nonsense.

I did 50 crunches after school, then spent an hour looking at no-makeup makeup tutorials on YouTube, because nothing could be more ridiculous than show-ing up at the pool at 9 a.m. looking like you thought you were going to a club.

I can't believe I used to go to work last summer without brushing my hair or even cleaning all the sleep boogers out of my eyes. I treated Grady like an annoying co-worker whose opinion didn't matter. What a fool I was!

He might not like me now, but we're going to be standing inches from each other for months. Maybe I can gradually worm my way back into his heart. He's a teenager—he won't be upset about Reese forever. Will he?

Saturday, June 3

Ummmmmm, GRADY IS A LIFEGUARD. What did he do, take a training course this winter and apply for the job in a timely fashion?? Who's that organized as a mere freshman? Wait—he must have done it so he and Reese could hang out together all summer, and now he's stuck working with the person who broke his heart. Poor guy.

I didn't even get to talk to him today. He sat across from the concession stand in the white wooden chair where Reese used to sit, leaning back with his arms crossed, yelling at the kids whenever they ran on the deck or dunked each other. Even wearing red lifeguard shorts and an orange waterproof watch, he looked like his skater self, with rubber bands around his wrists and his hair sticking up. He had on mirrored sunglasses, so I couldn't see his eyes.

I was working with some girl named Nadia who's going to be a freshman next year. She was shy and I think a little scared of me (possibly because I'm almost an upperclassman [!!!]), and I wasn't helping her out, conversation-wise, because I was so preoccupied by Grady. She saw me staring at him and said, "Who is that guy? He's cute."

"That's Grady," I said. She waited for me to elaborate, but I didn't want to get into it. Finally she said, "I wonder if he has a girlfriend."

"He doesn't," I barked, and she cowered in fear. I feel terrible. I'm going to be nicer to her from now on.

Sunday, June 4

I had a nightmare that Mom came home in the middle of the night and tried to steal me.

I've been telling myself I haven't heard from her because she's given up on the idea of shared custody. But I don't really believe that.

This morning I went downstairs and found Miss Murphy sitting at the island, reading the *New Yorker*. She looked up and asked me if I was OK.

"Yeah. Actually, no. I'm worried something bad might happen," I said.

"Want to talk about it?"

"Not really, if that's OK."

"Well, remember, 'sufficient unto the day is the evil thereof.'"

"What does that mean?"

"Think about today's problems today and tomorrow's problems tomorrow. If something bad happens next week, or next year, you can cope with it then. And it might not happen at all, so don't waste your energy worrying in advance."

It's good advice, and I'll try.

Monday, June 5

Even as I write these words, Reese and Zach are at junior prom. I got a shock when I opened Instagram and saw their selfie. He's wearing an ironic powder-blue tux; she's wearing a silver floor-length dress with one shoulder strap. Immediately, without thinking about it, I called Hannah. My heart was racing as I waited to see if she'd pick up. Then she did, and as soon as she said, "Hi, Chloe," she started crying.

"They're awful," I said. "This is beyond the beyond."

"I'm so embarrassed," she said. "I had my dress altered. I can't return it. I bought these shoes with hearts over the toes. . . ."

I knew what she meant. It's painful to think about your younger self doing something earnestly and hopefully, not knowing her efforts are doomed and she's headed for disaster.

"Reese and Zach," I said. "Their couple name can be Reek."

"You're not helping," she said, and she was still crying, but she was laughing, too.

I'm glad I called her. I'm still mad at her for ditching me all year, and for what? For this backstabbing boyfriend-stealer. But I realize I don't I have any right to complain, when I did exactly the same thing to her last year. If Mac so much as raised his eyebrow at me, I would cancel plans with Hannah in case he decided he wanted to hang out. So, really, I should be more understanding. I must have made her feel last year like she made me feel this year: Unimportant. Boring. Old news.

Tuesday, June 6

Tris and Elliott and I sat in the courtyard for a while after school today. Tris was on his phone, not paying attention to us, so I asked Elliott if he's been reading anything good.

"I started *On the Road*, but I can't stand it."

This caught my attention. Elliott looks like exactly the kind of guy who would fall for *On the Road*.

"Nothing happens," Elliott said. "There's no plot, and I'm sorry, but I think the writing is terrible. He says things like 'What a night it was!' It's like reading someone's aunt's Facebook comments."

We complained about Kerouac together for the rest of lunch. Tris looked up from his phone, figured out what we were talking about, and fell back into his phone again.

I love Elliott!

Wednesday, June 7

I love Elliott

Yeah so I noticed

You should love him too
OK?

I really really
like him

You are the Roy/Mac
of this relationship

I know

You have all the power

I know

Isn't it sad to realize this is
the way Roy and Mac felt
about us?

"Cute, fun to hang out
with for now, but actually
I DGAF"

So sad

Is it more fun to be the
Mac or the Chloe?

The Chloe

Definitely

I would rather be sick to my
stomach but super in love

Well that's the situation I'm
in right now and it sucks

Try to enjoy it

Easy for you to say

*Why don't you nut up
and tell Grady you
like him?*

                    *Believe me it would be an
                    exercise in humiliation*

                    *You should see the way he
                    looks at Reese*

What if you're wrong

                    I'm not

Just try talking to him

                    Maybe

Maybe.

Thursday, June 8

I don't know how the teachers expect us to study for finals when it's 85 degrees outside, our summer jobs have already started, and we're trying to write and memorize a script for a potentially life-changing conversation with the loves of our lives.

Friday, June 9

After Nadia and I cashed out, I pretended to be searching for something in my backpack. Finally she left, calling good night to me and Grady. I walked over to him. My heart felt like a kicking rabbit trapped in my chest.

"Hey," I said.

"Hey." He was still wearing his sunglasses, and I couldn't get a read on his expression.

"We haven't really talked yet this summer, somehow."

"Yeah, true." He crouched down, doing something with his water-testing kit.

"It's cool you're a lifeguard this year," I said. "I bet you don't miss the concession stand."

Say you miss it, I ordered him silently. *Say you miss it.*

"This is better, I guess," he said.

"Ha! Yeah, I can imagine," I said.

He didn't say anything else. The silence stretched on and on, like a vast windswept plain.

"Well, I gotta go," I said. "Have a good night."

"You too."

Horrible! Horrible. Stilted, awkward, emotionless, polite. And that was my very best attempt! That was me sticking to the script I worked on instead of getting ready for my tests!

Saturday, June 10

I ate two bites of dinner, studied for finals, and went to bed at 8:30 p.m. Miss Murphy came in to ask if I was sick, but I said no, just sick of myself.

Sunday, June 11

When I came downstairs at 9, Miss Murphy had my coffee and granola waiting for me. I thanked her, and she said, "Hurry up and shower. We're going out."

"I can't," I said. "Finals."

"You've been studying plenty," she said. "And this won't take too long."

She took me to the Emily Dickinson Museum, which is in the actual house where Dickinson lived. We took the 45-minute tour, creaking up and down the stairs and finishing in Dickinson's bedroom, where she wrote most of her poems. The walls were papered in a pattern of green leaves and pink roses. The twin sleigh bed is the one she really slept in. I couldn't believe I got to stand inches away from it. Across from the bed is a fireplace, and next to the fireplace is a reproduction of the tiny desk Dickinson wrote on. It's smaller than my nightstand, but that's all the space she needed to change the whole course of poetry. The view looked a lot like the view from my bedroom: trees and more trees.

The tour guide kept saying "Emily," which annoyed me. If she were giving us a tour of Hemingway's house, would she have called him "Ernest"? She also said no one knows for sure, but some scholars think Dickinson had a boyfriend or even boyfriends. Maybe E. D. was sick with love, like me, but she didn't let it take over her entire mind, like I do. She knew what was important: her work. I want to be like that. I'm not sure what my work is yet, but that's part of the problem. I need to find out, then do it.

Monday, June 12

I know being a grown-up is hard, and you have to support yourself, pay taxes, do a job you hate, etc., etc., all the stuff they complain about, but at least adults don't have to sit in front of a geometry final for two hours, sweating bullets.

Tuesday, June 13

Hannah and I are saying stilted hellos to each other in the hall, so that's something. Reese is completely ignoring both of us. Grady and I give each other a smileless *what's up* nod, or sometimes pretend not to see each other. Walking from class to class is exhausting—it's like fighting your way through a brambly forest of feelings. Only three school days left, then the water park trip on

Monday, then summer. Although it's not like summer will be much better, what with being forced to watch Grady ignoring me every day at work.

Wednesday, June 14

Whattttt I saw Noelle and Reese talking today! They were standing next to Noelle's locker. Their voices were low. Their faces were serious. As I walked by, Noelle saw me and gave me a look like, *I'll tell you later.* As soon as I was around the corner, I texted her, *?!?!?* An hour later, she wrote back:

*She stopped to say hi and I
couldn't turn her away*

It's not like we made up

> *What were you guys
> talking about?*

Hannah actually

*Reese is really upset about
what happened*

> *Hmmmmm*

Unless Reese is planning to prostrate herself at Hannah's feet and beg for forgiveness, I'm not that impressed.

Thursday, June 15

If I don't get an A+ on my English final, I'll eat my flip-flops. I was confident about the answer to every multiple-choice question, and I had a great time writing an essay about whether you can interpret *The Great Gatsby* as a feminist work. (I said you can. Jay and Nick don't see Daisy as a three-dimensional person, but that doesn't mean Fitzgerald doesn't.)

Tris and Elliott and I ate lunch outside after my test. I bragged to Elliott about my essay, and he said it sounds amazing. Tris confessed he's never actually read *Gatsby*, just watched both movie versions, and Elliott and I both said, "TRIS!!" Elliott said, "You had time to watch two movies but not to read the book? It's under 200 pages!" He's starting to be more like himself around me. And I could tell Tris was enjoying being ganged up on by his best friend and his boyfriend.

Friday, June 16

I wasn't planning it, but when I saw Grady in the hall after school, I changed course and walked right up to him.

"Are you going to work?" I said.

"No, I have the day off. You?"

"Nope. Just gonna sit at home alone, looking at my phone for hours. Nonstop excitement." I wish I could speak with earnestness and enthusiasm instead of being sarcastic all the time.

He closed his locker and put his backpack on. He wears it with the straps on both shoulders, and sometimes he even fastens the clasp across his chest. Everything he does is fascinating to me. All of his quirks are so endearing.

When he turned to leave, I followed him. "What's it like working with Reese?" I said.

"It sucks."

So he misses her and it's painful for him to be near her. Exactly as I suspected.

He stopped and said, "I forgot something in my locker. See you at the pool, probably."

"Be there or be square," I said, because I was nervous and upset, and so a Dad-like remark that made no sense popped out.

Chloe, accept the facts. He doesn't like you. He's pretending he left something in his locker to get away from you.

Saturday, June 17

It took me until 5 p.m. to remember that Father's Day is tomorrow. Thank God for Miss Murphy. After I asked her for help, she told Dad we had a lady situation, which wasn't technically a lie—I am a lady, and the situation is that I forgot about Father's Day—and drove me to CVS so I could buy a card.

Sunday, June 18

Celebrated Father's Day by getting into a fight with Dad. I worked up all my courage and said, "Do you have time for some driving practice?" and he said "Oh. Sure" in the same tone of voice he'd use to say "Oh. Sure, I have time for some Russian roulette." I said, "You sound terrified," and he said, "I'm not *terrified*, honey, but you have to understand why I'm wary after what happened on Memorial Day," and I said, "I *am* going to crash the car. Even you think so," and then went up to my room to be scared all by myself.

Monday, June 19

Last day of school! We went to Make a Splash, a water park 45 minutes away. Kind of a risky field trip, since it could have been 70 degrees today, but maybe the administration was counting on climate change, and they were right to, because it felt like mid-August.

It was horribly awkward but also very exciting to see everyone in their bathing suits. Nadine Wallach has an interesting birthmark on her torso, for example, and Chris Fortier has a dad bod already. I spent most of the trip sitting on a bench with Tris and Elliott, watching people rocket down the biggest water slide, plow into the flat part butt-first, and then attempt to subtly pick their giant wedgies.

Eventually I felt like a third wheel and told them I'd be right back. I wandered over to the fake river and watched strangers float by on inner tubes. Some of these strangers were cute boys from other schools, which made me think about the fact that there is an entire world of teenagers who do not attend MH and that it's crazy to act like Nadine and Chris and Grady and Reese, etc., are the only people in the universe and to get so wrapped up in our little dramas that I entirely forget the existence of other kids, not to mention refugees and political prisoners. Then Hannah tapped me on the shoulder and I forgot my insight immediately.

"Do you have a second?" she said.

"Sure."

"Thanks for calling me during the prom. That was nice of you."

"No problem."

She took a deep breath. "Chloe, I want to apologize. I'm so sorry I . . ." Her eyes filled up with tears, and she covered her face with her hands. I scooted closer to her and put my arm around her. Her shoulders were warm from the sun and oily from sunscreen. I knew she was about to give me a big speech, and I was interested in hearing it, but it was also superfluous. As soon as she said she was sorry, the last bits of my anger burned off.

"You were right," she said. "Reese is awful. I saw her being cruel to other people, but I always had an excuse for her. It didn't bother me until she stole Zach. And that's terrible! If I were truly Christian, I'd feel other people's suffering as strongly as I feel my own."

"Don't be ridiculous," I said. "What are you supposed to do, lie on the couch taking painkillers every time a friend of yours gets her wisdom teeth out? Of course you're going to be more upset when you're the one having a hard time."

"I was mean too," she said. "I was as bad as she was. That time we went to the Bowline? I knew she was intentionally making you feel left out, and I helped her do it. And it felt *good* to be mean. That's the scary part. Can you forgive me?"

"Of course I forgive you."

"Why?"

"For one thing, I did exactly the same thing to you last year."

"I guess you sort of did."

"I totally did! I ditched you for a jerk. For months! So what kind of hypocrite would I be if I held a grudge now?"

"But it's almost worse to ditch you for a friend."

"No way," I said. "Besides, every girl in our class

would do exactly what you did if Reese singled her out."

"You think?"

"Yes! I know *I* would! I'd be ignoring you at the Bowline so hard you'd think you were a ghost."

She still looked miserable, but she smiled at this.

"And you were right, when we had that fight," I said. "You *are* allowed to make new friends, and have a boyfriend, and ignore me if you want to. You know? There's no law that we have to be close for the rest of our lives."

"But I want to be close!" she said.

"Me too."

We smiled at each other.

"Has Reese tried to make up with you?" I asked.

"No. She says 'Hi, sweetie' to me in the hall, like everything's fine, but that's it."

"Are you sad about Zach?"

"Yes. I'm so sad."

"How did you find out, anyway?"

"Someone saw them making out at a party, and it got back to me. And honestly . . ." She trailed off and watched three little kids splashing along, kicking their legs and laughing. "I wasn't that surprised. Reese was always grabbing Zach's arm and teasing him. I told myself she was being nice to him because he was her friend's boyfriend, but I knew that wasn't it."

"They deserve each other," I said.

"I want him to be happy," Hannah said, and she started tearing up again.

I held my hand up like a stop sign. "He did this too, you know. He's half to blame. It's not all Reese's fault. Get mad at him."

If I know one thing for sure, it's that listening to "Someone Like You" on repeat and thinking about how wonderful your ex is and how much happiness he deserves is NOT the way to get over him. What Hannah should do is focus on the fact that Zach is a poisonous pile of raccoon poop. But of course she won't. Tris didn't. I didn't. No one can, at least not right away.

We walked back over to Tris and Elliott. I could tell Tris was shocked to see us together, but he said hi to Hannah like nothing was out of the ordinary.

Hannah and I sat next to each other on the bus on the way home, and when it was time to say goodbye, we hugged and hugged before she got in her mom's car. Her belly was pressed against mine, and I could smell her familiar smell and feel her shoulder blades under my hands. I'm so glad we can be friends again.

Tuesday, June 20

As bad as it is working across the pool from Grady all day, it's infinitely worse when he's not there and I'm working across the pool from Reese. I can't stand silence for more than two minutes—I have to turn on the radio or talk to Nadia. But Reese sits there for hours at a time without her phone, without a book, without anyone to talk to, looking like a queen even in her sunglasses and baseball cap, wearing a little smile on her lips, probably plotting her next battles.

I do admire her in some ways. Zach comes to pick her up after work a lot, and it's like ballet, the way she runs her fingers through his hair or nudges him with her hip. Even the mothers watch her in awe.

Wednesday, June 21

Nadia is so eager and optimistic. It should make me like her, but instead I want to put on noise-canceling headphones every time she starts talking. Today she was asking me how many extracurriculars I think she should do, and if the Love Notes ever accept freshmen, and if most people at MH have real relationships or just hook up, and I had to stop myself from shaking her and saying, "HIGH SCHOOL IS HORRIFYING. STOP LOOKING FORWARD TO IT."

On the other hand, I've never had a more willing audience for my Mac stories. Not only does Nadia listen to them, but she interrupts me to ask for more details.

Thursday, June 22

When I got home from work, Noelle was sitting on my front steps, looking at her phone. She glanced up when I called her name, and I jogged across the lawn to her.

"How did you get here?" I asked as we hugged hello.

"I borrowed my mom's car."

"You have to stop," I said. "You're going to get in an accident or arrested."

"Listen, I need to tell you something," she said, and pulled me down next to her on the steps. "Reese and I are friends again."

"*What?* Are you serious? How did that even happen?"

"She called me crying and said she misses me so much and she can't stand to lose me. She promised everything will change."

"And you fell for it?"

"Not necessarily."

"What does that mean?"

She shrugged. "Maybe she's sorry. Maybe she's not. Maybe she needs me now that she's on the outs with Hannah."

"So you're taking her back even though you don't trust her and she told everyone you're a slut."

"Don't be mad."

"I'm not *mad*. I'm shocked. She spread rumors about you! She kicked you out of her clique!"

"Keep your friends close and your enemies closer, right?"

"I'm serious, Noelle."

She slapped a mosquito that had landed on her arm. "She can be awful. But there are things you don't know about her. She pretends nothing gets to her, but it's not true. She has a lot going on with her family."

"We all have a lot going on with our families," I said.

"Yeah." We sat on the steps in silence, looking at the street.

"I shouldn't admit this," Noelle said, "but I kind of like all her drama. It's interesting."

I refused to say so out loud—I was a little mad at Noelle—but I understood what she meant.

"And you know I miss being popular," she said.

Something occurred to me, and I gasped and grabbed her arm. "You're going to disappear from my life!"

She rolled her eyes. "Don't be ridiculous."

"No, you are. You're back in the squad now, and Reese will never let you be friends with me."

"Would you stop? I'll be friends with whoever I want."

"You say that now."

"It'll be fine. You'll see."

I really don't think it will, but I'll hope for the best. Noelle and I aren't kindred spirits, but I do love her.

Her bravery and her prickliness and her honesty and her toughness—I would miss it all so much if Reese took her away.

Friday, June 23

Reese came over to the concession stand on the pretext of buying water and asked me how Hannah's doing.

"She's good," I said.

"Tell her I miss her," Reese said, and pooched out her lower lip, making a Sad Face.

"I definitely will," I said. Nothing has changed. Reese is still pretending to be nice and I'm still kissing her butt. I wonder if I'll manage to grow a spine before college.

She readjusted her ponytail in a businesslike way, and I could tell something else was coming. "So I know you and Noelle got tight this year," she said. "That's sweet."

"She's great," I said.

"Isn't she? I'm so lucky she's my best friend," she said, and stared into my eyes. I knew what she was implying—Noelle was her friend, not mine, and I'd better back off—but it was impossible to confront her, because what she'd actually *said* was so unobjectionable. Finally I couldn't handle the pressure of making eye contact with her, and looked away. She'd won again.

"So what's new with you?" she said cheerfully. "Are you dating anyone?"

As if she didn't know I'm not. Every person in our school is aware of the precise relationship status of every other person—who's sexting some guy from two towns over, who's flirting with whose girlfriend, who went down on her brother's friend in his basement.

"Nope," I said.

"You've had an epic dry spell this year, huh?" she said. "I'm not worried for you. You'll find someone sooner or later." She patted my hand and gave me a sympathetic look while I tried to smile. It's death to let her know she's getting to you. You have to at least pretend to be nonchalant.

Saturday, June 24

This is the first day I've worked with Reese *and* Grady, and the awkwardness levels were off the charts. Normally lifeguards sit at opposite sides of the pool during busy times, but on the same chair when it's quiet, so they can talk. But Grady never walked over to Reese's chair, and the few times she came to his, he got up and moved to the one she'd just left. I was trying not to stare at either of them, but it wasn't possible, and finally I gave up and watched them like they were a TV show. Nadia said, "Does Grady not like Reese or something?" and I took pity on her and explained their history. It was like teaching a small child her colors or something.

She was fascinated and asked a million questions. She doesn't know I like Grady, because I'm not about to confide in a random freshman, so she couldn't know she was punching me in the heart by saying stuff like, "But they look so cute together," "I can tell he's upset," and "I wonder if they'll ever get back together."

Sunday, June 25

Miss Murphy was gone when I woke up today. It turned out her mother had a bad night, and Miss Murphy had to leave first thing in the morning. The house felt quiet without her.

After he went for a run and took a shower, Dad came out to the deck, where I was reading, and asked if I had a minute to talk.

"I was considering asking Marian if she'd like to come to the Cape this year," he said. "But I wanted to talk to you about it first."

"Oh, I assumed you already asked her," I said. "It's fine with me."

"Really? I have such strong memories of going there with you and your mom. I wondered if it would feel strange, having someone else there with us."

"Are *you* OK with inviting Miss Murphy?"

"I think it'll be nice," he said, but I could see him thinking.

Good grief, he's not missing Mom, is he? I mean, I guess it would be fine if they . . . got back together.

She's my mother. I shouldn't feel sick to my stomach at the thought of living in the same house with her again.

Monday, June 26

I woke up early this morning and ran down to find Dad before he left for work.

"Did you invite Miss Murphy yet?" I asked.

"Not yet."

"You should call her this morning," I said. "We're going in less than two weeks. She probably has to hire someone to take care of her mom while we're away."

He looked surprised, probably at my sound reasoning, and said he would. I'm going to text him in an hour to see if he did.

Tuesday, June 27

Worst-case scenario: Dad dumps Miss Murphy and begs Mom to come back. She does, because she's sick of washing the floor of the yoga studio, and everything goes back to normal: she misses my school events because she's "writing," she has three glasses of wine and starts screaming at Dad for being passive-aggressive, and she occasionally remembers I exist and makes me feel like the center of the universe for half an hour. That wouldn't be SO awful, would it?

The good news is, Miss Murphy is coming to the Cape. I'm going to sprinkle rose petals on the master bed and suggest she and Dad go out for romantic dinners alone.

Wednesday, June 28

EUREKA! I'm going to invite Grady to our Fourth of July barbecue! I know he needs space, he's still not over Reese, etc., etc., but I have to subtly remind him of how fun and interesting I am, and what better way to do it than over cheeseburgers, while wearing my American-flag T-shirt and smallest cutoffs?

Thursday, June 29

I did it!! I planned it perfectly so we left work at the same time, and asked him in the parking lot. He said he thought he could probably come. Tris and Elliott and Hannah are coming too, and Miss Murphy, of course. This could be perfect!

Friday, June 30

Nadia asked me what I'm doing for the Fourth, and I told her about the barbecue. She looked at me longingly, but I stayed strong and didn't invite her. I refuse to let her *All About Eve* me.

Saturday, July 1

Well, I've invited Nadia. She was asking me if we light sparklers in this wistful voice, and I couldn't take it. She jumped up and down with happiness, and I felt guilty for not asking her sooner.

Sunday, July 2

Miss Murphy FaceTimed me for the first time in our history to show me her outfit options for the party. I couldn't figure out why she was stressing about it, but then I realized—some of Dad's college friends are coming in from out of town, and she must be nervous about meeting them. Grown-ups: they're just like kids! (I voted for the blue linen sleeveless dress.)

Noelle texted me saying she can't make it, because she's going to the beach with Reese and her family.

And so it begins

Would you stop?

Don't believe anything she says about me

CHLOE

I sent her an American flag and a sad face, and she texted me a yellow face rolling its eyes.

Monday, July 3

Miss Murphy spent the morning making a cake that looks like an American flag, with raspberries for the stripes and blueberries for the field behind the stars. Dad and I cleaned the backyard and hung up red, white, and blue lights. After dinner, Miss Murphy and I put on green tea face masks, and I made her take a selfie with me. I should go to bed, but I'm too nervous to sleep. I can't stop thinking about Grady, and what might happen tomorrow.

Tuesday, July 4

Oh my God. Oh my *God*. Mac came to the party.

It had been going for only half an hour, maybe 45 minutes. I was standing around with my friends, kind of listening to them but mostly looking to see if Grady had arrived yet. And then Tris's face changed, but before I could ask him what was wrong, I felt two hands clap over my eyes.

"Who is this?" I said, reaching up to grab the fingers. When I turned around and saw Mac grinning at me, honestly, my heart sank. I was so disappointed it wasn't Grady.

"Party at Chloe's!" Mac said. "Whoooo!"

Tris and Hannah were openly glaring at him, so I pulled him over to the shed to talk.

"What's the problem, Chloe Snow? Do I embarrass you?"

"What are you doing here?" I asked.

"What am I *doing* here? How about 'Nice to see you, Mac,' or 'Would you like a beer, Mac'?"

"Sorry. Nice to see you."

"I'm just messing with you, kid. I didn't realize you had a shindig going down. I'm home for the long weekend and wanted to see you, that's all."

I felt guilty I'd been rude, so I said, "I'm glad you came. Do you want something to eat?"

"I have a better idea. Let's get out of here and head to my house for a while."

Last year I would have ditched my friends and family at the speed of sound. Here was Mac, smiling down at me, his biceps practically ripping open the sleeves of his T-shirt, asking me if I wanted to go hook up with him. But I didn't want to. I had no desire to leave my backyard, which was full of sunshine and freshly cut grass and the smell of grilling meat, to dry-hump Mac on his dirty sheets next to a fish tank full of piranhas.

"I should hang out here," I said.

"Oh, *man*! You're still that mad?"

"I'm not mad."

"It's OK, Chloe Snow. I respect your game."

"It's not a game, I swear."

"Walk me out, at least?"

Dad and Miss Murphy were laughing in a circle of off-duty attorneys. I could tell by the way they were whispering and frowning that Hannah and Tris were filling Elliott in on the Mac situation. It seemed OK to sneak away for a minute.

When we got to his truck, we hugged goodbye.

"Sorry the timing was bad," I said.

"No sweat. See you next time I'm back, maybe."

He got in his truck and turned it on, then turned it off and got back out.

"What do you need to hear from me, Chloe? You want me to say I'll be your boyfriend?"

"Do you *want* to be my boyfriend?"

"I want to be your buddy."

"What, like my buddy with benefits?"

"If you want to put it like that."

"I want to put it like *this*," I said, and did jazz hands, for some reason.

"You're a nut," he said.

We smiled at each other. We do have fun together, I must admit. But standing there, watching him lean against his truck, I saw him for real, not through the bubble of delusion I walked around in last year. He's not the evil idiot I thought he was when I was so mad at him last summer, but he's also not the god in human form I thought he was before that. He's just a confident bro who would only ever make me unhappy.

"I like someone else," I said. "And I don't want a buddy. I want a boyfriend for real."

He looked at me.

"Also, I want to be a virgin for a while longer," I said. "I still feel like a kid."

He laughed. "You're a funny bunny."

"I'm serious."

"I know you are." He jingled his keys. "I'm not giving up on you yet."

"Give up on me!" I said. It was a relief that I'd said what I wanted to say, he wasn't angry, and we were already joking around again.

"How things have changed, Chloe Snow." He got in his truck again, turned the key in the ignition, and rolled down the window. "See you around, right?"

I leaned through the window to give him a kiss on the cheek. "See you around."

He tousled my hair and smiled, and for a second I felt a pang of regret about sending him away, but it faded fast. Then I turned around and saw Grady riding into the driveway on his bike, and my heart seized up.

"Sorry to interrupt," he called as Mac backed up and pulled onto the street.

"You weren't! That wasn't—there's nothing going on with him and me."

He got off his bike and laughed. "Yeah, I can tell."

Mac chose that moment to beep his horn while blowing me a kiss.

I turned back to Grady. "I know it probably—"

He cut me off. "It's cool, Chloe. You don't have to explain yourself to me."

"I know. But I'm serious."

He nodded. "Got it. Is there anything to eat?"

We were eye to eye. Well, almost. He's taller than me now. I could tell my face was rigid with anguish. His was calm and friendly. He'd just seen me lean into the truck to kiss Mac, and he didn't care at all. He was more interested in finding a burger than in listening to my denials.

I led him around to the back. He ate a big plate of food and laughed with Tris and Elliott while I whispered miserably to Hannah. Nadia came and chirped away to everyone. She was disappointed to hear she'd missed seeing Mac in person. Before Grady left, he came to thank me for having him over and gave me an awkward hug, the kind where only your clavicles touch and you pat each other weakly on the back.

That's that.

God I'm sad.

I was telling myself I had no shot with him, but I never believed that was true. Now I know it is.

Wednesday, July 5

Reese stares into the pool, Grady stares into space, I stare at Grady, and Nadia flits around darting interested glances at everyone and laughing merrily at her own jokes. Give her another year and she'll be dead inside, like the rest of us.

Thursday, July 6

I've already packed my bags for the Cape and put them by the front door. "Kind of excited for vacation?" Dad said.

Friday, July 7

Some nights it's like I can pull my head above water for a second and get some perspective. I look around at the blue sky and the white clouds and realize nothing is actually wrong; everything's wonderful and my life is charmed. I'm healthy. My father loves me, and so does my mother, in her own ridiculous way. I'm not marginalized; in fact, I'm privileged AF. I go to a highly rated high school and will probably get into a halfway decent college. Yes, the boy I currently love doesn't love me back, but life is long and I'm at the very beginning of my dating years. I get to sit on a cedar deck next to a green lawn, slapping mosquitoes and listening to the crickets chirp as the sky gets dark.

If only I could keep my head up and never put it under the water and start obsessing about jellyfish again.

Saturday, July 8

We're heeeeeeeeeeeere! My phone doesn't work and the air is soft and smells like salt and I can hear the waves as I sit here writing! Heaven, I'm in heaven!

Sunday, July 9

Dad was right—it is a little odd having Miss Murphy at the Cape. We only come to this cottage once a year, and somehow that makes the memories I form here more permanent. When I look at the breakfast nook, I remember sitting there playing cards with Mom. When we eat hot dogs for dinner, I think about her saying, "Do you know what they put in those things? Lips and anuses, for starters." When we lie on the beach, reading, I remember the time she got so mad at Dad, she grabbed his beer out of his hand and threw it into the ocean. I'm not saying my memories are so great and I'm missing her. I'm saying she's on my mind.

Monday, July 10

I noticed Miss Murphy standing at the top of the wooden stairs today and called up, "Miss Murphy! Can you please bring down the sunscreen when you come?"

When she made it down to the beach and handed me the bottle, she said, "At some point you should probably stop calling me Miss Murphy."

I squinted up at her, shading my eyes. She sat down next to me so I wouldn't have to stare into the sun. "What am I supposed to call you?" I said.

"How about Marian?"

I tried to imagine it. *Marian, can you please bring down the sunscreen?* Impossible.

"I can't," I said.

"Her mother calls her Murph," Dad said. I'd thought he was asleep. He was lying on his back with his hat covering his face.

"How about MM?" I said. "That way I can think 'Miss Murphy' in my head, but it won't sound so formal."

"Or how about M&M?" Dad said. "Because she's so sweet?"

"Dad!" I can't take it when he flirts with her in front of me. It's nothing to do with Miss Murphy. It's the general horror of realizing my father has a sex life (barf!!!!!!).

Tuesday, July 11
Dad and I went for a walk on the beach after lunch. The tide was out, and sandpipers were tearing across the wet sand, occasionally stopping to peck. Dad was being

quiet, and I knew he was gearing up to talk to me about something. I don't like the way parents are allowed to spring difficult conversations on you whenever they want, and you have to listen and respond even if you're getting a migraine or feeling queasy or just not in the mood to have a big thing.

Finally he asked, "Has your mother emailed you recently?"

"Nope."

He kicked a clump of seaweed out of his way. "Me neither."

My heart sped up. "Is everything OK with you and Miss—MM?"

"What? Yes, fine."

What were we talking about, then? I thought he was bringing up Mom because he missed her, but that didn't seem to be it.

"I wanted to talk to you about where your mother is," he said.

He sounded so strange that I panicked. "Is she OK? What, is she *dead*?"

"No! No. I'm sorry. I didn't mean to scare you. Listen— you know we've been struggling to agree on the terms of the divorce, right?"

I nodded.

"I don't want to give you more information than you

need, but essentially we hit a wall, and Veronica wasn't willing to continue talking about it. I decided to move ahead, so I filed for divorce. Because she's in Mexico, I had to go through the central authority there to transmit the letters rogatory—the details don't matter. The point is, the court clerk there attempted to serve her with papers, but she's no longer at her old address."

"So where is she?"

"I'm not sure."

I stopped walking. It was too difficult to take in what he was saying and coordinate my legs at the same time.

"I don't get it," I said.

"I think she moved to avoid getting served. If you officially acknowledge receipt of the papers, it sets the divorce in motion, and I believe she's stalling."

"Why?"

He sighed. "She sees the writing on the wall. She knows she's not going to get custody of you, and she knows she won't get other concessions she's asked for, so she wants to run away from the whole thing. And I'm speculating here, but I think she may regret the path she's chosen."

"Like, she regrets leaving you?"

"It's possible. She sounds unhappy. I don't know if her life there is what she imagined it would be."

"Is she still with Javi?"

"I'm not sure. I don't ask."

"Do you think she's even in Mexico? She could be in Bali. She could be HERE!"

"It's true that she's not necessarily in Mexico anymore."

I looked out at the ocean. The sun was making diamond crescents on the water.

"I realize this is upsetting," Dad said. "I wish I had more information for you."

"It's OK," I said. I was having a hard time listening to him, because I was trying to understand what he'd told me, and the shock of the information was freezing my mind.

We walked back in silence. I knew I should have questions for him, but they weren't coming to me. All I could think about was Mom in Tokyo, or Minnesota, or Bucharest. All of the possibilities canceled each other out, and it felt like she'd disappeared entirely.

Walking up the stairs to our cottage shook my thoughts loose, and when we got to the top, I said, "Does this mean you can't get a divorce?"

Dad shook his head. "I can proceed without her cooperation. It'll take longer, that's all."

"How long?"

"I'm not sure."

Wednesday, July 12

I slept terribly, and when I woke up, I threw on yesterday's clothes and ran downstairs. Dad and Miss Murphy were eating breakfast. I could tell by the way they looked up that they'd been talking about me. I poured myself some coffee and stood by the sink drinking it until Dad headed up to take a shower. Then I sat down next to Miss Murphy and said, "You know about my mother, right? That she disappeared, or whatever?"

She nodded.

"Are you going to break up with Dad?" I asked, and to my surprise, my eyes filled with tears.

She looked shocked. "No. Why do you ask that?"

"The divorce is going to take forever. Maybe you'll get sick of waiting."

She squeezed my hand once, hard. "I won't."

"What if you want to have kids? Don't you have to do that soon?" As I asked this, I looked at the tablecloth instead of at her.

She sighed and said, "Yeah, probably."

I couldn't help darting my eyes to her face. I'd thought she might say, "Everything in due course," or "I'm not even sure I want children," or "You're the only kid I need." I don't want to admit this, but I was upset and shocked to hear she does want babies, and with my father, and soon. *What about me?* was my first thought. *I'll be replaced! They'll love this baby more than they love me!* But my second thought was about Bear, and how cute and smart he is, and how much I love talking to him. Maybe it wouldn't be so bad.

"How would you feel about having a half sibling?" she said.

A suspicion jolted through me. "Are you pregnant???"

"No!" she said. "Really, no."

I thought about the idea of a new baby. A little person waking me up screaming at night. Dad cooing over someone else's face. Miss Murphy breastfeeding!! (Am I a prude if the thought of seeing her boobs makes me want to die?)

"It would be weird," I said. "Having a half sibling."

"Yeah. It would definitely be weird." She sounded deflated.

"Would you try to get pregnant even if my parents are still married?"

She was looking at my face but without seeing it. Then her eyes snapped back into focus and she said, "I would really rather not do that." So she's thought about doing that!

The beach was no fun today. I didn't get through a single page of my book. Instead of lying on my towel, I sat bolt upright with all my muscles tensed, thinking hard about everything that's happened and everything that might happen.

Thursday, July 13

The only way I could get to sleep last night was by fantasizing about Grady coming into the concession stand and saying, "Chloe, I have to tell you something: I'm in love with you," and then hugging me as tightly as he could. I fell asleep imagining the feeling of his arms around me.

Friday, July 14

Man, screw my parents and Miss Murphy for ruining the best week of the year. This is the one time when I can focus on my surroundings and not my thoughts. I hear the waves, I feel the sun warming up my hair, I taste the salt on my lips, and that's it. I don't zone out, oblivious to the world around me, thinking only about whatever's worrying me, like a brain in a jar. Except this year I am zoning out. I walk along the beach and I might as well not be there. I'm not taking any of it in. I'm obsessing about Dad's imaginary new baby and Mom's current whereabouts.

Saturday, July 15

Dad said Mom's fine, but how does he know that? OK, she said she'd be out of touch, but she could have said that and then been abducted, or had a heart attack, or drowned.

Sunday, July 16

Mom,

Dad told me you probably moved. Where are you now? Are you OK? Please write.

—Chloe

Monday, July 17

Back to work today, and it wasn't even that painful. I could hardly see Grady or hear Nadia. My head was so full of my mother, I had no room to think about them.

Tuesday, July 18

I rode my bike to Pop's to meet Tristan and Hannah. God, it was a relief to see their faces. Tris was stressed out because he detagged himself in a bunch of pictures Elliott posted and now Elliott's accusing him of being ashamed of their relationship. "But that's not it!" Tris said. "It's that I have a double chin in every picture he takes of me!" Hannah was stressed out because Reese and Zach are all over every social media platform, announcing their love to the world. There are selfies of them sharing the same ice cream cone, forming a heart shape with their hands, lying on the grass with their heads touching, and sitting on playground swings and leaning past the chains to kiss each other, to give just a few examples. They have the same profile picture on Instagram: the words "Zach <3 Reese" carved into the sand. "Everyone must be pitying me," Hannah said. "It's so embarrassing."

"It's not!" Tris said. "And if everyone's pitying you, that's nice. You're the good guy!"

"I'm the pathetic guy," she said.

"Everyone's too busy throwing up at how cheesy these pictures are to think about you," I said.

"But they get so many likes!"

"Likes mean nothing," Tris said. "People are so desperate to stay on Reese's good side, they'd like anything she posted."

Eventually I told them about Mom, and they felt terrible for complaining about their internet problems when my mother's run away again. But they shouldn't have felt bad. First of all, internet problems are real. Second of all, it felt so good to stop thinking about myself for an hour and focus on social media disasters.

Wednesday, July 19

Chloe,

I'm in good health and am living in Mexico City. Attempts to find me will prove fruitless, I assure

you. I'm sorry you and your father have driven
me to these lengths, but driven me you have.

—Veronica

Oh, thank God, thank God, thank you, God, if you
exist. It feels so luxurious to be angry that she signed off
"Veronica" instead of "Mom"! Now I can keep despising
her without worrying that she's dead.

I instantly forwarded the email to Dad and then called
him at work to see what he thought. He was furious with her
but pretended not to be. I asked him if he was going to try to
find her, and he said that would be expensive and probably
impossible. I said, "Do you think we'll ever see her again?"
and he said, "I'm sure we will." But why is he so sure?

Thursday, July 20
I wasn't on the schedule today, so Noelle came over and
we had lunch on the deck. After we finished, she put her
feet on the railing and lit a cigarette. "So what's going on
with Grady?" she said.

"I think—" I started, and then remembered: she's
friends with Reese again. It's not that I think she'd ever
spy for her, but what would stop her from gossiping about
whatever I said? Talking about people behind their backs
is what every normal human does.

"I think it's not meant to be," I said.

"Really?"

"He's not into me. It's fine. I'm over it."

She studied my face and said, "You're not holding out on me because he's Reese's ex, are you?"

"Noelle! No."

She ashed into her empty Diet Coke can. "OK. Just asking."

I felt slightly nervous for the rest of the afternoon. I don't think she did, but she never feels nervous. She's Noelle.

Friday, July 21

Now that I know Mom's OK, there's nothing mentally blocking my view of Grady. There he is, across the pool from me, looking tan against his white chair. Sometimes he leans forward and puts his elbows on his knees. Sometimes he leans back and lets his head rest against his interlaced fingers. When the sun shines in his eyes, he squints, which would make him look like a cowboy if he weren't also wearing a black baseball cap. When he's bored, he adjusts his rubber bands, takes off his hat and rubs his hair violently until it's sticking straight up, or juts out his jaw and massages it with his fingertips. Usually he keeps his shirt on, but sometimes he'll take it off, and then I can hardly look at him, he's so beautiful to me. Although he's grown a few inches at least, he's still skinny, wiry, which I thought I didn't like, but it turns out skinny and wiry makes my legs turn cold with lust. When the kids act up, he blows his whistle and bellows at them in a confident, deep voice. During adult swim, he stands in the lifeguard shack checking his phone. Sometimes youngish mothers come over to flirt with him, and he smiles and laughs, but not in a gross way. You can tell all the little girls are in love with him, which is only natural.

He's distant but polite to all of us—me, Reese, Nadia, and the college kids on staff: Jeff, Quentin, Angela, Phoebe. He's never late. Even though he's allowed to close the pool when it's raining, he almost never does, I think because the kids beg him not to and he doesn't want to let them down. Sometimes when the pool has just opened and no one's arrived yet, he'll get out his notebook and sketch.

I'm stalking boys from other schools online, and I've tried to force myself to develop crushes on Jeff or Quentin, even though Jeff sniffs violently every 10 minutes and Quentin covers his entire face in white zinc. Nothing works. I love Grady, only Grady.

Saturday, July 22

Dad grilled chicken to go with a salad Miss Murphy made.

"I put in cranberries, avocado, feta, and bacon," she

said as she brought it out. "I just *went* for it."

"When it comes to salad, M&M doesn't hold back," Dad said.

I was setting out napkins and silverware. It felt like I was seeing my father and Miss Murphy through the wrong end of a telescope. I can't relax and joke around with them, knowing the divorce might take a long time and Miss Murphy may or may not get pregnant and may or may not be my stepmother. I can't stand not knowing what's going to happen, which is kind of a problem, since the whole crux of life is that you don't know how everything will turn out.

Sunday, July 23

Dad sat me down after breakfast and said, "Chloe, it's very important that you try to get over this fear of driving. I don't want you to be limited later in life because you don't have your license. What if you don't wind up living in an urban area? You could find yourself trapped by a decision you made when you were a teenager."

"I'm not deciding anything!" I said. "It's not like I want to be afraid. I just am."

"Let's go out to the car right now," he said. "I'll back it up for you. We'll drive down the street—that's it. You can go as slowly as you want to."

I tried as hard as I could. I lectured myself as I walked

outside and as I watched Dad position the car for me. I breathed deeply and thought about calming things (Snickers, swimming, chatting with Tris). It didn't work. As soon as I got in the car, my heart started pounding and my vision got foggy. Dad looked at my hands, which were shaking on the wheel, and said, "It's not safe for you to drive in this state. Let's try again another day." He was trying to be understanding, but I could hear frustration in his voice. I don't blame him. I wish I could fix whatever's wrong with me.

Monday, July 24

I didn't have work today, so I went over to Tris's house to hang out with him and Elliott. It was meltingly hot, so Tris dragged his old *Blues Clues* kiddie pool out of the basement, and we inflated it with a bicycle pump, filled it with water from the hose, and then sat on beach chairs with our feet in it.

Elliott and I talked about books for a while and decided to have a two-person book club. He suggested *The Handmaid's Tale*, and I gave his idea two thumbs up (a real-life like!). Then I very casually asked him how Grady's doing.

"He doesn't seem that great, honestly."

"Really?"

"Yeah, he's gotten super quiet and moody."

"Do you think he's still upset about Reese?"

"Probably. I've asked a few times, but he says he doesn't want to talk about it, so I don't push him."

It doesn't matter whether or not he's over Reese. The point is, he's not into me.

Tuesday, July 25

I kind of hate being alone between the end of my shift and Dad's arrival home. It was fun the first dozen times, but now I'm used to it, and after about 20 minutes I start hearing a high-pitched buzz in my ears. It's probably juvenile tinnitus. Maybe it would be OK if Miss Murphy and her baby moved in.

Wednesday, July 26

Rode my bike to visit Hannah at Strawberry Hills Ice Cream Parlor, where she's working this summer. I thought she'd be able to sneak me some free scoops, but she charged me full price for my mint chip cone, and she wouldn't come around the case to sit down with me for a minute, even though I was the only customer in the shop. That's Hannah for you. I missed that rule-abiding schoolmarm of a high school kid so much.

Thursday, July 27

It was overcast today, and you could hear occasional thunder, although it never wound up raining. The parents and nannies must have been worried about a storm, because no one showed up. Reese was working alone, and eventually she got sick of her phone and came over to talk to me and Nadia. She went on and on about Zach, which was bizarre, since she stole him from one of my best friends. Either she doesn't know Hannah and I made up, or she doesn't remember, or she doesn't care, or two of the three.

"He's incredibly good-looking—Nadia, you've seen him, right? Yeah, so you know. His body is unreal. He's spending the rest of the summer doing this super-exclusive music program in California. He's all stressed out, like, 'You won't forget about me, will you?' and 'You'd never cheat on me, right, baby?' I think he's worried about leaving me alone with Grady."

"But you dumped Grady for him," I said.

"So?"

"So isn't Grady mad at you?"

Reese laughed and stroked her own hair like it was a little pet. "You know what guys are like."

What does that mean?! I don't know what guys are like! Is she saying she could get him back with one expert BJ? Is she saying she *wants* to get him back?

I knew it was a bad idea, but I called Noelle on my bike ride home and said, "Is Reese still into Grady?"

"I thought you were over him," Noelle said.

"I am. I'm curious, that's all."

"Why are you out of breath?" she said.

"I'm on my bike. I have earbuds in."

"Hmm, this sounds like a pretty urgent question!"

"Noelle, just tell me."

"Don't take this the wrong way, but I don't think I should. I don't want to get in the middle of this. I'm friends with both of you and I want to keep it that way."

"So she does still like him."

"Chloe, come on."

She wouldn't tell me, but it was the same thing as telling me.

At least she said she's friends with us both. I don't think it'll last, but I'm going to enjoy it while it does.

Friday, July 28

Oh my GOD. Nadia was distracted all day today, and finally, at a slow moment, she said, "Do you think I'd ever have a shot with Grady?"

"With *Grady*? Grady the lifeguard?"

"Yes," she said, looking hurt.

"I honestly have no idea," I said as I looked at her analytically for the first time. She's cute, dammit. She looks like an adorable little squirrel you could train to sit on your shoulder and eat nuts from your palm.

"I was thinking of telling him I like him. Would that be crazy?"

Yes, I thought, that would be crazy. To put yourself out there like that, to say the words so nakedly and open yourself up to rejection—that would be crazy.

"I don't know what to say," I said.

She wasn't even listening to me. She was busy staring across the water at him. He looked down and rubbed some sunscreen into his abs and a wave of longing knocked into me.

You know what, if I have to watch him and Nadia fall in love, that's what I deserve. I had my chance, I blew it, and he's done with me. It's my fault, and I have no right to be this upset.

Saturday, July 29

Tris and Hannah and I went to Walden Pond today. I'd written about 10,000 words in a group text convincing them to walk around the water with me so we could soak in Thoreau's aura, but it turned out to be a hollow victory, because I didn't enjoy our hike at all. I was jumping out of my skin and had no patience for contemplative silence or Mother Nature. It was hot and humid and mosquitoes were whining in my ears. We walked in single file, me in front, Tris and Hannah yelling at me for bringing them on this death march, me yelling back that I was very sorry and I'd never suggest doing something spiritually enriching ever again.

It was better once we got back to the beach and ran into the water. I'd promised myself I wouldn't bore them with my Grady problems, but as soon as we were on our towels, I told them Nadia was going to make a move on him and I was almost positive Reese regretted breaking up with him.

"I don't know if that's awful to hear, Hannah," I said. "Maybe I shouldn't have told you."

"It would make me very happy if she dumped Zach," Hannah said. "I know that's uncharitable, but it's true."

"But she can't get back together with Grady!" Tris said, horrified.

"Why not?"

"You have to stop her! And what about Nadia?"

"What about her?"

"She could be hitting on Grady right now, as we speak!"

I flopped facedown. "I know," I said into my towel. "It makes me want to throw up."

"So put on your shorts and go talk to him," Tris said. "Right NOW."

I shook my head. "I missed my chance," I said. "You saw him at the Fourth of July party. He couldn't be less interested in me."

Tris paused. I guess I was hoping he'd contradict me, but he didn't.

"What do you lose by telling him how you feel?" Hannah said.

"I lose my dignity," I said. "It would be like handing him a knife and asking him to stab me."

"That's a ridiculous comparison," Tris said.

"And I'm trying to be a better person," I said. "Less selfish. I don't want to cause more drama. He used to like me, he doesn't anymore, and the mature thing to do is accept that. Maybe he'll be happy with Nadia, or even Reese. I'm not going to interfere when I already know what he's going to say. Telling him how I feel would be a relief, but only for me. It would annoy him and stress out whoever his next girlfriend is going to be, so I can't do it."

"OK," Tris said sadly. "I get it."

"I do too," Hannah said. "I think you're doing the right thing, Chloe."

I'm crying as I write this, but I think I'm doing the right thing too.

Sunday, July 30

Reese forced Grady to give her a hug hello this morning and then sat so close to him she was almost on his lap. Nadia went over twice and looked up at him shyly through her eyelashes. I couldn't tell what they were talking about, but he was smiling. I breathed in through my nose and out through my mouth and bit the inside of my cheek whenever I thought I might lose it.

Monday, July 31
!!! x INFINITY

My hand is shaking, but I have to write.

I can't believe this.

I CAN'T BELIEVE this.

It was just the two of us working today. I spent hours staring at him longingly, willing him to look at me, saying *Grady, I love you* silently across the pool to him. He had his mirrored sunglasses on, like he always does, and I couldn't read his expression.

Bear came to the pool for the first time all summer and stood pressed against Grady's leg for an hour. During an adult swim, I saw him pointing to me and asking Grady something, and then the two of them walked over to the concession stand, holding hands.

"Bear, it's so nice to see you!" I said. "Where have you been?"

"At day camp," he said. "But tomorrow we're going to visit my cousins."

"Who is?"

"Me and my mommy and daddy and Grady. He's my brother."

"Right," I said.

"I have my bathing suit," Bear said. "It has fire trucks."

"I have my bathing suit too," I said. "It's green."

He nodded solemnly. "The water is cold, but not too cold."

"That's true," I said. "Especially in the shallow end. Are you thinking of going in?"

"Yes. I have my floaties. You see that?" He held out his arms to show me.

"I do."

"My babysitter can come with me." He pointed to a middle-aged woman wearing nylon shorts and chatting with some moms.

"Have fun," I said. "If you wave to me from the water, I'll wave back, OK?"

He smiled and they walked away. Grady and I hadn't said a single word to each other. *It's not just that he's not into me*, I thought. *He actually doesn't like me.*

Bear waved to me every few minutes from the pool, and I waved back every time, even while taking orders and making change. Before he left, he walked back over to see me, by himself this time. "I have to go home now," he said.

"Come back soon," I said. "Do you remember my name?"

"Yes! Chloe. You're my friend. I like you."

"I like you, too," I said. "So much."

At the end of the day, people trickled away until it was just me and Grady, and we shut down like we always do. I swept up and cashed out. Grady put away the lane dividers, checked the chemical levels, cranked down the umbrella, and locked up the shack. I packed my bag, rolled down the shutter, and closed and locked the concession stand door behind me. The sun had set, and the trees looked dark against the lavender sky. I called good night to Grady without looking at him, then headed out to the bike rack. I was riding out of the parking lot, thinking about Bear, when suddenly I screeched to a halt, dropped my bike on the gravel, and ran back as fast as I could.

Grady was putting his notebook in his backpack. He looked up, startled. "What's wrong?" he said.

"Grady, I like you. I like you so much. I always have; it just took me a while to realize it, and I'm so sorry. Mac is a cartoon someone drew on a napkin compared to you. You're a real person. You're interesting, and funny, and I have such a good time with you, or I used to, before everything that happened this year. And you're hot, OK? You're so hot. I sit across from you every day and I'm dying, Grady. I'm dying to—to be your girlfriend. I would give anything to be your girlfriend. I know you can't stand me now, and I know you're probably getting back together with Reese or already going out with Nadia, and I'm very sorry if it's annoying to hear me say all this stuff, but I had to tell you, Grady, because you have to know the truth."

He'd been listening to me without moving a muscle, and my whole body was prickling with fear, but when I got to the part about how hot he is, he started grinning, and a tiny spark of hope floated into my heart, and when I'd finished, we looked at each other, and he was still grinning, and I said, "Say something, Grady, Jesus Christ," but he didn't. He just stepped toward me and then he was hugging me so hard I thought my ribs would break, and then he was kissing me, and I was kissing him back, and we were kissing each other like we were trying to eat each other alive, and then we almost fell into the pool, and then we lay down on the grass and made out for an hour without pausing, until we were both thirsty and the grass had gotten cold, and then we drank some water from his thermos and made out for another hour, until we had to go home before our parents called the police.

We walked out to the parking lot with our arms around each other, squeezed together as tightly as we could squeeze while still being able to move our legs. Then we made out in the driveway for a while. My bike was still lying on the gravel, where I'd left it an eternity ago. I never wanted to move it. It was a monument to the moment I'd come to my senses.

"My mom's going to kill me," he said, still kissing me.

"My dad's probably walking around with a flashlight right now," I said, kissing him back.

"We're going to visit my cousins tomorrow," Grady said.

"Bear told me, remember? When are you coming back?"

"Not until Wednesday."

"Like, in two days?"

"No, a week and two days."

I was freaking out, but I wasn't going to say anything—I don't want him to think I'm weirdly obsessed with him already. Then he said, "Maybe I can jump out of the car when my mom's not looking and run back here," and relief flooded through me. He was upset about leaving too!

"She probably wouldn't notice," I said.

We had agreed for the sixth time that we had to leave, and then Grady said, "Tell me again about how hot I am."

"You're a brat."

"You love me."

"Stop."

"You love me so much you want to marry me."

"You want to get married?" I said.

"I would love to marry you," he said. "I'd marry you tomorrow."

"OK, we're engaged," I said.

And then we really did go home, after making out for another 20 minutes or so.

Grady, Grady, Grady, Grady Grady Grady Grady Grady!!!!!!!!

Tuesday, August 1

I hardly slept last night, and when I did sleep, I dreamed I was back at the pool, kissing Grady. I tried to eat breakfast, but I was too sick with excitement to choke down more than a bite of toast. In a strange way, I'm glad I won't see him for a week. Last night was so perfect; I wish I could put it under glass, like a snow globe, and live in it. If we keep going, if he turns into my boyfriend, we'll inevitably get in fights and be rude to each other and jealous of other people. If I keep sitting here writing in my diary forever, I'll never ruin what happened yesterday.

Wednesday, August 2

HE CALLED ME! He's in upstate New York, and tomorrow he'll be in Canada. He snuck out of his motel room and called me at midnight, and we talked for hours. It was like we were two detectives trying to crack the case of our own idiocy.

"Why did it take you so long to tell me?" he said.

"Because you were so moody and quiet all summer!" I said. "I thought you were devastated about Reese."

"I was devastated because you never talked to me!" he said.

"Is that why you were sulking every time we worked together?"

"Yes!"

We were quiet, and then I said, "*Were* you upset when Reese broke up with you?"

"No. Kinda. It was embarrassing mostly," he said. "I knew everyone in school was talking about it."

"Were you mad at her for cheating on you?"

He laughed. "A little. It wasn't like she broke my heart."

"But did you ever like her?" I said. "How could you stand to be with her for so long?" My heart was pounding. It was the question I most wanted to ask him, and also the scariest question to ask him. He didn't answer for a minute, giving me time to start panicking about what he was going to say.

"I never liked her like I like you," he said. "But, I

mean, you weren't into me. What was I going to do, sit around waiting for you to change your mind?"

"But why Reese? You could have found someone else."

"She found me, I guess. And—you don't want to hear this."

"No, tell me."

"I know she can be mean, but when she's nice to you, it's, like, a relief, and you feel amazing. It's fun to be around her. Scary, but fun."

"Oh my God. I know who she's like."

"Who?"

"*My mom.*"

"Oh, wow."

"My mom's exactly like that. Exactly."

"And you love her, right?"

"Did you love Reese???"

I could almost hear him roll his eyes. "No! I'm saying you understand the appeal of people like that."

"I guess. But part of the appeal of Reese is that she's so sexy, right?"

I felt sick, waiting to hear what he'd say.

"Chloe, I don't think we should talk about Reese anymore."

"Good idea."

"I'm serious. I don't want to think about it, you don't

want to hear about it, and talking about it will only make both of us upset."

"Wait, upset because you still like her?"

"No, you loon. Because I wasted a whole year being with the wrong person instead of with you."

Dad knocked on my bedroom door and asked me if I was planning on going to sleep anytime soon. After I'd gotten him to go away, Grady said, "So why were you kissing Mac that day?"

"I wasn't *kissing* him." He made a skeptical noise, and I said, "I gave him a peck on the cheek."

"Whatever you want to call it."

"He came over basically to see if I'd hook up with him, and I said no, so he was leaving. I felt nostalgic or something. That's all. Why didn't you believe me when I told you nothing was going on?"

"I'd just watched you kiss him. He was rubbing your head—I don't know, it looked so obvious something was up with you guys. And you were going out with him a few months earlier, so . . ."

"I wasn't going out with him!"

"You guys were making out in the Bowline."

"Oh, that. Yeah. That was a mistake. I completely ignored him after that."

"Really? Ha!"

"Why is that funny?"

"I was really upset in February. I thought you were his girlfriend again."

I remembered that, how rude Grady had been to me during rehearsal. It was so satisfying, realizing he'd actually been upset about Mac.

"Wait," I said. "In the driveway that day, on the Fourth—if you thought I was back with Mac, why did you act like you didn't care?"

"Duh. I was trying to be cool."

"I was like, he hates me. It's never happening with us."

"I'm an amazing actor."

"Oh! Wait! I know what I have to ask you! Do you hate my singing?"

"What? No. You have a sick voice."

"I *knew* it. I have to say one more thing about . . . you know who."

"Go on."

"She told me you think I'm a terrible singer."

"She made it up. I swear."

"I believe you."

Grady said, "You know when we started being friends again, during the musical? When we were talking about your parents a lot for a few days? Why did you disappear on me?"

"Did you like me then? You were with Reese!"

"I've always liked you," he said.

"I'm kissing you through the phone," I said, and he laughed and then said, "So why did you? Disappear?"

"Because I realized I liked you, and I didn't trust myself to be around you."

"What, like you were worried you'd jump me?"

"Yep. Basically."

"What made you tell me?" he said.

"For one thing, watching Nadia and Reese throw themselves at you."

"You were jealous?"

"Yes! Obviously. But mostly I think it was Bear," I said. "When he visited the other day, he told me he liked me, and the way he said it was so—I don't know, so pure. I had all these complicated reasons for leaving you alone, but suddenly I thought, 'What's so hard and confusing about just telling Grady you like him?'"

"I'm going to buy Bear an actual fire truck," he said.

Then we talked about all of it again, with more details this time. It's so fun, being our current happy selves and thinking about our confused and upset former selves!

Thursday, August 3

He's in Canada now. He can't use his phone. That's why he's not calling me: because he's in another country, not because he's suddenly stopped liking me.

What was all that nonsense Tris and I came up with about how fun it is to be sick with love? This isn't fun. This is torture. (But it *is* fun. I hate it, and I love it.)

Friday, August 4

Dad got home early from work today, and Miss Murphy came over a few minutes later. I could tell he was gearing up to talk to me about something, and I was busy worrying it was bad news about Mom when he said, "How about trying some driving?" He was attempting to sound cheerful. It wasn't working.

Then Miss Murphy said, "Why don't the two of us go, Chloe? I drove the Jeep over."

Dad stared at her. I could tell they hadn't discussed this plan yet.

"I don't know if that's the best idea, Marian," he said.

"Has Dad told you I'm terrified of driving?" I asked her.

"He mentioned it."

"And you still trust me with your Jeep?"

She grabbed her keys from the island. "Yep."

We went outside. I got in the driver's seat. It happened right away. Shaking, darkened vision, the whole thing.

"OK, start 'er up," Miss Murphy said.

"I can't," I said. "My hands are shaking too much."

"I don't think it's a problem," she said.

"What if I crash?"

She shrugged. "You won't."

"My vision is weird, too."

"Key in the ignition," she said. She was so calm and so sure of herself, and I'm so used to taking orders from her and not arguing back, that I found myself putting the key in the ignition and turning it.

"Throw it in reverse," she said. "Arm over the back of my seat. Give it a little gas. Turn the wheel to the right. More gas. Whoa! OK, that was good."

I was still shaking. I still couldn't see well. But I was doing what she told me to do.

"Foot on the brake. Whoops, the brake! There you go. Straighten the wheel out. Put the car in drive. One more click. There you go. And step on the gas. That's it! Want to take a right here? Push the wand up. Other side of the steering wheel. You got it."

I was doing it. I was DRIVING! I was still shaking and my heart was still pounding, but I hadn't crashed yet.

Miss Murphy turned on the radio. It was a song I didn't know, but she did, and she started singing along. Her voice is beautiful.

"What if the music distracts me?" I said. I could

barely talk, I was so focused on gripping the wheel and remembering which pedal did what.

"You're good," she said. "I'm not worried."

She sounded so genuinely relaxed that I relaxed a little. She trusted me. I could do it. I *was* doing it.

We kept going around the neighborhood. I was driving 20 miles an hour. Whenever a car came in the opposite direction, I slowed down to 10. A few times I pulled over and stopped so someone behind me could pass. Sometimes Miss Murphy said stuff like, "A little close to the lawn there," or "Try to make almost constant tiny adjustments to the wheel, rather than occasional big ones," but mostly she sang along to the radio and looked out the window.

We did a loop, then took a left and drove into the new development. We doubled back and took Ross Lane up the hill and around by the fields. After half an hour, Miss Murphy said, "Getting hungry?" and I nodded. I was still too tense to speak.

After I'd pulled into the driveway and turned off the car, she looked over at me, and her eyes were full of affection.

"You did it," she said.

"I did it!" I said. I was exhausted, but my heart wasn't pounding anymore, and my hands weren't shaking, and I could see.

"And you did well," she said. "I knew you would."

She didn't make a move to get out of the Jeep, so I didn't either.

"Do you know what scared you so much about driving?" she said. "Scared," past tense. I felt a surge of pride that I'd gotten over my fear and tried this thing I was so petrified of.

"How dangerous it is," I said.

She nodded.

I said, "And I always picture Dad dying in a car accident. Like, blood in his hair. How his body would look if his neck broke. Sick stuff like that. So then I thought, if I'm driving, I could kill him, or someone like him, or myself."

She nodded again.

I looked out the window at a bee floating through the air and thought about Mom leaving. I never expected it. It shocked me. And now it feels like I have to be on the alert for other terrible surprises. I trusted the world before. Now I don't. Now I know people can disappear.

Like she'd read my mind, Miss Murphy said, "I started worrying about death after my dad left."

"How did you make yourself feel better?" I said.

"I tried to comfort myself with statistics. I still do. It's overwhelmingly likely that we'll die of old age after living long, happy lives. We're extremely lucky. And most people we love won't run out on us. Even if they do, we'll be OK. 'Sufficient unto the day is the evil thereof,' right? If I ever got a tattoo, that'd be it."

I want to know the future so badly, because I want to know that no one I love will die young, or decide to leave me. But I can't know. Maybe Miss Murphy and Dad will get married. Maybe they won't. Maybe they'll have a baby. Maybe they won't. I have to be OK with waiting to find out, and in the meantime, I have to feel so grateful that my dad's girlfriend thinks about me, and worries about me, and believes in me so much that her belief seeps out of her and into me.

"SHE DID IT!" Miss Murphy told Dad when we got inside. She sounded so proud.

Saturday, August 5

Dear Mom,

Obviously things aren't great with you and Dad, or with you and me. I will admit I'm still angry at you for leaving. I'm also angry at you for trying to get custody of me when it's not what I want, and now for vanishing into Mexico City. I don't know if I'll ever forgive you for doing these things, but you're still my mother, and you always will be. If you want

to email sometimes (and I don't know if you
do), I'll be happy to write back.

Take care. I hope you're doing OK.

Love,
Chloe

I don't know if it's good or bad for me to have a relationship with my mother. Maybe cutting her out of my
life completely is the right thing to do. For now I think it
will make me feel worse to ignore her than to email her
occasionally. And if anything goes wrong, I can ask Miss
Murphy for help.

Sunday, August 6

I'd texted Hannah and Tris every detail of the Grady
situation, but today was the first time I got to talk to
them about it in person. They came over and we sat on
the deck and gossiped while eating Popsicles.

"I love everything about him," I said. "Like, I love
the smell of his spit."

"Oh my goodness," Hannah said.

"That's how I felt about Roy," Tris said.

"Poor Elliott!" Hannah said.

Tris waved his Popsicle in the air dismissively. "Oh,

Elliott's fine. He's not going anywhere. I like having him around."

"Very romantic," I said.

"At least you have a boyfriend, Tristan," Hannah said. "I don't think I'll date anyone else until I get to college."

Tris and I both burst out laughing, and Hannah looked wounded.

"Sorry, Han," I said. "It's just that you've been single for about two weeks total since we started high school."

She gazed off into the backyard. "Do you ever wish we weren't so obsessed with guys?" she said. "I think about them more than I think about school, or my parents, or anything else in my life."

"I do wish that," I said. "But it feels out of my control. I try to stop obsessing, and I can't."

"Please," Tris said. "We're in high school. Of course we think about boys all the time. Soon we'll be old and we'll have to think about our mortgages, or whatever, and we'll look back and wish we'd relaxed and enjoyed this part of our lives."

I am enjoying this part of my life. I really am. I don't want it to ever, ever stop.

Monday, August 7

"I miss Grady," Nadia said today. "He gets back from Canada on Wednesday. I don't know if you knew that."

"Um . . . ," I started to say, but she kept talking.

"As soon as I see him, I'm going to tell him I like him," she said. "I get the feeling Reese wants him back, and I have to talk to him before she tries anything. Don't you think?"

"I have to confess something," I said.

She cocked her head at me and looked alert.

"Grady and I are together," I said. She frowned in confusion, so I elaborated. "I mean, he's my boyfriend." Now she looked downright disbelieving. "I should have said something earlier, but I didn't think anything would happen, so it seemed pointless."

She studied me for a second and said, "That's interesting." It was obvious she didn't believe me. Mere weeks ago she was scared of me, and now she was coolly insinuating I'm a liar right to my face. And she was so unbothered, and so sure of herself, that I panicked. Does it mean something sinister that I haven't heard from Grady in days? OK, he's in another country, but if he liked me, wouldn't he call, or at least text? Did he text Nadia? Is that how she knew he'd be back on Wednesday? And *is* he my boyfriend? Yes, we were joking around about getting married, but that's so obviously hyperbolic. If you really wanted someone to be your girlfriend, you wouldn't talk about getting engaged, because you wouldn't want to scare her off.

I'm being crazy, right? It's terrifying to like someone this much. I take it back: I want to be Tris, not Elliott. I want to be Mac, not me!

Tuesday, August 8

Tomorrow's the day. God, I can't wait, I can't wait, and God, I'm so terrified to see him again. What if I'm right— what if there's something wrong? I have a bad feeling. What if he changed his mind? What if he met someone in Canada? What if he spent his trip realizing he likes Nadia? What if he walks into the pool tomorrow with a serious expression and says, "We need to talk"? What if he's chilly to me in front of Reese?

I can't eat. I'm shaking with hunger and fear. Grady, Grady, Grady!

Wednesday, August 9

Reese and I were on the morning shift, and Nadia and Grady were working the afternoon, so I had to gut it out for six hours, watching Reese preen and apply lip gloss and stretch her legs out like a cat. At ten of two, Nadia walked in and practically skipped over to the concession stand.

"I'm so excited to see Grady today!" she said, and as I was wondering whether to try to convince her, again, that he's not available, he walked in. When he saw me, he raised both of his arms in the air like he'd scored a touchdown, then dropped his bag on the grass, whipped off his hat and his T-shirt, *dove into the water*, swam the entire length of the pool without coming up for air, hoisted himself onto the deck, reached into the concession stand, and *pulled me out* over the counter. I was laughing and screaming. "Grady! You're insane! I'm getting soaked. Oh my God, my LEG! GRADY!"

"This is my girlfriend!" Grady was shouting. He had me over his shoulders in a fireman's carry. I was dimly aware of Nadia staring at us with a shocked expression, Reese glaring from across the water, and all the mothers and nannies looking at us indulgently.

"I'm going to marry this girl!" Grady yelled, and then he jumped into the water with me still on his shoulders. I came up choking and laughing and screamed, "Grady! This is the second pair of my sneakers you've ruined, you maniac!" Then I swam over to the ladder and sat on the second rung, and he swam over to me, held on to the handrails, and stared into my face.

"I *missed* you!" he said.

"I missed you so much," I said.

"Would someone report me to Mrs. Franco if I kissed you right now?" he said.

"Definitely," I said.

"OK," he said, looking at my mouth. He was inches

away from me, and the sun reflecting on the water lit up his beautiful skin, and his small overbite, and the pen strokes of his eyebrows, and his thick eyelashes.

"Let's stay in the pool," I said.

He nodded, looking serious, and said, "Let's stay in forever," and then he did kiss me, and I kissed him back, and I felt the sun on our heads and the water all around us, and when I opened my eyes, he was already looking at me, looking at me like I'm precious to him, and although I knew we'd have to get out eventually, and I knew we'd have to keep growing up and messing up and struggling along through our days, it felt like if we tried hard enough, we could stay in our snow globe, frozen in this moment, floating in the pool of our happiness, for the rest of our lives.

Acknowledgments

Thank you, Jesseca Salky.

Thank you, Melissa Albert, Sydney Navarro, Suzi Pacaut, Lauren Passell, and Emily Winter.

Thank you, Patricia Anne Chastain, David Chastain, Carl Chastain, and Laura Emmons.

Thank you, Liesa Abrams, Mara Anastas, Chriscynethia Floyd, Caitlin Sweeny, Alissa Nigro, Vanessa DeJesus, Katherine Devendorf, Jessica Handelman, Sara Berko, Mike Rosamilia, Jessica Smith, Christina Pecorale, Karen Lahey, and the whole team at Simon Pulse/Simon & Schuster.

Thank you, Jared Hunter, Wesley Hunter, and Malcolm Hunter.

I love you all so much!

Emma Chastain is a graduate of Barnard College and the creative writing MFA program at Boston University. She lives in Brooklyn, New York, with her husband and children.

#HASHTAGREADS

Bringing the best YA your way

TOMMY WALLACH
MORGAN MATSON
ROBYN SCHNEIDER
CASSANDRA CLARE
CLARE FURNISS
DARREN SHAN
HONOR & PERDITA CARGILL
#R
C.J. FLOOD
SOPHIE MCKENZIE
STEPHEN CHBOSKY
AMY ALWARD
JENN BENNETT
PAIGE TOON GAYLE FORMAN
BECCA FITZPATRICK
SCOTT WESTERFELD
S.J. KINCAID

Join us at **HashtagReads**,
home to your favourite YA authors

Follow us on Twitter
@HashtagReads

Find us on Facebook
HashtagReads

Join us on Tumblr
HashtagReads.tumblr.co